# WHEN WE WERE
## Saints

# WHEN WE WERE

*Saints*

# HAN NOLAN

Harcourt, Inc.
ORLANDO    AUSTIN    NEW YORK
SAN DIEGO    TORONTO    LONDON

www.HarcourtBooks.com

Library of Congress Cataloging-in-Publication Data
Nolan, Han.
When we were saints/Han Nolan.
p.   cm.
Summary: Inspired by his grandfather's last words and guided
by a girl who believes they are saints, fourteen-year-old Archie
sets out on a spiritual quest that takes him from southern
Appalachia to the Cloisters Museum in New York City.
[1. Spirituality—Fiction.   2. Mysticism—Fiction.   3. Sick—Fiction.
4. Emotional problems—Fiction.   5. Grandparents—Fiction.
6. Christian life—Fiction.   7. Cloisters (Museum)—Fiction.
8. Appalachian Region—Fiction.   9. New York (N.Y.)—Fiction.]
I. Title.
PZ7.N6783Wh   2003
[Fic]—dc21       2003004346
ISBN 0-15-216371-9

Text set in Sabon
Designed by Cathy Riggs

First edition
A C E G I K J H F D B

Printed in the United States of America

*For my husband, Brian,*
*and*
*my brothers and sisters:*
*Jim, Mike, Lee, and Caroline—almost saints*

## Acknowledgments

Many thanks to my husband, Brian Nolan, for his love, encouragement, and patience—always.

Thanks to my editor, Karen Grove, for her clear vision—it has made all the difference.

Thanks to my agent, Barbara Kouts, for her support when I needed it most.

Thanks to Lee Doty and Kathleen Rose, for their knowledge and help with this story.

Thanks to my wonderful writing group: Sue Bartoletti, Lisa Fraustino, Dianne Hess, and Ann Sullivan, for listening to earlier, stranger versions, for the laughs and encouragement, and for the star-spangled pants.

# PART ONE

*"Enter by the narrow gate;*
*for the gate is wide and the way is easy,*
    *that leads to destruction,*
*and those who enter by it are many.*
*For the gate is narrow and the way is hard,*
    *that leads to life,*
*and those who find it are few."*

MATTHEW 7:13-14

# CHAPTER

# 1

ARCHIBALD LEE CASWELL had named the still he and his best friend, Armory Mitchell, had built in the basement of his grandparents' home The Last Hurrah, in honor of Armory, who was moving with his family to Washington, D.C. He couldn't believe that a still they had made with their own hands would really produce any alcohol. That's why he agreed to the scheme when Armory showed him the instructions for building it. How could a few copper pipes, some scrap metal, a hose, and Armory's Coleman stove produce real alcohol? So Archie went along with the plan, and for a week the two of them carried the bits and pieces they had found for the still past the living-room windows, where his grandparents could have looked out and seen them at any moment, to the bulkhead and down the steps to the basement. But there they stood, to Archie's great surprise, facing each other with their first mugfuls of the homemade brew in their hands.

They were an odd-looking twosome. Archie was tall for his fourteen years and lanky, but his freckled face and wide blue eyes still had the look of a little boy in them. Armory, also fourteen, was three inches shorter than his friend and built like a truck, with a voice that carried like a truck's horn. He had small dark eyes that glinted with mischief.

Armory held his mug out toward Archie's and said, "Here's to our friendship. Long may it sail. Hurrah!"

Archie clinked mugs with Armory and waited for his friend to take the first sip, but Armory said, "No, let's drink it together. Down the hatch in one big gulp."

Archie sniffed the brownish liquid in his mug. It smelled like a toilet. "Are you sure we didn't overheat this stuff? The instructions said to keep..."

"I know what the instructions 'said.' You were the one looking at the thermometer every five seconds. You tell me."

Archie sniffed again and shrugged. "I guess it's all right."

"You wouldn't chicken out on me now, would you, Cas? The last hurrah and all that?"

"Have I ever?" Archie asked.

Armory chuckled. "Well there was that cliff face you and your bike didn't seem to want to go down a while back."

"I went, didn't I? And I beat you down it, too."

"Yeah, on your face. What did you call that maneuver you did off the front end of your bike? The arc and splat?"

Armory hooted and Archie shushed him. "My granddaddy will hear us."

"He's gotta know we're down here. He'd be more suspicious if we were quiet. So come on"—Armory lifted his mug—"to the last hurrah!"

Archie hesitated a second while the memory of the broken arm and ribs he had gotten from his ride down the cliff flashed through his mind. *What's the worst that could hap-*

*pen this time?* He lifted his mug and said, "To the last hur-rah!" Then he and Armory drank the bitter liquid down, each in one long gulp. When they had finished, they looked at each other and laughed.

Archie said, "Shh, he'll hear us." Then he laughed again and added, "This stuff's terrible. It tastes like we scraped the mold off these basement walls." He looked at the musty walls of the old basement and felt a sudden gripping pain in his gut. He clutched his stomach, and then the pain was gone.

Armory turned back to the still. "Let's go one more round."

"Are you kidding?"

"Come on, Cas, it'll put hair on your chest."

"More like my *tongue*," Archie said, feeling another sharp pain in his stomach. "This stuff's not sitting too well."

"Of course not. You never drank before. You're inex-perienced, that's all." Armory held out his hand. "Give me your mug, Cas, come on."

Archie handed it over and wondered how he could get out of drinking another mugful. He didn't want to wimp out on his best friend on their last day together, but he didn't think he could keep another round down.

Armory handed him back his mug, and Archie took it without looking into the cup or sniffing the brew this time. Again Armory held up his mug and said, "To the last hurrah!"

"To the last hurrah," Archie said without enthusiasm. He took a deep breath, closed his eyes, and swallowed a big gulp. He heard his friend laughing, and he opened his eyes.

"Caswell, I can't believe you drank that. This isn't brew, it's hair tonic." Armory shot forward and dumped his drink on Archie's head. Archie howled and emptied the rest of his brew onto Armory. "You lunatic!" he shouted.

"What y'all doing down there? Archibald?"

Archie heard the cellar door open and he froze. "Nothing, Granddaddy, we'll be quieter." He heard his grandfather coming down the steps and felt both panic and alcohol rising inside himself. He turned and looked wide-eyed at Armory, who wore an expression of surprised delight. Archie turned back in the direction of the stairs and saw his grandfather appear in front of him.

It took the old man no time to figure out what they had been up to, and Archie saw his face turn purple with rage. "What?" his grandfather shouted, grabbing the front of Archie's shirt.

"Granddaddy, it—it's not what you think. It's..." Archie couldn't speak. He could feel the alcohol rising and rising. He tried to swallow it back down.

His grandfather shook him and shouted, "This here is the last straw! You are in the clutches of the very devil himself! I'm gonna tan your hide, boy. Makin' a still in my own home. Drinkin'!" He shook Archie again, and Archie couldn't hold back any longer. He vomited all over the front of his grandfather's shirt and pants.

Armory laughed and shouted out, "The last hurrah! Caswell, you did it!" As though Archie had vomited on purpose.

Archie was stunned. He looked at his grandfather, whose body shook with rage. The old man clenched his jaws and bared his teeth as though he wanted to rip into Archie and shred him to pieces. Archie tried to speak, but the words wouldn't come out. Then his grandfather's expression changed. In an instant it went from rage to alarm. Archie watched him wide-eyed as he fell forward onto his knees and then down to the floor, where he curled up into a tight ball.

Armory stopped laughing.

Archie dropped down beside his grandfather and touched his shoulder. "Granddaddy, are you all right? What should I do?"

"Get your grandmama, boy," he whispered. "Get your grandmama. I'm dying."

# CHAPTER

# 2

THE CURTAINS WERE drawn in the living room, where Silas Benjamin Caswell lay dying. The room had a gray-green cast to it and smelled faintly of boiled collard greens. Neighbors sat around his bed in chairs brought in from the kitchen and dining room, and as the end drew near more friends arrived, bringing with them lawn chairs, as if the death of Silas Caswell were an event like a summer band concert. Emma Vaughn Caswell sat closest to her dying husband, and her grandson, Archibald, sat next to her. Emma Vaughn was singing low, "Just as I am, without one plea, but that Thy blood was shed for me, And that Thou bidst me come to Thee, O Lamb of God, I come, I come."

Archie studied his grandfather's face. All the familiar wrinkles and creases had been drawn to the sides, leaving the areas around his nose and mouth, and between his brows, smooth and pale from so many months of lying on his back. The only sign of life left that Archie could see was the movement of his grandfather's eyeballs beneath the closed purple lids. He knew if he was going to say something to him—apologize, or ask his grandfather for forgiveness—it had to be soon. He looked around the room at all the faces gazing upon his grandfather. He looked at his grandmother, frail and sad, her eyes ringed with fatigue. She would want him to say something. He should do it for her, but still, Archie remained silent. He couldn't do it, not in front of all those people, and anyway, he believed it was his grandfather who should speak to him. That's what he really wanted. He wanted to hear his grandfather say "I forgive you," or "I love you"—something that let him know that his grandfather didn't hate him.

Emma Vaughn stopped singing and hummed. The neighbors hummed, too. Archie remained silent, watching the end of a life and reminding himself that his grandfather's illness was not his fault. It was not his fault that his grandfather was dying. Clyde Olsen had told him that, and Clyde knew Archie and his grandparents better than anybody. He had grown up living next door to them, and had been a playmate and best friend to Archie's father. He worked on the Caswells' farm, having taken it over and hiring Archie to help when Silas could no longer run it.

Clyde had found Archie crouched down in the ruins of his parents' old farmhouse the day Silas Benjamin Caswell came home from the hospital and demanded that Archie haul his bed down to the living room so that he could die looking out through the picture window at Caswells' Mountain.

"Hey, son, what you doing down there?" Clyde had asked when he'd come upon Archie.

Archie squinted up at Clyde. The stone foundation where he hid was all that was left of the old farmhouse that had collapsed on his parents more than thirteen years before, killing them and leaving Archie's grandparents to raise him. Looking up, Archie could see the sky, the sun, the trees, and Clyde, who leaned over the edge of the foundation, his leathery face etched with concern. Archie rose to his feet but didn't speak.

"Maybe you ought to come on up out of there, son," Clyde said.

Archie climbed out of the ruins and stood in front of the older man, feeling awkward and embarrassed. He knew the man could tell that he had been crying. He looked down at the pine needles beneath his feet and stuffed his hands into the back pockets of his jeans, not knowing what to say.

"I seen your granddaddy come home today," Clyde said.

Archie nodded and kept his head down. "He's dying. It's my fault."

"Is that so?"

"We had a fight, Clyde." Archie looked up into the man's face and saw him break into a smile.

Clyde chuckled. "Well now, that's nothing new. You two been going at it near about since you could talk."

Archie shook his head. "This time was real bad. I really did it this time."

"If it was 'real bad,' then I'd say your good buddy Armory had a hand in it. Isn't that so?"

Archie backed up to lean against a pine tree. Clyde stayed where he was, but he pulled his oil-stained work gloves off his hands and tucked them into his back pocket, a signal to Archie that the man was willing to stay and listen to what he had to say. He nodded at Archie.

Archie knew Clyde was waiting for him to speak. He crossed his arms and tucked his hands under his pits, the way Armory always did. "We wanted to do something big, you know?" he said to Clyde. "He was moving all the way to Washington, so we wanted one last hurrah before he left. That's what we called it—the still, that is. The Last Hurrah, we called it."

Clyde raised his eyebrows and nodded. "The still. I heard about that, and I'm surprised at you, Archibald. Making your own alcohol's illegal in this state, even today."

"Armory got the instructions off the Internet. He said it was easy. He said it couldn't be illegal if you could get the directions off the Internet."

Clyde wagged his head. "Son, why you always had to follow after that boy I'll never know. He's gotten you into more trouble with your granddaddy. Maybe it's good he's moved away."

Archie rubbed his left arm, moving his hand over the area where Armory had tried to tattoo the words *Live Fast, Live Dangerously* with a razor blade and colored Sharpies. His arm still felt sore and swollen from the infection he had gotten from the dirty blade. His grandfather had been furious with him for that, too, but it was nothing like the anger and fury he had when he discovered the still.

"It's my own choice what I do," Archie said. "I can't be blaming Armory for everything. It's not his fault me and Granddaddy don't get along. It's me. It's my fault." Archie stared off into the woods on his right. "Granddaddy has never liked me." Archie's voice was a whisper. "Not in the way he liked my father."

Clyde cleared his throat and said, "I suspect your

granddaddy got awful sore over that still, but he loves you every bit as much as he did your father. It's not your fault he's dying, son. No matter how much you and him goaded each other, that didn't cause his liver problems."

Archie raised his brows and looked back at Clyde. "'Liver'? It's not his heart? He didn't have a heart attack? That day he found us in his basement with the still—he was so mad." Archie shook his head. "He's never been that mad. His whole body shook. And then—he just keeled over." Archie felt tears stinging his eyes, and he blinked them away. "He hasn't talked to me since, except when he got home and wanted his bed brought down to the living room. He didn't say one word to me when I went to see him in the hospital. He blames me, all right, and so does Grandmama."

Clyde stepped closer to Archie, his muddy work boots shuffling through the blanket of pine needles. "That doesn't sound like your grandmama. Did she tell you she blames you, or are you just imagining that's how she feels?"

Archie shrugged. "Grandmama never tells me anything. Why didn't she tell me it was his liver?" Archie answered his own question. "She hates talking about painful things. But still, she blames me. She has this look, you know? You ever seen her look when she's disappointed in you? She doesn't have to say anything; her look says it all. You ever seen it?"

Clyde shook his head.

Archie pushed himself off the tree, then fell back against it. "Yeah, well, it makes you want to just curl up and die, and she's been looking at me that way ever since Granddaddy took sick. And Granddaddy, if he looks at me at all, gives me his mean, squinty-eyed look, like he's plotting out seventy-five ways to get even with me."

Clyde set a calloused hand on Archie's shoulder. "I'm not saying they aren't upset about the still; maybe they are, but they aren't blaming you for that bad liver. Your granddaddy's been suffering with liver trouble for a long time now. Maybe what your grandmama wants is for you and your granddaddy to talk things out. Son, you don't want to let him die before you two have had a chance to say what needs to be said to each other. You understand?"

Archie looked into Clyde's gentle eyes and nodded. "Yes, sir."

"Once he dies those things can't be said. Now, maybe it's up to you to be the bigger man this time and speak up first. You think you can do that?"

Archie had told Clyde that he thought he could. He knew he had to say something to break the ice and come to some kind of understanding with his grandfather before the old man died, but Archie never did muster up the courage—and so there he sat, with his grandmother and all the elderly people in the town, watching his grandfather breathe his final breaths. Instead of speaking up, he waited for his grandfather to say something first. He just wanted to hear one word, one word of encouragement.

The neighbors waited, too. They hoped for one last word from the old prophet. Silas Benjamin Caswell had been the town prophet long before the small southern village hidden in the mountains had become an artists' colony where people from all over the country came to buy handmade pottery, landscape paintings, dulcimers, and finely crafted pieces of furniture. In the early years people took his predictions of famine and locusts and tornadoes seriously, but as he grew older and times and the population in the mountain village changed, his predictions became quaint, and the summer people, sitting out on their decks and balconies, would point as Silas passed by calling out to them and shaking his finger, and say to their guests with a chuckle, "There goes the prophet, warning of hellfire and damnation." The people gathered at his bedside now were his old friends, the ones who remembered how it used to be.

The day grew grayer, the room darker. The friends waited and hummed. Then Archie stood up. *It is now or never,* he decided. He had to say something. He knew he would regret it for the rest of his life if he didn't. In spite of what Clyde had said, he felt he was responsible for his grandfather taking ill when he did. All he had to say were two words: *I'm sorry.* Heads turned toward Archie when he stood up, but the humming continued. The heads turned back to the dying man. Then, just as Archie opened his mouth to speak, his grandfather, Silas Benjamin Caswell, opened his eyes. The humming stopped. He lifted his right hand and pointed. One thick yellow fingernail pressed into Archie's stomach. Silas Benjamin looked at his grandson, and Archie looked at him.

"Young man, you are a saint!" his grandfather said.

His raised arm flopped back down by his side, his eyes closed, and with the release of one last dry breath, he died.

CHAPTER

3

ARCHIE THOUGHT IT was fitting that it was pouring
rain on the day of his grandfather's funeral. He believed it
was the old man's way of raining hellfire and damnation
down on his head one more time. He let the rain soak
his good wool suit as he walked alone from the church to
the graveyard and waited for everyone else to arrive. His
grandmother and friends rode in cars following the hearse
the half mile to the graveyard. The rain and the need for
umbrellas and the waiting for people to get to their cars and
line up had slowed everyone down, so Archie had a good
twenty minutes to stand alone at the empty grave site.

His grandmother had given him an umbrella to hold
and the site had a canopy over it, but Archie didn't take advantage of either of those things. He felt he deserved the
punishment of the cold rain. He looked out past the deep
pit with the fake-grass rug pulled over it to the gravestones
just beyond the Caswell plot and discovered three stones
standing side by side, one with the word BACK written in

block letters, the next with the word STREET, and the third with THRASHER written on it. Before he knew what he was doing, Archie had invented a new character for the comic strip that he had been working on: the Back Street Thrasher, a daredevil mountain biker with a penchant for murdering people and archenemy of Mountain Mike the Mountain Biker. When Archie realized what he was doing—and how angry his grandfather would have been to know that at his very funeral he was working on the comic strip his grandfather had forbidden him to do—he felt ashamed of himself and kicked the mud at his feet.

"Look at you, Archibald, all soaking wet," his grandmother said when she caught up with him. "I gave you that umbrella to put over your head, not to use as a walking cane. Now come on, you're standing up front with me, and take this camellia." She handed him one of the two white flowers she held in her hand. "I want you to lay it on his casket after Brother Will's words."

Archie took the flower and stood with his grandmother beneath the canopy. The rain beat down hard, so that Brother Will had to yell to be heard over the noise. It slanted in and pelted Archie's legs. He stepped in closer to his grandmother, hoping to protect her legs from the cold water. His grandmother patted his arm in thanks. While the pastor spoke, gesturing toward the casket, Archie looked out to the three strange gravestones that stood in the fog that rose up from the leaves covering the ground around them.

He noticed someone standing beneath the oak tree just beyond the stones, directly across from him. It was a woman or a girl; Archie wasn't sure which. She was tall and slender; that much he could tell, but she held her umbrella so low,

Archie could not see her face. She was dressed all in black, from her boots and tights to the dress that came down to just above her knees. Two slender, young-looking hands gripped the umbrella. Archie wondered who she was and why she wasn't standing with everyone else. It looked almost as if she was deliberately standing in front of him, watching him from beneath her umbrella. He stared out at her and felt for a moment that he was seeing some kind of ghost rising out of the fog, and he determined that when the service was over, he would go and find out who she was. He knew that if Armory were there he would call out to her, and probably even would have done so in the middle of the service.

Remembering Armory made Archie's heart sink. He missed his old friend. He turned his attention back to the service, but when it was time to bow his head for one last prayer, Archie kept his head lifted and his eyes fixed on the figure still standing beneath the tree.

After the service Archie followed his grandmother's example and kissed his flower and placed it on top of the casket. Tears welled up in his eyes, taking him by surprise. He had yet to cry for the loss of his grandfather. He thought to say something, anything to make up for not speaking before the man had died, to make up for all the ways that he had hurt his grandfather over the years, and all the fights they had had with each other. He thought again to apologize for the still and for vomiting on him, but what was the use? His grandfather was dead, and anyway, an apology wasn't enough—but what was? Becoming a saint? Was that what his grandfather's final words meant? Was he saying, "It'll take your being a saint the rest of your life to make it up to me now, boy"?

His grandmother's friends had their own ideas about what the words had meant, and after the service, when Archie was trying to get away and catch up with the stranger beneath the tree, they held him back and gave him their take on Silas Benjamin Caswell's final words.

Miss Nattie Lynn Cooper shook her finger at him and said, "You listen to me, child, your granddaddy's last words were a warning. Take care, Archibald, and sin no more— that's what the old prophet was saying!"

Mrs. Wally Hoover said, "Nonsense, Nattie Lynn, don't you go scaring the boy half to death. Old Silas was just having a heraldic vision. It had nothing to do with Archibald at all."

Archie looked out past the women and saw the figure still standing in the same place, as though she was waiting for something. He wondered if maybe she was waiting for him. The thought made chills run down his spine. He still considered the idea that she was some dark spirit a real possibility.

Then Miss Callie Butcher stepped forward and argued with the others, taking hold of Archie's hand. "With old Silas so close to death, he was not of sound mind. The fool was just speaking gibberish," she said. She shook Archie's hand in hers and added, "Don't you think another thing about it, Archibald."

Archie couldn't help noticing that nobody, not even him, believed his grandfather's words meant just what he had said—that Archie was a saint.

At last the women moved on, and Archie hurried out toward the oak tree before any more of his grandparents' friends could catch hold of him. As he jogged he saw that the dark figure was moving. Then he realized she was coming toward him, and he thought of the Back Street Thrasher, wondering if he had conjured up some kind of evil spirit. Archie slowed down, then stopped. The figure kept walking. The rain and wind whipped her dress about her knees and beat upon her umbrella. She held the umbrella so low over her head that Archie wondered how she could see where she was going. As she approached him, Archie began to back away. Then he heard her speak in a soft voice.

"This is for you, Archibald Lee Caswell," she said. She placed a small laminated card in the palm of his hand.

Archie looked down and read the words on the card:

*Who are you, Almighty God of goodness and*
*    wisdom,*
*that you should visit me and judge me worthy,*
*I who am lower than the worms in the soil,*
*and most despicable?*

"What's this supposed to mean?" Archie looked up and saw the figure retreating.

"Hey!" he called. He started after her, but then he heard Clyde yelling to him. He turned and saw Clyde and his grandmother gesturing for him to come on, it was time to leave. He looked back for the girl—he was certain she was a girl and not a woman—and saw her already across the cemetery, heading toward town.

Archie looked down at the card in his hand, squeezed it, and then set out across the graveyard to join Clyde and his grandmother.

# CHAPTER

# 4

Archie looked for the strange girl as he rode through town on his way home from the funeral, but he didn't see her. Then for several days afterward, he rode his bike the nine miles into town, or on days when his grandmother, who didn't see well, needed to run some errands and Clyde couldn't drive her, he drove her in his grandfather's truck, even though at fourteen he had no license, and searched for the girl while his grandmother went about her business. He didn't have much to go on, no face and no name, but still he wandered in and out of the shops and boutiques that lined Main Street searching for her, wanting to find out who she was and how she knew his name, and why she had given him that card. What had those words to do with him?

It was early April and not yet the high tourist season there in town, so Archie had hoped that she would be easier to find, but although there were a number of tall, slender girls with soft voices, none of them seemed right to him.

He either knew the girls already, or if not, they didn't show the least bit of interest in him. The girl at the cemetery had known his name. He figured if he spotted her, she would startle or draw in her breath or in some other way show him some bit of recognition.

The girl and the card with its unusual message weren't the only things on his mind. Archie felt that his grandfather haunted him as well. He had written an e-mail message to Armory about it, but Archie decided something had to be wrong; his best friend hadn't written him back in over a week, and they had promised to e-mail each other every day. Archie decided to call Armory, and after getting permission from his grandmother, he did.

Armory answered the phone laughing, and Archie felt so happy to hear his friend's deep voice on the other end, he laughed, too.

"Hey, it's me, Cas. How are you? I've been e-mailing you like we promised, but I haven't heard back from you. Everything okay?"

Archie heard Armory whisper something to someone and then Armory said, "Cool!"

"Huh?"

"Oh, sorry, Cas. What did you say?"

"Are you okay?" Archie spoke louder, as if Armory had trouble hearing him.

"Yeah, sure, great. Well, you know how it is, getting used to a new school and all. Oh, wait." Armory laughed. "Sorry, I guess you don't, being *home*-schooled all your life. How's that going, anyway? Your grandfather giving it to you as usual? Still trying to convince you the South won the Civil War? Man, I'm glad to be out of Hicksville."

*Who is he talking to?* Archie wondered. It sounded as if Armory was saying everything for someone else's benefit. As if he was putting on a show for someone. And what had happened to his voice? He sounded like a Yankee.

Archie took a deep breath, feeling irritation rising in him. "Armory, I wrote you—he died. I told you that. You wrote back, remember? You said, 'Cool!' Remember?"

"Oh yeah. Oh yeah? So what's that like, having the old buzzard out of the way? Are you, like, going wild, or what?"

Archie heard his friend whisper again and then laugh. The conversation was going about as well as the e-mails. "Who's there with you?" he asked.

"No one—anymore," Armory said. "So go on; what were you saying?"

Archie took another deep breath and pushed on. "I think my granddaddy is haunting me."

"Cool! Like a ghost or something?"

"No. His words, his last words keep bugging me. I looked up 'saints' on the Internet and read this article that said that they used to throw saints to the lions or stone them to death, or they cut their heads off just because of their beliefs. Ever since I read that, I've been having all kinds of nightmares. You think Granddaddy Silas wants me stoned to death? Saints are Catholic, right? You know how Granddaddy never did abide by anything Catholic. You know what he was like. There was only one religion—his. He meant to insult me, take one last jab at me, right? Make me feel guilty for what we did?"

"Clyde's Catholic, isn't he?" Armory asked. "Old Silas liked him enough to let him run the farm."

"That's different. He was like a second son to Grand-daddy. He knew Clyde since Clyde was two."

"Well, I think it's cool dreaming about getting your head cut off. Chop, chop. You get all the luck, man."

"Yeah, thanks. I don't feel so lucky. Remember I wrote you how when Granddaddy died, he poked me in the stomach when he spoke those words? Remember I said he dug his fingernail into my stomach?"

"Uh—well—okay."

Archie could hear him snickering, as if what he was saying was so funny. Archie didn't know what to do but continue. Armory was his best friend, after all—or he had been. Archie said, "It's weird, I know, but I can still feel my granddaddy's poke." He rubbed his stomach. "It's like this dull pressure just above my belly button. It's here all the time, like a warning or something."

Archie heard someone giggling. There was someone on the other line. It sounded like a girl. Then the giggling turned to laughter and the girl spoke. "Who is this clown talking? Armory, do you hear him drawl? What a hick. I can't believe you used to know this dude."

Archie said, "Who is this? Armory? What's going on?"

Then he heard Armory's deep laughter along with the girl's. "Cas, meet Darcy, my girlfriend. I said she could listen in on the other line. She wanted to hear you talk with your accent."

"What accent?" Archie asked. "You know I don't have much of an accent."

"'Whut ac-see-nt?'" the girl said, imitating him. "You sound so corny."

"Told you," Armory said.

Archie didn't know what was going on, but he'd had enough. Without making a sound he hung up the phone and then sat staring at it for several minutes. He didn't know what to think about what had just happened. How could Armory have humiliated him like that? He felt he had just lost his best friend, and he didn't know what to do about it. He wanted to talk to someone, but who could he talk to? He and his grandmother never talked about those kinds of things, and Clyde was busy on the farm. Archie should have been, too, but Clyde had told him to take some time off from work because he had been too distracted lately, and that made him dangerous around all the machinery. It felt like nobody wanted him around.

Archie headed outside and aimlessly roamed the farm. His grandparents owned more than two hundred acres of fields and pasture and woods, two large ponds, a stream, and behind their home, a mountain: Caswells' Mountain.

He walked into the woods and through the fields, past the grazing sheep and cows. He pitched rocks into the stream that ran down the steep slope of the mountain, then climbed to the top of the mountain. He lifted his head to the sky and spoke to his grandfather, asking him, "Have you blessed me or cursed me, Granddaddy?" Archie's answer was a dull pressing sensation just above his belly button. That night he returned home and went to bed without dinner.

The next day he woke up feeling strangely calm and still dreamy after a night of dreams he couldn't remember, but he knew they had been pleasant for a change. He awoke early and again climbed to the top of the mountain. He sat down on a boulder and sucked on a lemon he'd carried in his pocket. He watched the cows grazing in a field below him. He watched them a long time.

The day had started out cool and sunny and calm, a day Archie had called a blue day. Every day, he believed, held a color; every day had a certain cast to it, blue or green or gold or pink. That day Archie had called blue, but after sitting for a couple of hours staring out at the fields, the light changed, deepening the colors about him to purple, and the wind began to blow. Right from the start the wind had felt uncommon, as if it had swept up from beneath him.

Archie tossed his lemon away and looked about. The cows that he had been gazing at only moments before seemed closer, clearer, as though he were looking at them through a telescope, and each hair on their brown-and-white bodies stood out in detail, perfect and alive. Everything, he realized, looked that way: the rocks, the patches of spring snow, the grass, the trees; everything was filled with a spirit and an energy that radiated out toward him. The wind blew harder and Archie's hair stood up on his head. He ran his tongue over his front teeth, licking the sourness off them. He saw the pines, a cluster of them bending in the breeze, bowing, beckoning.

Archie stood up and experienced a strange sensation of weightlessness. He could not feel himself. He could not sense where his legs and feet ended and the ground began. His whole body had no beginning and no end. The sky, the air, the sun, the earth, and the trees belonged as much to his body as his skin and bones. He walked toward the trees. He felt light and transparent. The pines swayed and bent, speaking with the creaking of their branches, the bristling of their needles, the thump of their cones as they fell to the ground. Archie listened, but it was like the speech of his grandfather when he spoke in tongues—foreign, and powerful. He felt the power and the energy of the trees course through his body. They were alive as he was alive, full of spirit and consciousness. He dropped to his knees and cried. Tears of joy and of worship flowed from his eyes. His heart, his whole being, filled with joy.

Archie stayed with the trees until the light faded and the wind died down and the voices around him grew silent. He did not know what had happened to him, or why, but as he descended the mountain, following the stream in the dark, he remembered the words on the card the girl had handed to him:

*Who are you, Almighty God of goodness and*
    *wisdom,*
*that you should visit me and judge me worthy,*
*I who am lower than the worms in the soil,*
*and most despicable?*

He had read the card over many times since the day of the funeral, but it was only then that he understood its meaning, and he wondered how the girl had known this would happen to him—and that the words would speak to his feelings exactly.

# CHAPTER

# 5

ARCHIE DIDN'T TELL anyone what had happened to him, but he wanted to. He wanted to know why it had happened. Why him, the lowliest of worms, as the card said? He had spent his life bedeviling his grandfather every chance he got, and in the end he vomited on him and caused him to have a liver attack and die. He knew he didn't deserve to feel so wonderful, so holy, so—so like a saint for that little while up on the mountain. Still, he tried to recapture the feeling again, that spiritual unity with all things, but it didn't happen. Each time he climbed the mountain and stared out over the fields and forest, the cows just looked like cows grazing in a distant field. The rocks and stones lay about him, hard and gray. The trees did not speak, and the wind and sky did not pass through him. Everything was as it had always been.

A few days after his experience on the mountain, Archie's grandmother caught him talking to the maple tree that stood outside their kitchen window, and later that same day she saw him talking to the rocks he held in his hands, and she stepped out onto the farmhouse porch and asked, "Archibald, sugar, are you feeling all right?"

Archie looked up, startled, and dropped the rocks. He opened his mouth to speak, thinking to tell her about his strange experience, but then he caught the look in her eyes, a look that said, "I can't cope with your problems right now, so please say you're all right." Archie knew she had thoughts of her own to dwell on, thoughts that caused the creases between her brows to deepen and that had made her burn the roux she was stirring on the stove a few nights before, so he nodded and said, "I'm fine, Grandmama. I was just studying those rocks and thinking out loud."

His grandmother nodded, a look of relief spreading across her face. "Well, that's all right then." She hesitated a moment and continued, "I just got a call from Lenice Oates down at the library. She says a book you wanted came in. I have some—some errands I'd like to get done, and Clyde is busy, so I thought you might drive me to town and pick up your book at the same time."

Archie looked at his grandmother. A pink flush rose up her neck, and her glance strayed from Archie's face to some distant something off to the left of her.

Was his grandmother uncomfortable about asking him to drive? He had been driving since he was twelve. All of the kids on the local farms learned to drive early, so he didn't think much of it, but he knew his grandmother believed in obeying the law, and he was driving into town, not just on the farm the way he had done before his grandfather died.

Archie was eager to get a look at the saints book he'd ordered, so he ignored his grandmother's behavior and told her he would run get the truck.

On the way into town, Archie's grandmother sat beside him, unsnapping and snapping her purse. Archie glanced at her and decided something other than his driving her to town was upsetting her, but he didn't say anything. She stopped fiddling with the purse and fussed with her dress instead, tugging at it and brushing her lap over and over again. Then when Archie pulled up in front of the grocery store, his grandmother told him to move on down the road a bit to the bakery shop. Archie did as he was told, and his grandmother climbed out of the truck and told him to pick her up in two hours. Archie blinked, surprised. What could take so long at the bakery? He looked at the other shops that lined the street—The Beanery, The Natural World, Century 21, a law office, and two art galleries. Maybe his grandmother was going to change her will.

Archie didn't say anything. He only nodded and waved good-bye. Then he drove on to the library, parked, jumped out of the truck, and ran up the steps, eager to see the book about saints that he had discovered on the Internet. He had read that the book had three hundred and thirty-two beautiful illustrations. The Web page he had found only showed four, but that was enough. Archie felt he just had to see the whole book. He had a passion for all art, even though he had enjoyed goading his grandfather with his love of comics, saying to him once when his grandfather tore up one of his drawings of Mountain Mike and called his art a waste of good time, "Why shouldn't I love drawing comics? After all, I'm named after a comic strip character, aren't I?" His grandfather had been livid. Archie had been named after Silas's own father, a war hero, and not the redheaded doofus in the comics.

When Archie reached the top of the steps, he yanked

open the library door, then tried to act nonchalant as he walked toward the counter—no need to look too eager over a book about saints.

Mrs. Oates saw him coming, pulled out a thick blue book from beneath the counter, and handed it to him. She smiled. "Is this for art or religion this time, Archibald?" she asked. Archie knew after his recent experience up on the mountain that it was for both, but he lied and said, "Just the art." Then he blushed, and he knew he had given himself away. He felt bad about the lie. Mrs. Oates was the only one who really knew and understood the depth of his passion for art. She was the one who told him about the interlibrary loan system, which made it possible for him to get hold of almost any art book he wanted, and who introduced him to El Greco and van Gogh and his other favorite artists, but still he couldn't admit to her something he could barely admit to himself: that he was interested in anything religious. That had always been his grandfather's territory, not his.

He took the book and sat down at his favorite table in the Art section and, with trembling hands, opened it. He hoped that maybe somewhere within the pages he would find a description, an explanation of what had happened to him up on the mountain. As ridiculous as he felt the idea was, he hoped to discover that his experience was common among saints and that his grandfather hadn't mocked him but had made a true prophecy.

He was drawn at once, though, to the many paintings inside—some of them colorful and beautiful and some of them terrifying, with illustrations of all kinds of evil creatures surrounding the praying saints. All the saints, male and female, wore long, flowing robes, and all of them wore halos. Some of the halos were bright gold discs that gleamed off the page at him. Archie ran his fingers over them to see if he could detect the difference in texture and color from the rest of the illustration. They looked so real to him. Other halos were not discs but just thin gold circles floating above the saints' heads, barely visible.

Archie read some of the text beneath the paintings and discovered that long, long ago, everybody worshiped the saints because they believed that saints could perform miracles. The book called this the cult of the saints. Archie closed the book and took a deep breath. He knew about cults. His grandfather had warned him that cults were dangerous, the work of the devil on earth, and he had sworn that he'd kill him with his own bare hands if Archie ever thought of getting involved with one. "It's soul danger, and we don't mess with that, ya hear?" Archie *had* heard, and he believed with all his heart that his granddaddy had meant what he said: He'd kill him with his own bare hands.

Archie stared at the book's cover, plain blue with black writing. Even the cover seemed like a deception. Looking at it he would never have guessed that the book held so many beautiful illustrations. One in particular caught his eye. It was a painting of the Virgin Mary holding the baby Jesus, the two of them surrounded by angels with blue-tipped wings. Most of the picture was painted in a deep, rich blue. It was a blue like he'd never seen before, and he wondered what colors the artist had to mix to come up with it. Not everything in the painting was blue. Jesus was wrapped from the waist down in a gold cloth and wore a gold halo. Mary, too, wore a halo, and the angels had hair of gold, but it was that blue in all the robes and in the wings that made him draw in his breath.

Archie thought surely a painting of Jesus and Mary would be all right to look at again. He reopened the book and found the picture. The blue was electric, and the charge ran straight through his eyes to his brain. He stared at the illustration a long time, and he felt something strange come over him. He didn't know how to explain it to himself. He felt the way he believed he was supposed to feel in church but never did: holy and close to Jesus. Archie couldn't help himself; he looked at more illustrations, read the captions, read the chapter headings, read the chapters—first one, then another, and another. "This is soul danger," he whispered to himself.

He read about the way Catholics prayed for the intervention of the saints on their behalf. They prayed for Saint Anne to protect pregnant women, Saint Apollonia to heal toothaches, and Saint Basil to protect someone unjustly accused. There were all kinds of rituals and prayers a person could offer up to each saint, and once the saint had granted someone's wish, the person was supposed to offer up still more prayers.

He read how to make a red sachet stuffed with laurel leaves and valerian and oregano, plus a piece of paper with the saint's name on it. The petitioner was supposed to burn the collection of herbs once the saint had granted the wish.

"Just like witches," Archie said. "Pure, unholy witchcraft." He closed the book again. He'd found nothing in the writings that told of an experience like the one he'd had, and he knew that his grandfather's last words were not words of praise but an accusation. "You have accused me, Granddaddy Silas," he whispered. "You meant to curse me with your words, didn't you?" His only answer was the dull pressing sensation in his stomach.

Archie stood up to return the book to Mrs. Oates and saw his grandmother's three best friends coming toward him in a line, their faces lit up with excitement.

Archie hid the book behind his back.

Mrs. Wally Hoover, short and plump, with cheeks that jiggled when she talked, was the first one to speak. "Archibald, we're all just so excited you and your grandmama will be coming to live with us. Won't it just be so much fun? And you'll love living in town. We've got the band concerts in the park, and the art festival. You'll be able to walk to them, and you know, I still play quite a mean fiddle. People always love cloggin' to my fiddle."

"Huh?" Archie looked from one to another of the women. *What is she talking about?*

Then Miss Nattie Lynn Cooper, a sturdy-looking woman who always carried her knitting stuffed in a back-pack she wore slung over one shoulder, the needles poking out like weapons, spoke up in a firm voice. "It's a good idea, Archibald. All of us have been rambling around in our big old houses all by ourselves now that our husbands and children are gone. It just makes good common sense to con-solidate and all live at my place, don't you know. And we can help one another out. I've got my heart, you know, and Callie her arthritis. It'll be good to be able look after one another."

"And don't forget, I play the fiddle," Wally Hoover said again.

"We're going to be living with y'all?" Archie asked, stunned. He imagined Wally Hoover with her fiddle, playing "The Devil Comes Back to Georgia" and shouting out to him, "Keep a-cloggin', Archibald!" He couldn't imagine how clogging the day away would make for a grand old time, especially since he couldn't dance worth a darn. And how could his grandmother sell the farm? Why hadn't she told him? Wasn't the farm supposed to go to him someday? How typical of her to do it this way, after the deed was done, and through her friends instead of telling him herself. She had gotten her friends to tell him the bad news the same way she had always gotten his grandfather to tell him anything important or painful. No wonder she had been so nervous in the truck. Archie looked at the three smiling women and felt helpless.

Miss Callie Butcher, the shortest and oldest of the three, said, "Won't it be wonderful, Archibald? We will all have the opportunity to raise you up in the way you should grow."

Archie was speechless. How could he bear to live with four women—four *old* women? Four voices telling him to wipe his feet and clean his room and study longer and turn out the light and get to bed. Four women wanting to know where he's going, where he'd been, what he's got hidden behind his back or down in the basement or out in the barn. No, he couldn't bear the thought of four women fussing over his cuts and tears and broken bones. His whole life would change. Nattie Lynn's house was close to town, which meant it had no land to speak of, just a few acres, and no woods, no ponds or streams, and no mountain rising up from behind the house like a giant hunchback—no Caswells' Mountain, his sacred mountain. How could his grandmother turn her back on her whole life, *their* whole life, and move away?

"Well, Archibald," Nattie Lynn said, "what do you think?"

Archie swallowed hard and looked at the women's smiling faces; they were waiting for him to speak, to say something, to tell them what a great idea it was. He opened his mouth but could think of nothing to say.

Callie Butcher shifted her cane to her left hand and Archie saw her hand shaking. His grandmother's hands shook, too. They always shook—from age or some secret illness, Archie didn't know, but they always shook. She was eighty-four years old. The other women were in their eighties, too; Callie, maybe in her nineties. He supposed it made sense for them to live together, just not with him.

Archie smiled as best as he could and said, "It sounds like a sensible idea, y'all living together. Me and my grandmama can talk it over later." Archie checked his watch. "But right now I got to get to some errands that need doing, so—so, if you'll excuse me." He scooted out from behind the table, nodded at the women, and hurried away, dropping the book about saints at the front desk on his way out the door.

He ran to the truck and climbed in. He pounded the steering wheel with the palms of his hands a couple of times and sat staring at the brick wall of the library, blinking back tears. Then he saw the women coming out of the library and started up the truck, backed out of the parking space, and sped off, unsure of where he was going. He wanted to go yell at his grandmother, but two thoughts stopped him. The first was that he had never in all his life known his grandmother to change her mind once it was made up, and the second was that he was afraid if he stormed into the bakery or wherever she was and yelled at her, she would collapse and die, like his grandfather had, and he couldn't live with that; things were hard enough already.

He drove through town, past the boutiques and the brick-front stores, not knowing where he was headed. Then at the end of one of the last blocks on Main Street, he noticed the only eyesore in town, a narrow, pale green home, three stories tall, with peeling paint and rotten windowsills and a sign outside that had a hand painted on it with the words PALMS READ written in bold black letters above it.

Archie had passed that house for fourteen years and had never given it much thought. His grandmother always said, "A fool and his money are soon parted," every time she happened to notice the sign or see the old woman who lived there rocking and fanning herself out on her porch. This time when he came to the house, Archie stopped. He didn't know what compelled him—a desire to get back at his grandmother by doing something he knew she'd disapprove of or a desire to know something of his future—but he turned into the driveway and shut off the engine. He stared at the sign a minute, took a deep breath, and said to the roof of the truck, "Lord, help me. What am I doing here?"

# CHAPTER

# 6

ARCHIE CLIMBED OUT of the truck and followed the arrows pointing to a side entrance. He came to a door that had the word ENTER, written on a piece of poster board, stuck in the glass window. Archie entered. Beads hung down like a curtain in front of him. He parted the beads and stepped into a hallway with a large round table in the middle of it. A bell sat on the table. Archie studied the bell. His body wanted to run, but his mind told him to ring it. He picked it up and rang the bell. A man called out, "Coming!" Archie was startled. *A man? Where is the woman?* They always saw a woman sitting on the porch, fat with long gray hair, and lots of jewelry on her hands.

He had just decided to leave, to bolt back through the beads and into the truck, when a door opened and a man stepped into the hallway. He was thin, with black hair and a long mustache that he wore waxed and turned up at the ends. Archie recognized the man. He'd seen him in town before, at the gas station and sitting on the bench outside Ye

Olde Country Store, reading the newspaper. He was wearing baggy black pants that were held up with red-yellow-
and-green suspenders.

"You want your palm read?" the man asked, smiling,
his deep-blue eyes looking eager.

"Maybe," Archie said. "I thought a woman did it,
though."

"Used to; now it's just me. You still interested?"

Archie shrugged. "I don't believe in palm reading."

The man smiled, exposing his crooked, coffee-stained
teeth. "Neither do I."

"Then why...?"

"Let's just say I'm perceptive. Anyway, people like
palm reading. I look at their palms and tell them what
the lines on their hands mean. They leave happy. Anyone
can do it. Go to the bookstore, buy a book—lots of them
around—spend about an hour studying the meanings of
the lines, and you're in business."

"'A fool and his money are soon parted,'" Archie said.

"People get their money's worth and then some, sonny."

"But you just said..."

The man looked impatient. He set his hand on the
doorknob as though ready to retreat back into whatever
room he had come out of. "I said I was perceptive. I don't
just read palms. I read *people,* but you can't put that on
a sign. Tourists wouldn't understand. They expect palm
readers in the South. They like to think they're doing something tacky and different, something they can go home and
tell their friends they've done. That's the first time. By the
end of the first visit, they're hooked—and they come back
every summer to get a reading."

grandmama's Ensure, drinking it with your meals. That hasn't worked, either."

Archie slid himself back in his seat. The man was making him uncomfortable. "You're just guessing," he said.

Mr. Simpson laughed. "Of course I am, but I'm right, aren't I?"

Archie didn't answer.

Mr. Simpson continued. "You don't like all the freckles on your face, do you? Don't worry; they'll fade when you're older. You've got an intelligent face. You're smart, but I'm not sure you read much. You're by yourself a lot, too, but you're not lonely—you just think you are. You think you ought to be lonely, but truth is you're your own best company."

Archie had never thought of that. He liked it. He liked someone telling him it was okay to enjoy being by himself. Wasn't that what Mr. Simpson was saying?

The man kept studying his face, concentrating on the eyes the longest. The way he studied him reminded Archie of the time his great-aunt, long dead, had him sit for a portrait. He'd had to hold still for hours. He was only eight. His great-aunt was surprised at how well he sat. "Some people pass out from sitting so long, but look at you, sitting just like a statue of yourself," she had said.

Archie didn't know if he was allowed to blink, but he couldn't help it, the lights in the room were so bright.

"You're a creative type, although you haven't had much of a chance to use your creativity in a big way yet." Mr. Simpson took one of Archie's hands in his and examined his long fingers. "Art?" he asked.

Archie shrugged again. "Yeah."

The man turned Archie's hand over and looked at his palm. "Calluses. Old ones."

"We rented out the farmland a few years back because my grandfather couldn't work it anymore. Clyde Olsen farms it now. I've been working for him but not lately, not since my granddaddy died."

The man returned to Archie's eyes. "You like cars. You like fast cars, sports cars. You like speed. You like baseball over football because you like the speed of the ball. You like the sound of the ball making contact with the bat. You like it because you can play it well. You can move around those bases fast, but you wish you liked football better."

"You can read that in my eyes?" Archie closed his eyes a second, then opened them again and saw Mr. Simpson still staring at him, his eyes squinting, his lips pursed.

"You're upset about something. Now I'd say it was your granddaddy, but that pain is already etched in your face; this is more recent, this is right here. You've heard some disturbing news today. Your grandmama isn't sick, I hope."

Archie flapped his hands. "What good is telling me stuff I already know? And no, she's not sick."

"Sometimes, son, we know what's happened, but we don't know how what's happened has affected us," Mr. Simpson said. "Then sometimes we don't know what we know, or how we feel about what we know. That's all."

"I could go to one of those psychologists if I wanted that kind of information."

"You could—for fifty dollars or more. Or you could talk to a friend for free. Just so happens, you came to me."

"My grandmama is going to sell our house and move us into Miss Nattie Lynn's house," Archie blurted out. "Do you know Nattie Lynn Cooper?"

Mr. Simpson nodded.

Archie told Mr. Scott Simpson, a perfect stranger, what little he knew of his grandmother's arrangements. The man didn't offer any advice; he just listened, but Archie felt better anyway. He didn't tell him about his experience up on the mountain. He thought he'd save that for another time, maybe, but then Mr. Simpson said, during a pause in the conversation that had grown too long, "Now there's something else, something... What do I see here? Something..." He paused and leaned forward to get a better look at Archie's face.

Archie resisted the urge to lean back. His heart pounded in his chest. He didn't want this stranger knowing things about him that even he was unsure of—but then again, he did. He wanted someone to know. He wanted someone to talk to.

Mr. Simpson sat up, raised his brows, and said, "You're spiritual!" He squinted at Archie and said, "Ah, but you don't like it; it scares you."

"It does? I mean, it does."

"So tell me about this saint business."

Archie was startled. He felt the pressure above his belly button and covered his stomach with his hand. "You heard about that?" he asked.

Mr. Simpson nodded. "I reckon everybody around here has heard about it. Is your granddaddy right? Are you a saint?"

Archie eyed the man, searching for a mocking glint in

his eyes, but he looked sincere. "I don't know," he said. "I don't even know what a saint is."

Mr. Simpson studied Archie, his blue eyes squinting, then not squinting, then squinting again. "I think you know very well what a saint is."

Archie turned his head away and got a shot of bright lights in his eyes. He looked down. "Anyway, I'm not a saint—far from it."

"That's too bad. The world could use more saints, don't you think?"

Archie looked at him. "I know what a saint is. I know what it feels like to be a saint," he said, recalling the minutes on his knees beneath the pine trees. He rubbed his stomach.

Mr. Simpson sat forward in his chair, as if he really wanted to know. "How does it feel?"

"It is a deep hungering and thirsting after God."

The words had slipped out of Archie's mouth before he even thought to say them. He didn't know that was what he knew until he said it, but that was what was in his heart—what had been in his heart ever since the time on the mountain.

"You know then," Mr. Simpson whispered. "You have that hunger."

"But I hate going to church on Sundays, and I've never even spoken in tongues like my granddaddy, and the only reason I'm saved is because it got embarrassing for my grandparents to stand in church every Sunday and see me just sitting there like a lump of candle wax stuck to the seat when they called the sinners to the front."

"Still, you have that hunger," Mr. Simpson said.

"Maybe," Archie said.

The two of them sat facing each other in silence. Archie was trying to read Mr. Simpson, but he couldn't.

Then Archie looked at his watch and stood up. "I got to go pick up my grandmama now, so—thanks for everything, and all," he said. "I reckon I got my ten dollars' worth."

Mr. Simpson stood up, too, and shook Archie's hand. He opened the door and let Archie out of the room.

Archie stepped into the hallway and saw a girl coming toward him wheeling a bicycle beside her. The room appeared dark to him after his sitting so long in such bright lights, and Archie could not make out the girl's face. She was just a shadow floating down the hallway.

Mr. Simpson spoke up behind Archie. "This is my daughter, Clare. Clare, this is Archibald Caswell."

Clare leaned her bicycle against her hip, shifted the apple she was eating into her left hand, and shook Archie's hand.

"I've never seen you before," Archie said, surprised, now that she was close enough for him to see her better.

Mr. Simpson said, "She's been living in North Carolina with her mama the past several years. She's living with me now."

"'Archibald Caswell,'" Clare said. "The saint."

Archie blushed and mumbled that he had to get going.

Clare grabbed his arm. Her grasp was firm, strong. "I want to talk with you."

"Yeah, sure. We'll get together sometime." Archie wanted to leave. He backed up toward the beaded curtain. Clare, still holding on, moved with him, the bicycle making a *click-click* sound as it rolled forward.

"Tomorrow," she said. She propped her bike against the wall and took another bite of her apple.

Archie shook his head. "Oh, well, I don't know. I've got stuff..."

"It's a Saturday. I'll ride out there in the morning. Be there round nine." She squeezed his arm and let go. "You'll be glad to know me, Mr. Archibald Caswell."

Archie drew in his breath, recognizing the voice. "You're the girl!"

Clare smiled, brushed past him, and said over her shoulder, "See you tomorrow."

# CHAPTER

# 7

ARCHIE AND HIS grandmother rode in silence most of the way home from town that afternoon. Then just before turning off onto the long dirt road leading to the Caswell farm, Emma Vaughn said to her grandson, "I've made arrangements with Century 21 to rent out the house for us until you're old enough to claim it for yourself. I have left it to you in my will."

Archie replied, "I'm going to the public high school next year."

The two Caswells understood each other perfectly. Archie knew it was too late to argue about the move; his grandmother had already set things in motion. Emma Vaughn knew that her grandson would no longer submit to being home-schooled, especially not by four elderly women, so nothing more was discussed by either of them that night.

Early the next morning Archie came in from mowing the lawn around the house and sat down to breakfast. He looked at his plate loaded with biscuits and gravy, bacon and eggs, and pushed it away.

"Sorry, Grandmama," he said, "but I can't eat this; my stomach is upset." He rubbed his stomach just above his belly button, where the discomfort was the greatest.

"Go fetch the Pepto-Bismol, sugar. It's in the upstairs-bathroom cabinet."

Archie stood up. "If you don't mind, I think I'll just finish up the chores you're wanting me to do. There's a girl coming to see me at nine. Her name is Clare. Clare Simpson."

"Oh?" Emma Vaughn's tiny mouth turned up. "Is this my grandson's first little girlfriend?"

Archie opened the napkin his grandmother had set by his plate and covered the food with it. Seeing all that bacon and gravy made the pain in his stomach worse. "I only just met her, Grandmama. And she's at least as tall as I am, so she's not 'little.'"

"Well, all the same, I think it's sweet." His grandmother paused and tilted her head. "*Simpson.* The only Simpsons I know live down yonder, in Talcum. Who's her daddy?"

Archie left the table and headed for the door. "You don't know him. His name is Scott—Scott Simpson."

Archie left the house and set out for the barn. Before he could get to it, he heard the screen door open. His grandmother called out, "Ivy Simpson's boy?"

Archie turned around and his body sagged. "I don't know, Grandmama," he said, the exasperation evident in his voice.

"Don't you be getting sly with me, Archibald." Emma

Vaughn came down off the porch and stood with her hands on her hips. The sun peeked out from a cloud momentarily, and Archie saw the pink skin beneath his grandmother's thinning white hair. It made him feel sad and his shoulders sagged some more.

"All I said was I don't know, Grandmama, and I don't."

"The palm reader's son?" Emma Vaughn said, tapping her foot in the mud.

"Probably." Archie picked up the hose he had used earlier that morning to rinse out the old pig trough and tried to look as if he had too much work to do to be standing around chatting.

"Did you go see that palm reader yesterday?" Emma Vaughn took a few steps closer. "Did you pay him to read your palm?"

"Grandmama!" Archie said, not wanting to admit to anything, knowing she wouldn't understand.

"Did you pay him?"

"It's my money. I earned it."

"I didn't raise a fool." Emma Vaughn shook her finger at her grandson. "You're going to go back there this afternoon and get your money back, or . . . I don't know what."

Archie threw down the hose and straightened his back. "I will not. Mr. Simpson earned it. He more than earned it. I am a satisfied customer."

Archie had never had a real argument with his grandmother before. If she'd had anything to say to him, she'd gotten Silas to say it for her. Both of them seemed to realize at the same time what they had just done, and neither one knew what to do next.

Archie stared at the mud puddles his hose had created earlier that morning, and his grandmother stared at the clouds.

Finally Emma Vaughn turned around and walked back toward the house. She stopped at the porch steps and turned around again. "You be sure to bring that Clare girl on inside and introduce her to me, you hear?" She made her voice sound firm.

"Yes, ma'am," Archie said, relieved that their first confrontation was over.

Archie worked hard the next two hours cleaning out the barn, a job he had promised his grandmother he would do a week earlier. It was a gray-brown day, according to Archie, cool yet clammy, and he was soon soaked with sweat, though the work felt good to him. His mind was so preoccupied by the argument with his grandmother and the impending move—and thoughts about the visit from Clare—that he didn't hear her come up behind him, and he jumped when he heard her say, "Good morning, Mr. Archibald Caswell."

Archie spun around and there she stood, with her bicycle leaning on her hip the way it had the day before. This time Archie could see her face, and he was surprised to realize that she was pretty. She was more than pretty. There was something extraordinarily attractive about her, although Archie couldn't identify exactly what it was. Her dark, shoulder-length hair was damp and lay flat against her forehead where her helmet had pressed down too hard. She wore no makeup, but her cheeks were ruddy and her eyes sparkled with an intense joy, as though nothing in the world was greater than that moment standing outside the barn in the gray-brown light with Archie. She was as tall as

Archie, which made her about five foot eight, and she stood with her back straight instead of hunched over the way so many tall girls Archie knew did. She had on tights and a shiny blue, form-fitting cycling shirt, and Archie could see the slender muscles in her legs and arms. Her violet eyes and her smile lit up her whole face, and Archie decided he had never seen eyes that color or teeth that white. He wiped the sweat off his face with a rag he had stuffed into his back pocket, took note of the bicycle, a Cannondale road bike, and said hello.

"Nice place you have here," Clare said.

Archie frowned. "All our land's been rented out. My granddaddy got too old to farm it, and soon the house will be rented out, too. Maybe your daddy told you that already."

Clare smiled. "No, he didn't." She looked around her and said, "I bet you're real proud of this place."

Archie looked out toward the pasture and said, "Yeah, I am—or, I was."

"You feel you belong right here," Clare said, nodding.

"Yup," Archie said, shifting his gaze to the woods and then to Clare.

Clare said, "I bet you even named all those cows out there, didn't you?"

"We got too many cows to name," Archie said, laughing. He caught a glance at Clare, blushed, and looked back out at the pasture.

"I can see you've got lots of cows, but still you've named them, haven't you?" Clare said. She pointed to the one closest to the fence. "What's her name? Bessie? Flowers? Pansy?"

Archie laughed again. "No, Freckles."

Then Clare laughed, too, a high, sweet laugh, and said, "You've named it after yourself, haven't you? I wonder why?"

Archie blushed. He didn't want her to notice his freckles, and he didn't want her to know he had named all the cows—but most of all he didn't want her to know he had named the cow by the gate (a female) after himself. Somehow he had managed in just a few seconds to give away two of his stupidest and closely held secrets. Still, he answered her. "That one's a troublemaker, just like me."

Clare tilted her head and studied Archie's face so intently it made him blush again, and he turned away. Then, realizing he was facing the wall of the barn and didn't know what to do about it, he turned back around and shrugged, keeping his eyes on the ground.

"No, I don't see you as a troublemaker at all. Quite the opposite," Clare said after she'd completed her examination of his face.

Archie lifted his head and jammed his hands into the back pockets of his jeans. "That's 'cause you don't know me," he said. Then he added, "But that card you gave me. That was you, right? How did you know...?" Archie shook his head, bewildered, not finishing the sentence.

"Oh, I knew," Clare said. "That's why I'm here, actually." She took a step toward Archie and said, "You feel like walking?"

Archie shrugged. "Okay. Want to hike up the mountain?" Archie stuck his thumb out and pointed behind him.

"Sure." Clare rested her bicycle against the barn and hung her helmet on the handlebars.

Archie led the way, speaking over his shoulder. "If you had a mountain bike, I could take you on some pretty twisted trails. They're not that long, but you can really bomb down this one steep one; it's got a pretty decent run out at the end. Oh, or would you rather walk around the fields, or go through the woods?"

Archie knew he was talking too much and sounding like an idiot, but Clare made him nervous. He liked her. He liked the way she looked at him, as though *she* liked *him*. No, it was more than that. She looked at him as though she knew all about him and loved him anyway. He'd never seen that loving expression before in anyone's eyes, not even his grandmother's. He wondered what she could have to say to him.

Archie glanced back to see if Clare was following, but she moved ahead of him as if she climbed Caswells' Mountain every day of her life and was showing him the way. She pulled a rubber band off her wrist and put her hair into a ponytail. Archie watched it swish back and forth in front of him as she walked, and he smiled. Then he noticed a price tag sticking out of her shirt, and he wondered if he should say something. It was just the two of them and he didn't care, but he had to introduce Clare to his grandmother later, and maybe she'd be embarrassed if she got home and realized she had been going around with a price tag hanging out.

Archie told her about the tag, and Clare stopped and reached back for it. She pulled it off and laughed. "My mother bought me a whole new wardrobe before I left to live with my father."

"Wow," Archie said.

Clare turned around to face him, and he saw a hint of sadness in her eyes. "She likes to know that I'm dressing appropriately at all times." She sighed and turned back around, and Archie heard her murmur, "Dear Mama."

Clare continued up the mountain, taking long strides up the steep rock-strewn path. Archie scooted to catch up with her until they were walking side by side.

"Archibald, I have come here because I believe you and I were meant to be," Clare said, knocking into Archie's side every now and again as the two of them tried to keep to the narrow path.

"Meant to be *what*?"

"Partners, soul mates, pilgrims on the same journey."

Archie cut his eyes sideways at Clare. What was she talking about? "No offense," he said, "but I'm not interested in any partners or pilgrims or whatever."

"We were predestined, Archibald. It's not about what we want; it's just the way it is."

Archie stopped walking. "Wait a minute. What are you talking about? And why did you give me that card?"

Clare stopped walking, too, and turned to face Archie. "I was told to give it to you and so I did."

"Who? Who told you?"

Clare smiled but didn't answer his question. Instead she said, "Do you know that my father had a vision about me just before I was born?"

"How would I know that? I don't have visions and I don't read people, like your father. I'm not a prophet and I'm nobody's soul mate. Sorry." He turned around as if to go back down the hill. The shining eyes he had thought were so beautiful moments before were creeping him out.

The girl was crazy. No wonder she looked at him the loving way she did. She was nuts!

Clare grabbed his arm and stopped him. "My daddy had a vision that I would someday illuminate the world—the world, Archibald. That's why he named me Clare."

"Well, that's real nice. Maybe you should go work for General Electric, become a lightbulb or something." Archie couldn't help himself. He wanted to get away, and he thought insulting her would be the quickest way to do it. He felt let down, disappointed. He realized that for a little while, when they'd been talking about the cow and she was looking at him and smiling with such love and gentleness in her eyes, that he had felt a surge of excitement. He thought maybe he'd met someone who could become a good friend. He needed a good friend.

Clare laughed at Archie's remark and didn't look insulted at all. "That's a good one," she said. Then she got serious again. "Your granddaddy's dying words were for you. He said you are a saint. Last words are important, especially ones made by a prophet."

Archie turned serious. "Do you know that all my granddaddy's predictions were of gloom and doom? They were all about sin and repentance."

"You have been *called*, Archibald. Do you dare refuse the call?" A gnat hovered near Clare's eyes. She blinked but didn't brush it away.

"I don't know what I 'dare' do. I don't know what you're talking about. What do you want from me?"

"Archibald, I am your answer. You've been searching, haven't you? You want answers. Why did your grandfather call you a saint? What did he mean? I am your answer. I am part of your journey to sainthood. Come on, let's walk and I'll tell you more." Clare set out again, taking the lead up the hill.

Archie didn't know why he followed her, except that she seemed so sure of herself, so certain, and he was so unsure about everything. He did want answers. He ran to catch up to her, and when she saw that he was with her, she smiled at him—and the smile was so welcoming and her eyes held such joy at seeing him that Archie relaxed a little and listened to what she had to say.

"Before my aunt died I used to visit her, and she had these books about the Virgin Mary and Jesus and the saints—stuff like that. I read them all. So I've known my destiny since birth practically."

"What 'destiny'?" Archie slowed down, but Clare kept marching up the hill.

"There is a Saint Clare. She was canonized—made a saint—in 1255. She was the female partner to Saint Francis of Assisi. Before she was born, her mother had a vision. And do you know what it was? That she would illuminate the world." Clare glanced back at Archie, her eyes shining. "I'm Saint Clare and you, Archibald, are Saint Francis. Those words on the card were his. Not his exact words. I translated them. He was Italian. But it's his thought—and yours, Archibald. Am I right?"

Archie caught the branch that flew toward his face after Clare brushed past it, and he sped forward to catch up with her. He grabbed her arm. "Look, I don't even know this Saint Francis. I'm not Catholic. I don't know any of this stuff, okay? My grandfather was just blathering. Sometimes he got his words mixed up. He once called a pencil a peanut! I'm sure what he meant to say was that I am a sinner, not a saint. He just got the words mixed up. Or he was just cursing me or mocking me, that's all."

"Saint Francis is one of the best-known and best-loved saints in the world!" Clare said, ignoring his words. She took Archie's hand from her arm, and she held it as she continued walking, pulling him along with her. "He was just a nobody like us till he got sick, and when he recovered, he went to pray in the church of San Damiano. That's where he heard Christ say to him, 'Repair my falling house.'"

"Sounds like he was still sick, then, if you ask me," Archie said.

"Archibald, listen." Clare smiled at him and squeezed his hand as if to say, "I understand your discomfort, but I'm here with you; it's okay." And Archie felt okay. He felt really okay. Out of the blue, just like that, with a squeeze from her hand, he felt more okay than he had felt in a long time, since before Armory had moved away and before his grandfather's illness. Archie continued up the mountain, walking hand in hand with Clare as if they'd walked that way for years, and he listened.

"In order to do what Christ had told him to do, Saint Francis sold everything he had, even the clothes off his back, and went to work on rebuilding the church. His father was so mad, because he was rich and his son was turning his back on all that; so his father disowned him and Saint Francis became like a pilgrim, traveling all through Italy, preaching about living simply and repenting."

Archie shook his head. "Okay now, I don't know what this is about, but I'm not going to tell people to repent, especially when I'm just as much a sinner as anybody. My granddaddy was always telling people to repent, and meanwhile he was rusting out his brain on liquor every day. He never had a vision sober."

Archie's eyes widened and he stopped in his tracks, pulling his hand away from Clare's. He hadn't intended to tell Clare about his grandfather. It was an unspoken promise in the family that no one would tell. Archie wasn't even supposed to know about his granddaddy's drinking. Did his grandparents think that he believed his grandfather was just filled with the Holy Spirit every time he staggered down the driveway shouting prophecies at the top of his lungs? Archie knew it was spirit all right, but it wasn't holy. He had let the information slip out in front of Clare without thinking, and he felt exposed and suddenly afraid, believing somehow that his grandfather would know and punish him for telling.

Clare said, "It's okay, Archibald. Come on—we're almost near the top." Again she smiled and looked at him with so much compassion and acceptance, his fears fell away. He blinked several times, surprised that he had to fight to hold back his tears. He didn't even know what he was feeling so tearful about—his grandfather's drinking, or Clare's loving acceptance of him?

Clare walked ahead and continued her story. "You see, Saint Francis set up a monastery and so did Saint Clare, only hers was for women, but they both took a vow of poverty and chastity and humility." Clare paused, glancing back at Archie. "Come on with me, Archibald."

Archie started walking again.

"He lived like Christ," Clare said when Archie had again caught up. "Now, weren't you always taught that nobody could be as good as Christ, and that we're all sinners, and only Christ was without sin? But the pope, I forget which one, a recent one, said that this Saint Francis was the best representative of Christ there ever was. What do you think, Archibald? Do you think it's possible for us humans to live a sin-free life? I mean never, ever sin? Could we do that?"

Archie answered, "I don't know. Maybe it was easier not to sin way back in the Middle Ages." They had reached the top of the mountain, and together they stepped out into the clearing.

"I don't think so. Hey, it's pretty up here," Clare said, turning to look around her.

Archie looked, too, feeling proud of his mountain. The sky appeared large and close, and the grass and wildflowers were beginning to poke up through the ground.

"It's so beautiful, isn't it?" Clare said, sounding delighted. She ran toward a large rock near the center of the mountaintop. It was where Archie liked to sit and think and eat his lunch. It was where he'd sat when the light changed, and the wind blew, and everything came alive and became part of him, and he a part of everything. Clare reached the rock and climbed on top.

"I'm queen of the hill!" she shouted, laughing. "Come on up!"

Archie joined her, and they stood together on the rock, looking out at the pines where Archie had fallen to his knees in worship. They were silent for a minute and then Clare spoke. "Saint Francis is also known as the patron saint of the ecologists, because he loved the earth and the animals. He spoke to them, and he believed they spoke to him. He called the sun and the wind his brothers, and the moon and water his sisters. See, he felt a kinship with all the earth." Clare turned to Archie, who stood with his mouth open. She put her hands on his shoulders. "You know exactly what I'm talking about, don't you? You know."

Clare looked at him, her eyes shining, and Archie nodded.

CHAPTER

# 8

ARCHIE DIDN'T KNOW what to make of Clare and
her strange stories. Was it possible that this Saint Francis
had had the same spiritual experience as he, and wrote
those words on the card afterward? Was it possible that he
and this girl were somehow really soul mates? What did
that mean? What did any of it mean? How could he be a
saint? His grandfather hadn't meant those words, not the
way Clare seemed to believe they'd been meant.

He gazed out at the trees. They looked somber and still
in the dull morning light. Ever since his experience, he'd
had a different feeling toward trees, as though they were
people, or at least living spirits. When he'd driven his grandmother to town the day before, he had seen men working
on the side of the road, sawing branches and limbs off an
old oak tree, and Archie had wanted to cry out for them to
stop. He'd felt the pain of the saw as if they were cutting
into his own limbs. He'd felt a sudden grief he didn't understand, as though his grandfather's death had happened

just that morning and not months earlier. He'd felt the pain most severely in his stomach, in the now familiar spot just above his belly button.

He felt the same spasm of grief every time his grandmother set down a plate of food. Until that morning he had never said anything about it to her, but each day it got harder and harder to face each meal and eat it. He would look down at a chicken breast and see the whole chicken, live and blinking at him. He'd see the pig, and the cow, and the lamb, all of them alive, and he couldn't bear to eat. When Archie was twelve his grandfather had taken him hunting, and he'd been proud to bring home his first buck, and his grandfather had been proud of him, too. A few months later he took over for his grandmother the job of selecting a chicken for dinner and wringing its neck. He had seen those as steps on the way to manhood; now the idea of hunting deer and killing chickens was physically painful to him, and he knew he couldn't do it anymore.

Clare broke into his thoughts. "Tell me what you know, Archibald. Tell me why you stare at those trees as though you're seeing Jesus Christ himself standing before you."

"I'm afraid if I tell, it will never happen again—the thing that happened, and I think—no, I *know*—I want it to happen again more than anything else I've ever wanted." He was surprised that those words had come out of his mouth. He didn't talk that way. That wasn't him. He felt his heart beating faster. He knew he would say more to this strange girl.

Clare jumped down off the boulder with a grunt. Archie followed, landing hard, too.

"Yes, Archibald, I know. You're not the only one it's

happened to." Clare grabbed his arms. "You've been given a gift, to see the world as it really is," she said, her stare and the sound of her voice intense. "You have heard the call. How will you answer?"

His eyes widened. "Has it happened to you? Have you felt the whole earth suddenly come alive? The trees and the grass, everything moved to the beat of my heart; we all had the same heartbeat, we were all one live being. Even the cows chewed their cud to the rhythm of my heartbeat. I didn't even have a body anymore, and the trees were spectacular—I can't even tell you. It's like they spoke, and they had this power and energy, and, I don't know, there was this love energy between us. It's wrong to worship trees. That's like that druid cult, worshiping trees and plants and things. But I can't help myself. I want it to happen again."

Clare shook his arms and smiled. "Yes! It can happen again. It will happen again. The Bible says God is in all things. It's not wrong to worship what's holy, and if God is in all things, then the trees are holy. You're worshiping God in them, not the trees. Everything is holy."

Archie took a step closer to Clare, excited to at last have someone with whom he could share his story. "Yes! I—I know that. I felt it. I felt that holiness."

"Archibald, it's happened to me, too. Many, many things have happened to me." She let go of Archie's arms. "See, we're meant to be together. I think that long ago most people had this kind of experience. I think it was natural. But see, now we live inside all day long and we don't know nature anymore. We don't know ourselves anymore. I think once upon a time we were all holy and we knew it, and we recognized it in one another."

"Yeah, maybe back with Adam and Eve," Archie said.

"But I believe we can know it again. I believe we can be holy again. We just have to break down the barriers we've built between the natural world and us. We have to break down the barriers between God and us."

*"Just?"*

"I know, it's not easy, but there are plenty of others who have done it. Jesus, for one, and the Buddha and Muhammad and the saints and probably others. Us, Archibald! We two are going to find the way to God. We will find a way to live so that every moment is like that moment you had up here with the trees. Every moment will be holy and we will be holy and we will see holiness in all things."

Archie stared wide-eyed at Clare. Her words, her energy, excited him. She knew what had happened to him up there on the mountain. She understood. It had happened to her.

Clare lifted her arms up to the sky. "We will live like Jesus. Jesus said the kingdom of heaven is within. We will go in search of that kingdom within. We will be pilgrims in search of God and God's pure love and holiness. We will be united with the universe. We will be saints!"

"How? How can we do this?" Archie asked, caught up in the spell of her words. He felt sure that she would know. She had the answers.

Clare lowered her arms and took Archie's hands in hers and said, "Saint Francis de Sales said, 'Sanctity does not consist in being odd, but it does consist in being rare.' You are rare, Archibald. Do you understand this? You are rare. We must live in God, not in the world, if we are to be saints."

Archie was eager to understand. "What does that mean? I don't get it. I live in the world because here's where I was born. Of course I live in the world. You say not to live in the world but in God. How? What does it mean to do that?"

"Being of the world is living in sin, Archibald. Doing sinful things and participating in a life that isn't dedicated one hundred percent to God. That's not us. We're different, you and I. We're rare. God has called us. God has chosen us. *You* have been chosen, Archibald. You can't turn your back on God's call."

Archie nodded. He knew that what he had experienced up there on the mountain was rare. He was sure it had never happened to Armory. The thought of Armory brought back the memory of their last day together down in the basement with the still, and Archie lowered his head and said, "You're the only one who believes that my granddaddy meant what he said, that I'm a saint. Even if I did have that experience, how can I believe? You don't know me—the stupid things I've done."

Clare blinked at him and touched his face, then dropped her hand by her side. "I don't need to know what you've done. That's what's on the outside. I try to look inside; you see better that way. Archibald Lee Caswell, you have been chosen."

Archie put his hand to his face where Clare had touched him and wondered, *Is Clare right? Have I really been chosen?* Maybe God had spoken through his grandfather on his deathbed. Maybe it was God who had called him a saint. Looking at Clare's beaming face, hearing her words, he felt anything was possible. His grandmother was always talking about people in the Bible who had led sinful lives, and then God touched them and they became holy people, saints even. Was he one of them? He looked at Clare. "But how are we supposed to live like Jesus? You mean exactly like Jesus, wearing sandals and toga things and preaching and wandering around and living in the desert?"

Clare sat down on the ground, pulling Archie down with her. The two of them sat cross-legged facing each other, leaning in toward each other. "I mean we give away all our possessions. We cannot serve two gods, and possessions are like gods."

"Wow!" Archie said, straightening up, shocked at the idea. "You're willing to give away your bike and stuff?"

Clare looked down and ran her hand over the grass between them. "I'm willing to give up everything for God." She looked up. "Aren't you?"

Archie thought about his bike, Giant's XTC NRS 1. It was *Mountain Biking Magazine*'s Bike of the Year and his all-time dream machine. It was the first time in his life that he felt he got the exact thing he wanted, not some cheap copy, not some used-up, make-do-for-now thing but the real deal—the same bike that Armory had. If his grandmother would let him, he would sleep with his bike—he loved it so much. Then there was his computer. He didn't have the same love for it as for his bike—it wasn't beautiful to him the way the bike was; it didn't thrill him just to lay his eyes on it the way his bike did—but it did keep him from feeling isolated. He did his schooling on it, and he got information on it, like the computer art programs he had discovered.

Archie thought about his art and then asked, "Drawing isn't considered a possession, is it? I love art. I've got to draw. I couldn't give that up. Believe me, my granddaddy tried that one already. Giving up the computer would be really tough, okay, but giving up drawing and biking—my mountain bike—that would be like giving up my life."

Clare took one of Archie's hands in hers and shook it. "But don't you see? Those are the first things you need to let go of then. We have to get rid of all the things that block us, that keep us from seeing God."

Archie pulled his hand away. "'Seeing God'?"

"Isn't that what's happened to you up here already? Maybe you didn't see an old man with a long white beard, but you did see God. Why else were you worshiping the trees? You want that experience again, don't you?" Clare scooted closer to Archie, and she spoke with whispered urgency. "What if we could feel that way, have that holy feeling all the time? All the time, Archibald, not just once. Don't you want that?"

Archie had watched Clare talking to him. He thought she was beautiful. She looked at him with such eagerness and earnestness that Archie couldn't resist her. She looked as if she was already seeing God before her, as if she could see God in him. He said, "I wonder what it would be like to have that feeling all the time? I wonder if it's even possible?"

Clare leaned forward and grabbed Archie's shoulders. Archie braced himself with his hands on the ground to keep from being pulled into Clare's lap. Still, their noses almost touched. "Yes! It's possible," she said, "and I know the way."

# CHAPTER
# 9

CLARE EXPLAINED HER vision to Archie. They would
give away all their possessions, and they would begin to
pray without ceasing. "I read it in a book," she said. "It's
called *The Way of a Pilgrim*. Only we will be saying a different prayer from the one in the book. We're going to say
it three thousand times, to start, every day. And it's best to
say it outside for now. We must be present to the real world
around us, not the artificial world of buildings and houses."

Archie felt overwhelmed by her proposal and listened
to her in stunned silence. He loved the way she looked at
him, as though he was someone special and wonderful, and
he loved her certainty about everything. He wanted that.
He wanted to feel sure about something in his life. With
Armory gone and his grandfather dead, nothing felt sure
anymore.

Clare said to him, "We will pray these words, *Be still
and know that I am God,* and each time we say the prayer,
we will think about its meaning. It's important to consider
what it means each time—three thousand times every day."

"Okay," Archie said, shocked to hear himself agreeing with her. Was he crazy? Was she?

"And we will dress simply without adornment, like monks, and we will eat simply—rice and beans and vegetables with nothing added, and no meat."

Archie rubbed his stomach. "That one shouldn't be too hard."

Clare stood up and dusted off her hands. "That's enough to start, I guess. Once we've done all that, I'll tell you the next stage."

Archie stood up, too. "'The next stage'? There are stages?"

"Of course." Clare pulled the rubber band out of her hair and redid her ponytail. She missed some of the hair, and it hung down around her small face, framing it. Archie wanted to fix her hair for her, not because he thought he could do a better job but because he wanted to touch her hair. He had a strong desire to feel in his hands the strands, warmed by the sun that had come out while they were speaking. He reached out to touch her hair, then decided the touch might be sinful, and he let his hand drop to his side.

They started back down the mountain with Clare in the lead and Archie trotting behind, listening to her plans. They were to call each other every day and report on their progress. They were to pick one outfit that they would always wear and give away the rest of their clothes. They would not watch television or listen to the radio. They would read only the Bible or other holy books of wisdom. They would get together and do their prayers every weekend until school let out, and then they would meet every day.

While Archie listened to all of this, a line from a song ran over and over in his mind: "It's the end of the world as we know it and I feel fine." Then he thought of all his CDs, all the great music he would have to give away if he actually followed Clare's plan, and he didn't feel fine at all.

When they reached the bottom of the mountain and Archie saw his house, he remembered with dread the promise he had made to his grandmother and asked Clare if she would come in and meet her.

"Oh yes, I need to tell her something. Thanks for reminding me," Clare said, leaving Archie to wonder what she could have to say to a woman she'd never met, and hoping that his grandmother wouldn't be rude to her.

Clare headed toward the house as though it were her home, striding ahead of Archie and walking through the door without hesitating or waiting for him to lead her inside. Archie scrambled to keep up and reached the foyer just behind Clare.

Clare took a look around, glancing left at the living room and right at the kitchen. She ran into the living room and said, "Look at all these beautiful flowers and all these plants!"

The plants stood on the coffee table, and the side tables, and in the two window seats, and lined up along the mantelpiece. Clare leaned over and smelled the Easter lilies that sat on the coffee table. "These smell wonderful. If I close my eyes, it's a warm sunny day out and the birds are singing and there's a waterfall in the distance."

Archie stepped forward. "You see all that just by smelling the flowers?"

"Mmm," Clare said. She went around the room, moving from plant to plant, flower to flower, like a bumblebee sampling the nectar. "Are these your grandmama's beautiful flowers?" she asked, her nose in the daffodils.

"Yeah," Archie said, surprised himself by all of the plants. When had his grandmother moved them out of the back room? "My grandmama used to just keep them in one room, the guest bedroom. My granddaddy didn't like plants growing inside. He said plants and animals belonged outdoors. I always wanted a dog. A farm needs a dog, but my granddaddy said he wouldn't let it inside, so I refused to have one." Archie sniffed one of the daffodils, noticing it didn't have much of a smell. "Anyway, as long as he didn't see them, my grandmama was allowed to have the plants in the house."

"Well, she has a real gift, doesn't she?" Clare said. "You know, I always think the most beautiful souls reside inside people who can make things grow like this, don't you?"

Archie was about to answer, but then his grandmother spoke from the doorway. "Why, thank you, honey. I appreciate that. You must be Clare."

Clare stepped forward and offered her hand. "And you're Archibald's grandmama, Emma Vaughn Caswell. I've been wanting so much to meet you."

Emma Vaughn looked surprised. "You have?"

Clare turned around and looked at all the flowers and plants. "They're such a comfort, aren't they—the plants. Like old friends, I would think," she said.

"Why, yes!" Emma Vaughn replied, and Archie noticed her face flush with pleasure and surprise. He, too, was surprised. His grandmother seemed just as taken with Clare as he was. She sat down on the couch and asked Clare and Archie to join her.

Clare sat next to Emma Vaughn and patted the seat beside her. "Come on, Archibald, and sit, so we can get to know your grandmama better."

Did Clare know how little he knew his grandmother, or was that just some figure of speech? Archie sat down beside her, wondering what she would say next.

"This is where Mr. Silas Benjamin died, isn't it?" Clare asked, turning to face Archie's grandmother. He sure hadn't expected her to say that. He watched his grandmother to see if she would break down crying or get upset with Clare for bringing up such a touchy subject.

"Well, yes, it is," Emma Vaughn said, her voice solemn. "I'm not sure I've done the right thing bringing all these plants out here, but it seemed such a pity to keep them in the back room, and like you said, they are a comfort."

"Of course they are," Clare said, glancing around again at the flowers. "And you've filled this room with life. That's important. A room needs that; a house needs it. Don't you think?"

"Yes, yes I do."

"And it's important that you do the things that give your life meaning, and I can see, Miz Caswell, that gardening does that for you."

Again a pink flush of delight spread across Emma Vaughn's cheeks. "Well gracious me, child, aren't you a surprise? Except for the kitchen herbs and these plants here, I haven't done much gardening in a long while. When I was much younger, I used to dream of creating a marvelous garden here on the farm."

Archie couldn't believe the expression on his grandmother's face. She had a faraway, enraptured look, as though she were seeing paradise before her. She told Archie and Clare all about her girlhood dreams, and for the first time in Archie's life, he saw his grandmother as a person, a real person with her own hopes and dreams and disappointments.

He had never heard his grandmother open up to anyone the way she was opening up to Clare. In a matter of minutes, Clare had her laughing and crying and divulging things Archie never would have guessed in a million years about his grandmother. She confessed that being married to Silas had been a full-time job, and she'd never had the time to create much of a garden. She said she had always loved cats. She had grown up with them as pets, and she had been so sad when she married and Silas refused to let her have any house cats. Clare even got her talking about his grandfather's prophecies and how sorry she felt for him. She told Clare how hard it had been for his grandfather to accept all the changes in the town he had loved so much, and she told her, almost whispering, that Silas drank too much.

Archie sat listening with his mouth dropped open in shock. By the end of the conversation, Clare had convinced his grandmother that she should return to her gardening and take over one of the greenhouses on the property to grow the camellias she loved so much. "But first," Clare added, "you need to get your leg looked at."

Both Archie and his grandmother looked flabbergasted.

Archie said, "What's wrong with her leg?" and at the same time his grandmother asked, "How could you know about my leg? I've told no one."

Clare smiled. "I saw you limping when you came into the room, and when you sat down you bit your lip like it hurt an awful lot to sit. It's your leg, isn't it? Your right one."

"I hadn't even noticed," Archie said. He leaned forward in his seat to get a better look at his grandmother. "Grandmama, is this true?"

"Well, yes. Yes, it is. I thought it was just my sciatica acting up."

Clare said, "But you know it isn't. That's why you've got so much worry. I can see it in your eyes. You need to take care of that leg and let a doctor look at it, and all your other worries will take care of themselves. You've got a greenhouse to fill and a cat or two to add to your household, and Archibald here to love."

Archie and his grandmother looked at each other, and Archie saw tears in his grandmother's eyes. He smiled at her and looked away, touched by the love he felt coming from her. At that moment he felt closer to her than he'd ever been before.

Before Clare left, Emma Vaughn had promised her that she would make an appointment with the doctor and would begin planning a garden and clearing out the greenhouse for her camellias. Archie wondered if his grandmother had forgotten her plans to move in with her lady friends. If she had, he wasn't going to remind her of it.

Archie walked with Clare out onto the porch, and when he had closed the door behind him so his grandmother couldn't hear, he asked her, "What did you do in there? Her face is all lit up like a Christmas tree. I've never seen her like that. I never knew all those things she told you." Archie shook his head in wonder. "I just never knew."

"I'm just seeing her, Archibald, and loving who I see. That's all." Clare hugged him good-bye, then ran to her bicycle and rode away, waving as she pedaled down the drive.

Archie waved back and watched her until she rode out of sight.

CHAPTER

# 10

THE DAYS PASSED AND Archie didn't do any of the things Clare had told him he must do. He thought about what he was supposed to be doing a lot, daydreaming instead of doing his schoolwork, asking himself if he could ever say that prayer three thousand times in one day, in one sitting. How long would it take him? He watched the television and wondered what it would be like not to see his favorite shows anymore, especially the old reruns of the Laurel and Hardy shows and *Star Trek*.

Archie looked at all the drawings he had taped up on the walls of his bedroom. While his grandfather had been alive, Archie had kept his drawings hidden in his closet because his grandfather had once torn up a whole morning's worth of work after he discovered Archie had been in his room drawing instead of out baling hay with Clyde and the other workers. Archie had tried to explain that he had lost track of the time, but that was no excuse. His grandfather grabbed the papers in his fist and shredded them and left them on the floor of Archie's bedroom for him to pick up. Because his grandfather was gone, Archie felt it was at last safe to take his drawings out of hiding and spread them all over the room by taping them to the walls. How could he give up the pleasure and comfort his drawings gave him, especially since he had the freedom to draw and display whatever he liked?

Archie sat at his computer and stared at the screen. He knew that if he and Armory were still writing back and forth, he wouldn't be able to give up the computer even for a day, but now he wondered. Armory hadn't written him at all to apologize or explain what had happened on the phone when Archie had called. Archie wrote him once to see if he could find out, but Armory had never answered him and so he gave up. He realized the friendship was over.

He wondered what Armory would think if he told him about Clare. How would he describe her? Armory wouldn't believe him if he told the truth. He'd tell Archie that Clare was crazy, that the whole saint scheme was totally insane. When Archie thought about trying to explain everything to his old friend, it did sound crazy, even to him, but when he thought of Clare's visit and the way he had felt when he was with her—special and accepted, loved, even, just the way he was; skinny, lost Archibald Lee Caswell—her vision made perfect sense. Didn't she say he had been called? Didn't she say he was rare? Why then was he hesitating? He wanted to do it, didn't he?

Archie couldn't get the memory out of his head of that day up on the mountain when he'd been down on his knees before the pines. He couldn't get rid of the memory of that feeling he'd had up there, and he wanted to experience it again—experience God. He wanted to see Clare again, too, but what if she was wrong? What if he wasn't "rare"? What if he hadn't been called, and it was just his grandfather's way of getting to him one last time? What if he tried to do the things Clare had told him to do and he failed? He hated the thought of disappointing her—and God. He wanted it to be as easy as the first time, but no matter how many times he biked up the mountain and sat on the boulder eating a lemon, that wonderful, holy experience never happened again.

The only thing easy for Archie was giving up meat. That was one rule he could follow. His stomach wouldn't let him eat it. He told his grandmother not to cook him any more meat or poultry or fish.

She looked horrified. "What will you eat then? You're already skin and bones. You need your protein; you're a growing boy."

"I'll eat grains and beans and vegetables," he said.

His grandmother set her hands on her hips. "Well now, why don't you just go on out there with the cows to do your grazing and I won't have to cook at all."

Emma Vaughn had changed. She had made a doctor's appointment, and although she had to wait until her doctor got back from his vacation, just making the appointment had taken a load of worry off her mind. She had also started cleaning out the greenhouse, and she whistled in the mornings when she cooked breakfast and sang in the bathtub in the evenings. The greatest change, though, was that she spoke her mind and in no uncertain terms, and even though that meant she got after Archie every so often, he was pleased with the change and grateful to Clare for the way she had helped his grandmother.

Archie tried to explain his troubles with eating meat without getting his grandmother too riled up. "Grandmama," he said, "I would eat meat if I could, but my stomach just has a violent reaction to it these days. I don't know why. But you don't have to do anything extra. I'll get the groceries and I'll cook my own food, too."

Emma Vaughn shook her finger at Archie and said, "I've been cooking for seventy-nine of my eighty-four years, and I'll be cooking till I die, Archibald Lee Caswell—and don't you forget it. You'll get what you get, and if it's not good enough . . . well, then I don't know what."

Archie got what he got, but he wouldn't eat the meat. He ate the vegetables and the rice, but if his grandmother made a meal with everything cooked together in one pot, like a stew or a casserole, he didn't eat at all.

Archie thought the stews were tricks his grandmother tried to get him to eat meat. He knew she couldn't believe he'd go without eating just because something had meat in it, but he did.

"You're a stubborn boy," she said to him one night when he once again refused her stew and got up from the table.

"No, Grandmama, you're a stubborn woman," Archie replied, "and I still can't eat the meat. I'm sorry."

Archie made up for the missed meals by going down to the kitchen after his grandmother had cleaned up and making a couple of peanut-butter-and-jelly sandwiches to eat in his room. He knew his grandmother had to know about it, since the peanut butter and jelly jars were emptying out more quickly, but she never said anything and neither did he.

Archie didn't call Clare that first week after they had gotten together, or the week after that, either, and she didn't call him to see why he hadn't called. He felt guilty about it. He remembered Clare's face, her radiance, that light in her eyes, and he felt ashamed, but he had nothing to report, so he didn't call. However, as the days passed, something inside Archie began to shift, and it shifted so slowly that he didn't even notice. It began with his schoolwork. He always did his work listening to music, but one day the music seemed too loud and he found it hard to concentrate, so he turned it down. A little while later the music sounded too loud again, and he turned it down some more. That kept happening until, by the end of the afternoon, he had turned his music off altogether. From that day forward he didn't listen to music while he studied.

A few days later he decided that his bedroom felt too crowded. All the time that he spent outside on top of the mountain made him more aware of the confinement he felt when he was in his room with the door closed. The old model cars he had collected over the years distracted him, and besides, he told himself, he was too old for model cars. He put them in a box and took them down to the basement. Archie had cleaned out every trace of the still while his grandfather had been in the hospital, but the memories of that afternoon with Armory and his grandfather were still vivid in his mind, and he set the box down and hurried back up the steps as fast as he could. His grandmother was standing with a puzzled expression at the top of the stairs.

Archie, believing she wanted to know what he was doing, told her he was packing up some things for the move, and she looked at him with her hands caked in dirt and her eyes shining and said, "Archibald, I'm confused." Then she wandered back out to the greenhouse, not saying why she was confused. Archie guessed it was because she was still making plans for the move with her friends to Miss Nattie Lynn's house, while at the same time she was planning her garden at home.

Archie returned to his room and looked at all the art and comic books he'd read and the piles of biking magazines. What did he need those around for, collecting dust and crowding him to distraction? He wasn't going to read them again. He loaded them into more boxes and carried the boxes down to the basement. But then there were all the empty shelves in his room waiting to be filled up again. He didn't want that, or he'd be right back where he'd started— all squished up with no room to move around. He wanted space. Suddenly he couldn't get enough space. He hauled off the shelves and all of his CDs and his radio/CD player. He took the television out of his room. There was one in the living room he could watch, he reasoned.

By the end of that third week since he had seen Clare, his room held a bed, a desk and chair, his computer, a chest of drawers full of clothes, and his art supplies. By then Archie realized that he had begun to do the things Clare had told him he should do, but still he did not call her. He hadn't done those things to get closer to God and become more of a saint. He had done them because the clutter and the noise bothered him. When he went to church with his grandmother, even on Easter Sunday, he still tugged at the collar of his dress shirt and fell asleep during the sermon, and he never felt saintly in the least while he was there. In truth, Archie didn't want to go to church anymore. He didn't know what he wanted, but he knew that whatever it was, it wasn't at the church. That was his grandfather's church, not his. He told his grandmother that, expecting an all-out war over his decision, but she surprised him, saying, "You're old enough to make your own choice about that."

Archie didn't attend any other church after his discussion with his grandmother. His church, he felt, was on the mountain. He spent more and more time up there, lying on his back in the grass, staring up at the sky and the tops of the trees, and occasionally saying the words Clare had given him to say, trying them out: *"Be still and know that I am God."* He thought about the prayer. That's what Clare had said they should do—think about what the words mean. Every time he thought about it, though, lying on the mountain with his eyes closed and whispering the words— *"Be still and know that I am God"*—the meaning was slightly different: *If I am still, I'll know who God is. If I'm still, I'll know that God is here, with me. If I'm still, I will know that God is everywhere. In the stillness, I'll feel God's presence. In the stillness, I'll feel God's presence in me and around me.*

Archie would think those thoughts for a while, and then his mind would start to wander, and before he knew it he'd fall asleep. He liked sleeping on the mountain and waking up to the late-afternoon songs of the birds or the warm sun on his face. One day, though, he awoke and said to himself, "It's time to call Clare."

He returned to his house. He looked around for his grandmother and then remembered Clyde Olsen had come by earlier to take her on her round of errands. He looked at the clock. It was after four. He knew Clare would be home from school by then, and in the back of his mind, he thought his grandmother should have been home by then, too.

He found Clare's number in the phone book and called her.

Mr. Simpson answered and Archie felt relieved. He would tell Clare who was on the phone. She could refuse to come to the phone if she was mad and didn't want to speak to him.

He heard Mr. Simpson call to her, and he heard him say Archie's name. Then there was a pause, and Archie's heart began to beat faster. Clare's voice said, "Hello," and he couldn't speak. He didn't know what to say or how to explain himself.

"Archibald, are you there? Archibald? How are you doing?"

"Uh—"

"Archibald?"

"I—uh—I'm trying to do all those things we talked about. I wasn't planning on doing them because . . . well, I thought maybe it would be really hard and maybe I wouldn't be good at it. I mean, maybe I'd fail—or something. But you know what? It's not so hard. I mean, I'm not doing everything. I'm not saying that prayer thing three thousand times, more like about thirty, but I've cleared out my room some, and I don't listen to music while I study anymore, and I'm hardly ever on the computer . . . I don't know; I think I want to get serious about this. I think I want to try it all and see what happens. If you're still willing to do this with me, I mean." Archie stopped talking and waited for Clare to say something. She didn't speak right away, so Archie said, "What do you think?"

"Of course I'm willing, Archibald. We're soul mates, aren't we? We'll say the prayer together. It's hard keeping count, isn't it? Why don't you just try praying for three hours."

"Three hours? Wow."

"You should try it first. Then you'll say *Wow.* Anyway, we could get together on weekends and say it together. School will be out soon; then we can get together more often."

Archie was about to agree with Clare's plans and arrange a meeting time when he heard the call-waiting signal. He said, "Clare, hold on, someone's on the other line."

It was Clyde Olsen and he sounded shaken.

"Archibald," he said, "I've been trying to call you for hours. I don't know how it happened, but I'm afraid your grandmama's gone and broke her hip. She's here in the hospital. Can you get yourself down here?"

Archie said, "I'll be there as soon as I can." He hung up the phone, grabbed his grandfather's keys off the counter, and ran out to the truck, forgetting all about Clare waiting on the other line.

# CHAPTER

# 11

C LYDE OLSEN WAS WAITING for Archie when he arrived at the hospital. Archie saw him, thin and haggard-looking, standing at the nurses' station in his overalls with his hat in his hand, looking out for him. Archie waved, and he saw relief spread across Clyde's face. Clyde said something to the nurse, and she came out from behind the counter and the two of them greeted Archie when he arrived at the nurses' station.

"I'm Mrs. Little," the nurse said to Archie, extending her hand.

Archie shook it, looking at Clyde, whose expression had changed back to worry.

"Your grandmother has broken her hip, which given her age is quite serious," the nurse said. She'd begun walking down the hall, so Archie and Clyde followed. "She's still groggy from the anesthesia, so you won't visit for too long, will you?"

"No, ma'am."

The nurse pointed. "She's right at the end of the hall, room three-sixty. When you're through, come back to the nurses' station and I'll have you fill in some of the blanks Mr. Olsen left on the insurance forms for your grandmother."

"Yes, ma'am," Archie said. He looked at Clyde, who only nodded.

"How did it happen?" Archie asked him once the nurse had gone.

Clyde shook his head. "I don't rightly know, Archibald. I had dropped her off at the post office while I went on to get some gas. When I returned she saw me and stepped off the curb, and in one split second I saw her face twist up with pain and her body just crumple beneath her. It was terrible. She was in such pain, and I just couldn't lift her. There wasn't any way without her crying out in agony like I was breaking her to pieces. I just couldn't move her. So I called the ambulance." Clyde finished his story as they arrived at Emma Vaughn's room.

Archie said, "Thanks, Clyde. Thank you for looking after Grandmama."

Clyde gave a quick nod and shook Archie's hand. "You need anything else, son? Need a lift back home?"

"No, I'm fine. I got the truck."

Clyde put his hat on his head and a soil-encrusted hand on Archie's shoulder. "Well then, I'm gonna head on home. I'll drop off your grandmama's groceries on the way, if that's all right. I'll set them on the kitchen table for you."

Archie watched Clyde walk down the hall a moment, then turned and stepped into his grandmother's room.

Emma Vaughn lay still in the bed on the other side of the room. Her eyes were closed, and the television was on.

A nurse was fussing with an IV bag and watching the TV. She pressed a button to turn it off and said, "I think she's sleeping."

"No, I'm not, either. Is that you, Archibald?" His grandmother opened her eyes and, seeing her grandson, reached out her hand.

Archie stepped forward and took it. "Hey, Grandmama, how you doing?"

"I'm doing all right for the moment, and I want to take full advantage of this bliss medication they got me on and get some good sleep, because I know when it wears off I'm going to be in a lot of pain, so I'm not going to talk to you long."

"Yes, ma'am."

His grandmother lifted her head off the pillow and leaned toward Archie. "You listen to me now, you hear? I want you to go on to Nattie Lynn's house and stay there. She'll take good care of you."

"Grandmama, you lay yourself on back down." Archie patted her shoulder, and she fell back on the pillow. "Now, I'm fourteen years old. I don't need anybody looking after me. I'll be fine at home. I'm practically an adult. Shoot, I'm driving, aren't I?"

"Listen, Archibald. I don't know how long I'm going to be in here. I reckon I shouldn't have waited for my doctor to get back from vacation and should have had this leg seen to sooner, but no use crying over it now. I'm here and here's where I'll be for a while, but when I get out, we're moving to Nattie Lynn's whether the house is rented out or not. So you might as well move on over there now. You do as I say, you hear me?"

"But what about your camellias and your big garden idea?" Archie asked.

"I can grow a flower garden at Nattie Lynn's just as well. It's more important that you've got people looking after you. Now you go on. Go on over there right now."

"Yes, ma'am," Archie said, but when he left the hospital that evening, he went straight home, put up the groceries Clyde had left, made and ate two peanut-butter-and-jelly sandwiches washed down with a can of warm Coke, and then went to his room to try three hours of praying without ceasing.

He closed his eyes and began praying. It was just as hard to do as he'd imagined, because his mind kept wandering. He thought about his grandmother and wondered what he would do if she died. She had always had so much energy and acted much younger than all of her friends that Archie thought of her as living forever, or at least until he was through college. But she looked old in the hospital, with her hair drawn back off her face and so much white surrounding her—white sheets, white blankets, white hospital gown. She looked just like a ghost, pale and weak.

Archie wondered if his grandmother had made arrangements with someone to take care of him if she died. He thought about Clyde Olsen. He was the youngest friend his grandmother had, but he was fifty and had never married, which his grandmother always thought was peculiar, so Archie didn't think she would choose him. All of her lady friends were worse off than she was, as far as Archie could tell, and he hoped that now that his grandmother was in the hospital, the whole four-ladies-and-Archie-living-together plan would be put on hold. But already the phone had rung three separate times that night, and after he answered the first call from Miss Nattie Lynn, who told him that she had expected him for dinner and asked him what he was doing at home, Archie let the answering machine pick up the other two calls.

Archie thought that if he legally couldn't stay on the farm by himself, then he would want to go live with Armory and his family. They owned a big, fancy townhouse in Georgetown, a neighborhood in Washington. They had plenty of room for Archie and plenty of money. Then Archie remembered he and Armory weren't friends anymore. How could he have forgotten that? He felt tears stinging his eyes and uneasiness in his stomach. How could he live without his grandmother? How could he even think of it? With her in the hospital, he realized how much he really loved her. He knew if anyone was a saint, she was, for putting up with him and his grandfather. Maybe, he thought, his granddaddy had really been pointing at her the day he died.

Archie didn't want to think about death anymore. He opened his eyes and looked at his watch. He had been ruminating on his situation for thirty minutes, and his prayers had been long forgotten. "Some saint I am," he said. He lay back on his bed and started again. He lasted more than an hour before he fell asleep with his prayer on his lips.

A few hours later he awoke to find himself outside on the edge of his grandfather's old tobacco fields. He stood fully clothed, except for his shoes, beneath the moon and the stars. He felt their light all around him, soft and misty. He looked up into the sky and felt so overwhelmed by what he saw—the millions of stars, the fat full moon so close he felt he could reach out and wrap his arms around it—that he fell to his knees in tears. Once again his body lost its boundaries and he became the stars and the moon and the whole sky, and the earth beneath him. Tears streamed down his face, but he didn't notice. He felt overcome with love for God and humbled by the strong feeling of God's love for him. Over and over he felt the words *I AM* beating in his chest, pulsing through him, pulsing through everything around him. "I AM," he said out loud. Then these thoughts ran through his mind: *We are connected to this earth. There is life in all things. There is God in all things. There is God in me. The trees are holy. I am holy. A saint is holy. I am a saint.*

# CHAPTER

# 12

IN THE EARLY MORNING Archie sat up in the field, and his surroundings appeared as they always had and his body felt as it usually did, separate, and heavy with weight. But things were different just the same. Inside he had been changed. He knew things he hadn't known before. He knew the Kingdom of God was in him. It was in all people. He had read about the Kingdom of God in the Bible before and had never really understood what the Kingdom was. But the night before he had felt it. Until that night he always had prayed to something "out there" or "up there" in the sky. He had never thought to pray deep inside himself, to the indwelling God. He'd never understood that the "I AM" of God was inside him. When he prayed he always prayed for God to give him something—an A on a test, or a dual-suspension mountain bike for Christmas, or for his grandfather to get well.

The previous night he'd realized that all the things that happened to him in his life were perfect, and were as they should be. Good or bad, it was all God, and all right. He wanted to hold on to the thought, to all the great feelings he had had the night before. He wanted to hold on to God. But when he returned to the house and took a shower, he could feel it all starting to slip away from him, and his worries about his grandmother and his future were moving in to take God's place. He had felt so full, so wonderfully full of God's love for him. Why couldn't he feel that always? Why couldn't that feeling stay strong and close, the way it had been just a few hours before? He had never felt anything so perfect and so good. Was it possible to always feel that way? Clare had said it was. She had said they just had to follow the way of the pilgrim. They had to say that prayer and focus on God. He thought of Clare's face. When she had looked at him up on the mountain and taken his hand, she had loved him. He wanted that. He wanted to see her again and to feel her love for him.

"Clare!" He had forgotten all about her. He'd hung up on her. *What will she think of me now?* he wondered. He ran to the phone and called her up. A very groggy and hoarse Mr. Simpson answered the phone.

Archie asked to speak to Clare.

"It's not yet six o'clock, on a Saturday, Archie. I doubt she's up. Let me go see," Mr. Simpson said.

A few minutes later Clare picked up the phone. "Archibald? What happened yesterday? Is everything all right?"

"I'm sorry I hung up on you. Clyde Olsen was on the other line. He said my grandmama broke her hip."

Clare's voice softened. "Oh, Archibald, I'm so sorry. What can I do? How can I help?"

"Can you come over? Now? I need to talk to you. I— I need to see you."

"I can come, but it will take me a while because I'm walking everywhere these days."

"Couldn't you ride your bike, just this once? I really need to see you as soon as possible." He didn't know why, but as he spoke he felt a lump form in his throat, as though he were trying to keep from crying—and he was. He felt ridiculously emotional.

"All right, I'm there," she said.

Archie said, "Thank you," then realized he was talking to the dial tone and hung up.

Clare arrived on her bike in less than forty-five minutes. It looked as if she was still in her pajamas. She wore a pair of baggy flannel pants with bands around the bottom of both legs to keep the fabric from getting caught in the chain ring and a worn-out long-sleeved Tar Heels T-shirt. She had thrown on an old tattered jacket with a broken zipper, over the shirt. When she took off her helmet, her hair was in tangles.

Archie thought he had never seen anyone look more beautiful in his life. He grabbed her and hugged her hard. "Thank you for coming." He let go.

"Well, look at you!" she said. "You're glowing."

"Really?" Archie blushed. "I think *you* are."

"Tell me what's happened, Archibald."

Archie told her about his grandmother's broken hip and how he had come home from the hospital and had tried to say the prayer for three hours, but he had been too worried over his grandmother to concentrate. Then he told her what had happened out in the tobacco field. When he had finished he said, "Nothing had changed, you know? Grandmama was still in the hospital, but I felt wonderful. I felt God's love, really strong inside me, and I felt everything was okay. I wish I could always feel like that, no worries."

"You can," Clare said.

"I tried to hold on to that feeling, but I couldn't. I want to. I mean, it's addictive, that kind of thing."

Clare laughed and placed her hand on the top of Archie's head. "You have been blessed," she said.

Archie nodded and looked into Clare's shining eyes. "I think I have. I don't know why, but I have."

Clare took his hand in hers. "Come on. Let's go climb your mountain and get praying."

Archie glanced at his watch. He had promised his grandmother he'd go by to visit and take her bed jacket to her after noon. It was only seven-twenty; he had plenty of time.

The two of them climbed in silence. The day was raw and gray—a pure gray, Archie called it. He had wanted the day to be sunny to match the way he felt, and instead it looked like it might rain. This time as they went up the mountain, Archie had no problem keeping up with and even passing Clare. At first he had followed behind her, noticing that she looked thinner than he had remembered. Then he felt he couldn't get to the top fast enough, and he surged ahead. Once they reached the top, Archie ran to the trees and dropped to his knees. Clare sat down beside him. Together they recited their prayer, over and over. As the morning moved on, the sky grew darker and it rained. Archie tilted his head up and let the rain fall on his face, big, heavy drops of water.

"This is perfect," he said, getting to his feet. "This will be my baptism. This is holy water pouring down on me."

Clare stood up, too, and lifted her face to the sky. "We will be purified. Our sins will be washed from our bodies and souls. We will go forward from this day and sin no more."

Archie kicked off his Nikes and, ignoring the cold, pulled off his socks, jacket, and shirt and spread his arms wide. "I'm ready, God!" he said, shouting to the sky.

The rain came down harder. Thunder rolled overhead. Clare pulled off her shoes and socks and ran with Archie over the mountaintop, the wind and the rain pushing against them. They cried out to the thunder and to the rain and to the wind and sky, calling them their brothers and their sisters. They ran toward the east, and toward the west, toward the north and the south. They climbed up onto the boulder and, clasping hands, raised their arms and let the rain bless them and purify them. Archie let out a howl, and Clare laughed until tears ran down her face.

After several more minutes, the rain began to slacken and the wind died down. The thunder rolled away and the sun pushed through the clouds.

Archie spoke in a whisper. "We have been purified." He turned to Clare and took her hands in his. "We are like Adam and Eve in Paradise." Clare squeezed his hands, and together they turned and jumped off the boulder. They walked hand in hand back to the trees and knelt on the ground. Again they said their prayer, the same line over and over again. Each time Archie said the words "I AM," he felt the power of the words in his body, and most forcefully in that spot just above his belly button.

Archie and Clare prayed and prayed until they felt emptied of all but the prayer. Then they grew quiet and still and remained that way until the sun burned the backs of their heads and Clare said it was time to leave.

Without speaking they took each other's hand and descended the mountain. When they reached the bottom and came out from behind the house, Archie spotted a familiar car in the driveway: Callie Butcher's hearse-mobile, as Armory liked to call it, an antique black Cadillac. Then they heard a woman's voice from inside the house exclaim, "There he is! Thank the good Lord!"

Miss Nattie Lynn and Miss Callie Butcher pushed open the screen door and stepped out onto the porch.

"Lord have mercy, child, you gave us a scare," Callie said, waving her cane at the two of them. "We saw that soggy bowl of raisin bran with the sour milk in the kitchen and thought...I don't know what. Where have you been? Your grandmama has charged us to look after you, and you were nowhere to be found. And look at you; you're soaking wet—both of you. Now, y'all come on in here and get out of those clothes before you catch your death, and let us fix you something to eat."

The two women turned back into the house, and Archie and Clare followed them.

Once inside, Callie, short and humpbacked, took over, ordering Archie to find some dry clothes for Clare and ordering Clare to take the clothes into the bathroom and to clean up and change. Then she told them both to hand over their wet things so she could wash them. They did what she asked. When they came into the kitchen, both of them clean and in dry clothes, Nattie Lynn set a plate of grilled peanut-butter-and-banana sandwiches down on the table and ordered them to sit. Then she poured them each a glass of milk and told them to eat.

Archie and Clare did as they were told. The two old women sat down between them, with their mugs of coffee, and Nattie Lynn said, "Now then, why don't you tell us who this young lady is, Archibald. I don't believe we've had the pleasure."

Archie swallowed a bite of sandwich and said, "This is Clare Simpson, a *very* good friend of mine."

Clare grinned at Archie.

*"Simpson,"* said Nattie Lynn, looking up toward the ceiling.

Callie said, "Mildred and Scott Simpson's little girl?"

"Yes, ma'am," Clare said, looking at her.

Callie shook her head. "Why, that just can't be. You were just a baby not too long ago."

Clare swallowed a big gulp of milk, then said, "I'm almost sixteen years old now, and I'm tall like my mama."

"Well, I declare. You're all grown up." Callie turned to Nattie Lynn. "Isn't she?"

"Oh my, yes indeed. Baby Doris—sixteen years old already."

Clare choked on a bite of her sandwich, and Archie patted her on the back. "Are you all right? Can you speak?" he asked.

Clare nodded, and Callie, seeing that she was fine, turned back to her friend and said, "Her name is Clare, honey, not Doris."

Nattie Lynn shook her head. "Oh no. I remember Mildred telling me her name was Doris. It's Doris. Isn't it?" She looked to Clare for confirmation.

Clare glanced at Archie, then said, "I am Clare, Miss Nattie Lynn."

"Well, I'm sure you're not," Nattie Lynn said.

Callie patted her friend's hand. "Honey, if she says her name is Clare, then her name is Clare. She ought to know. Anyway, there's no use going on about it."

Nattie Lynn frowned and stared down at her hands wrapped around her mug.

Clare rested her hand on Nattie Lynn's shoulder. "I'm sorry I've upset you, and here you have gone to such great trouble to fix us this lunch and make me feel so welcome."

Nattie Lynn looked up at Clare's shining eyes. "Nonsense," she said, "it's just a sandwich."

Clare shook her head. "Not 'just a sandwich'; there's a secret ingredient you've added to it, something special. I'm not sure what it is, but I bet you make all your meals special."

Nattie Lynn blushed and waved her away. She looked at Callie, who was smiling across from her. "I reckon I do have a way with food."

Clare turned to Callie. "And Miss Callie, what do you love?" she asked.

"Me? Why I love animals," Callie said, her brows raised; she was surprised by the question.

Clare smiled and nodded. "I believe God has prepared a special place in heaven for people who have been so good to the animals."

Callie's face turned sad and she lowered her head, her humped back looking even more bent. "I've had animals all my life. I grew up on a farm, and then when I was on my own, I always had cats and dogs and my parrot, Sugar Pie." Callie looked up at Clare. "She died last year, you know. Now I have no more animals, just my dear friends." She reached out and patted Nattie Lynn's hand, and Nattie Lynn smiled.

"Have you ever thought of volunteering down at the animal shelter? They always need people to love the pets."

Archie didn't know what to make of the whole scene. Within minutes Clare had Miss Callie excited about working at the shelter, and Miss Nattie Lynn sharing the secrets in some of her famous recipes for the first time in her life. Clare kept talking to them, and never once did Archie hear them complain of heart problems or arthritis the way they usually did when the women got together.

Clare asked them odd questions. She asked them what their strongest held belief was. She asked them why they thought they were put on this earth, and what did they feel was the cross they were given to carry through their lives, and what was their greatest joy.

By the time Clare told them she had to get going, Callie and Nattie Lynn were so fired up with energy, they offered to drive her home, and the two women set out toward the barn to fetch her bike as though they were going to lift it into the trunk of Callie's hearse-mobile themselves. Archie refused to let them lift the bike. He loaded it into the trunk and waved good-bye to them as they rolled down the driveway, relieved they had forgotten that they had come there to try to convince him to return home with them.

When they had gone Archie stood staring after them and wondering what had just happened. He thought about the way Miss Nattie Lynn had confused Clare's name, thinking she was someone called Doris. The woman had been upset by the confusion, but Clare had managed to make her forget about it and had redirected her thoughts. Clare seemed sincere with her compliments and her interest in the two women, just as she had with his grandmother, and with him, too, but Archie wondered if it was just Clare's way with people, or had she manipulated them on purpose, to get herself out of an uncomfortable situation?

# CHAPTER

# 13

WHEN ARCHIE RETURNED from visiting his grandmother that night, he fell into his bed exhausted. The hospital had drained him. His grandmother's room had seemed airless. She had slept most of the afternoon, and the rest of the time she'd tried to convince Archie to go and stay at Nattie Lynn's house, but Archie had refused. He turned on the television to try to distract her, but the sounds of the voices coming from the box and the flashes of light as the scenes changed annoyed him. Television, he realized, was just one more obstruction between him and God, and right then he vowed never to watch it again. He turned it off and stared at his sleeping grandmother. He tried to pray, but he couldn't concentrate. He felt tired and restless at the same time. Later he watched her eat dinner, and then said good-bye and rode home on his bike. It had felt good to get out in the fresh night air. The temperature had dropped, and the cold air blew down on him from the mountains. It kept Archie awake and alert, but once home he felt the fatigue and couldn't wait to climb into bed.

Lying on the bed Archie closed his eyes and prayed. He wanted God. He wanted to feel the bliss, the ecstasy that he had felt in the tobacco field and again up on the mountain with Clare, being baptized by God's holy water. He didn't want to worry about his grandmother. He didn't want to keep wondering what would happen if she died. She had looked so frail that afternoon, lying in the bed, doped up on pain medication. Seeing her that way scared him.

Archie prayed. "Use me, Lord. I want to serve you. Show me how to serve you. Please, God, show me." Tears fell from his eyes; his desire was so great, and so was his fatigue. He was tired, yet he couldn't sleep. He grabbed his wool blanket, rose from his bed, and went outside to sit in the rocker on the porch, where he rocked and prayed until at last he fell asleep.

Over the next two weeks, Archie spent as much time as he could each day praying and meditating on the mountain. When he came down in the evenings, he would find messages waiting for him on the answering machine. His grandmother's friends called to check up on him and to let him know they had been by to see him. Other callers just wanted to know how his grandmother was doing. Reverend Fox asked why he hadn't seen Archie in church lately and offered to find him rides to church and to the hospital. Bruce, Art, and Mr. Flyte from his baseball team wondered why Archie hadn't shown up for tryouts, and two friends from his home-schooling group wondered where he had been and if he still planned to go on the camping trip to the Smokies with them. Archie deleted the messages. All of those people seemed like friends he had known in another lifetime. They had nothing to do with him now.

Sometimes at night he would sit down at his desk and draw. One night, though, he picked up his colored pencils and tried to finish his drawings for another story about the Back Street Thrasher, but the story seemed stupid to him and his illustrations a waste of time. He sat with his work and stared at the frames on the page. He had drawn the sequence like a comic strip, just like the other illustrations he'd taped to the walls of his bedroom. He looked at them and wondered how his stupid drawings served God. He drew a tree in the space he'd left blank on the page, then tore the whole thing up. Nothing felt right to him anymore, except praying and waiting for God. He'd told Clare that all he wanted to do was pray, and she had said that he could then move on to the next stage and instead of saying "Be still and know that I am God" for three hours, he should say "Be still and know that I am" for *four* hours, and spend the rest of the time in silence and stillness.

Archie was surprised that taking away the word *God* and just saying "Be still and know that I am" changed the prayer's meaning. Instead of thinking about God's presence in all things, he thought about God's existence. "In my stillness I will know that God exists," he said, and he knew that it was a knowledge that would come from within and not because someone in church told him so.

Every day he said the words and waited for the transformation. He lived for the ecstatic experience of God's presence in him. Each time he sat down to pray, he tried to find his way back to that place within, but the harder he tried, the more elusive it became. He spoke to Clare about it after trying for several days, and she told him to fast and to pray six hours a day saying "Be still and know." Those words, he believed, opened a whole new world to him. "In my stillness I will know all things," he said, and he believed it was true. The more he was able to still his mind and thoughts, the more he would understand his purpose and the way in which he could best serve God.

With this new sense of knowing all things, Archie no longer believed he needed Clare to guide him through the stages. He knew what he had to do. He fasted every few days, only drinking water and eating a couple of slices of bread. His only showers were when it rained and God could wash him clean. He wore the same pair of jeans and the same sweatshirt every day and slept only two or three hours a night, spending the rest of those dark hours seeking God. In the mornings he went to the hospital to visit his grandmother. She was not getting better, and the doctor told him she could not yet move to the rehabilitation nursing home. On the day she was supposed to leave the hospital, she'd come down with a urinary tract infection, and the nurse told Archie she would have to stay another couple of days.

Archie believed he had caused her illness, and he feared it would be just like his grandfather's death all over again. Every time he went to visit his grandmother, she became more distressed. He still refused to move to Miss Nattie Lynn's. He told her he was doing just fine, but she wouldn't listen.

"You're not doing fine, sugar," she said to him. She shifted on her bed and tried to get comfortable, but Archie could see that all her shifting wasn't working. Beads of sweat had formed on her forehead, as though all the restlessness was exhausting her.

She pushed off the top blanket and gestured to Archie. "Look at you. Your hair needs cutting and a good washing.

It's so dirty and greasy it looks brown—a brown rat's nest. And look at your clothes. You wear the same old ratty jeans and holey sweatshirt every time you come, and I hate to say it, Archie, sugar, but you don't smell sweet. But even worse, you look ill. You're skin and bones, and those pretty blue eyes of yours look like someone took Clorox to them. And you've got deep, dark hollows going all around them. It scares me to see you like this. Your granddaddy used to look like that anytime he took sick. Now, I want a doctor here to take a look at you."

"Grandmama, I'm just fine. I'm worried about *you*, that's all," Archie said, and he was. He spent many of his hours in prayer with her in his heart. He patted her hand. "I love you, Grandmama," he said.

Emma Vaughn blushed and gave a little nod. Then she pulled the blanket back up and shifted on the bed again. "If you would just go to Nattie Lynn's and let them look after you. That's all I ask. Couldn't you do that for me? My friends have gone up to the house several times to leave you dinner and bring you groceries, and they come back and find you haven't touched any of it."

"Grandmama, please."

"They say you've been spending most of your time with Clare."

Archie nodded. "Yes, ma'am."

"She's a sweet girl. She's come by to see me a few times here in the hospital, you know."

Archie didn't know, but he was pleased because he could see it pleased his grandmother.

She nodded at him. "It's all right, you two spending time together, just as long as you do it with Nattie Lynn's supervision. How about that? You move into town and you can see her more often."

Every time Archie came to visit, they went back and forth over the same argument. Then his grandmother got pneumonia. The changes the illness made in her shocked Archie. The nurses had put all kinds of IV fluids into her veins, and they seemed to need to draw blood from her every few hours, so her arms and hands were bruised all over, and she had oxygen tubes in her nose that ran to a tank by her bed, and there was a heart and blood-pressure monitor hovering nearby as well, beeping and making all kinds of other noises. Archie was sure it was the stress of seeing him and arguing with him all the time that did that to her, and he decided it was best he didn't visit her anymore. He felt it would be better if he prayed for her instead; so he stayed on his mountain and did not go to the hospital.

Clare came when she could in the afternoons after school, and together she and Archie prayed on the mountaintop, sitting in the shade of the pine trees. Archie had prayed so much his voice was hoarse, and Clare told him not to worry, that soon he would not have to pray out loud at all. "The prayer will be in your heart all the time, and no matter what you're doing and what you're saying, your heart will be praying. You will be talking to God always."

"Is that how it is with you?" he asked. "Is it always in your heart?"

Clare smiled and bowed her head and whispered, "Yes, Archibald."

Archie looked at her sitting beneath the pine trees, at the top of her head, the curve of her long back, her delicate-looking hand smoothing out the clump of pine needles by her side, and he wondered where on the road to sainthood she was. Was she farther along than he? Sometimes he thought so, because of the way she knew things, as if she had been at this saint business for years, but then she talked as if they were doing everything together—each wearing one set of clothes all the time, giving up possessions, fasting, and both praying together for the same length of time.

Archie asked Clare about that, and she looked up at him with such sadness in her eyes, he couldn't bear to look at her. He lowered his head.

"Where am I on the path?" Clare replied. "You want to know? Too far to ever turn back. Too far for my mother to comprehend. That's why I moved here to live with my father. He's like me, so he doesn't ask too many questions. It's best, Archibald, not to ask too many questions."

Archie didn't know what to make of Clare. He did have questions. Where then on the path was she? How far was "too far"? Why, if she was so far along, did she bother with him? But before he could speak and ask her any of those things, Clare said, "I think you're ready to expand the prayer now. You can pray to these words, *Be still.*"

"'Expand'?" Archie asked. "Don't you mean *shrink*?"

Clare shook her head. "Every time we remove words, we open the prayer up wider. Don't you see that? To pray *Be still* is to be present to all the possibilities God has to offer you. To add words adds meaning, until the meaning becomes much more narrow and so does the prayer. You'll say *Be still* eight hours a day until you feel ready to just stay silent and listen, and after that you will be praying all the time and you will need no words."

Archie couldn't wait until he was praying as she had said, with his heart. He decided that maybe he still needed Clare's guidance after all, and he looked forward to the next stages she had in store for him.

Then one day Clare arrived freshly scrubbed, wearing new clothes and carrying some CDs in a backpack, and Archie objected. "No, this isn't right. This can't be the next stage. There can be nothing standing between God and us." He pointed at her. "Why do you look like that? And what's with the CDs? Music is a distraction."

Clare said, "My mother's in town checking up on me, so I have to go underground for a while."

"'Underground'?" Archie asked.

"I have to wear nice clothes and eat big meals or she'll take me back home with her." She held up her backpack. "And even the saints chanted, you know. Some even wrote music for God. The right music can become another path to the Lord. Don't you think, Archibald, that we should explore every pathway?"

"'Explore every pathway'?" This was not part of what Archie "knew," and he was reluctant to give in to her, but at last he did. He went down into his basement and dug out his CD player, and they carried it up the mountain with them. Clare put on the last movement of Suite no. 2 of Respighi's *Ancient Airs and Dances*. Archie thought they would sit and meditate to it, but Clare put the music on and stood up and danced, raising her arms above her head, her palms open to the sky as though she were calling God down to her. The music was light and joyous, and Clare, keeping her arms high, her face to the sun, spun and leaped about the mountaintop and called to Archie to join her. "It is a way of praising God; come on."

Archie wanted to keep watching her. He was fascinated and awed by the graceful way she moved. Her hair shone in the sunlight; her eyes, her face, her body, everything on her glistened. Archie knew it was the light of God within her, and he wanted that same light for himself. He wondered when the light would begin to shine in him that way, and watching her dance, he felt jealous. The feeling surprised him. He had thought he was above that kind of emotion by then. No wonder he didn't have the light. He shook his head as though he were shaking out the thought and jumped up to join her for the grand finale.

They held hands and spun with their faces to the sky, and the music resounded with its final bursts of exuberance. They spun until they fell laughing onto the ground. Archie looked at Clare's beaming face and wanted to kiss her and touch her and hold her. Then, ashamed of his thoughts, he stopped laughing. He turned away from her and retreated to the trees. He dropped down on his knees and fell forward on his face. He wanted to eat the dirt, punch his fists into a rock, or pound his body with his fists. How, he wondered, could his mind turn on him that way after so much prayer and devotion to God? How could it happen—first jealousy and then lust, in a matter of minutes? How? How could he feel a desire for anything but God?

Clare came up behind him and spoke to him. "Are you all right?"

Archie lifted his head but didn't look at her. "No more music," he said. "No more dancing. I think you should go now."

"I don't understand."

"Come back tomorrow," he said. "I'll be okay by tomorrow."

Clare knelt down beside him, and he lowered his face back to the ground.

"Maybe we're going too fast with all this, Archibald. Maybe you should back up a little; maybe pray only three hours a day for a while and eat more."

Archie rose up and glared at her. "Eat more! Pray less! I need to pray more, much more. I'm no saint! I'm a sinner, Clare. A sinner." He turned his head and looked across the mountain. The grass was getting longer and greener. A breeze ran through it and the blades slanted away from Archie. "Remember when you asked me if I thought we could be like Jesus and be sinless? Remember you asked if people had that capability?"

"Sure, I remember."

"Well, I want to find out. I want to find out if I can be pure in my thoughts and my words and my actions. I want to see if it's possible to really be like Jesus. Otherwise..." Archie looked at Clare. "Otherwise, there's no hope at all. I mean, what's the point of trying to be good if it's not humanly possible—if in the end we're always going to sin?"

Clare didn't answer him right away. She picked up a pine needle and sniffed it, then twirled it in her hand. She laughed and looked up at the sun, and a tear ran down her face.

"Clare?" Archie said.

Clare knelt down beside Archie and took his hand. "We *are* soul mates. I have waited so long for you, Francis."

Archie laughed. "I'm not Francis yet."

Clare let go of his hand and said, "Someday soon, Francis, we will go on our pilgrimage. I know now that someday you will be ready."

Archie's face brightened. "A pilgrimage? Like a trip? When? Where would we go? Would we walk? What kind of pilgrimage?"

Clare brushed her hair back off her face. "There is a place," she said. "I will take you there, but not yet, not now. You have to be ready for it."

Archie rose up on his knees, barely listening to her words. A pilgrimage was the answer to his prayers. He knew that many people went on pilgrimages to pray for healing and were healed. He would go and pray for his grandmother. "Yes!" he said. "This is brilliant! This is a brilliant idea!"

Clare laughed, and Archie grabbed her hands and pulled her up with him and spun her around. "Clare," he shouted, "you are perfection!"

# CHAPTER

## 14

When Archie had not been to see his grand-mother in three days, Nattie Lynn called him and left a message that she wanted to see him to discuss a very serious matter. Archie knew what the serious matter was and he didn't want to go and face Miss Nattie Lynn, but out of respect for her wishes, he went anyway. His hours spent up on the mountain every day had changed him. He felt a love for all things, and all people. He loved Miss Nattie Lynn, he realized, and he would go and talk to her and show her his love. He had convinced Clare that riding their bikes for transportation should be acceptable, at least until school let out, so Archie climbed on his bike and rode to Nattie Lynn's house.

As he rode he noticed patches of the sun's light striking the mountains in the distance, and closer, the tiny wild-flowers springing up on the sides of the road. He noticed all the colors of green in the leaves of the trees, and all the shades of brown in their trunks. He felt such love for the flowers and the trees and mountains and the sun that shone down upon them on the golden day that he had to stop several times so that he could take it all in. The love he felt pouring from him was overwhelming to him. His chest expanded with emotion; his eyes filled with tears. The world was so beautiful, he didn't know what to do.

A car passed behind him and Archie felt something hit his back. A teen's voice yelled from the car, "Get out of the road, clown!" and sped past. Archie turned around and found the Coke can that had been thrown at him. He picked it up and examined the red-and-white design on the silver can. Even the can, with its crushed center, looked beautiful to him. He climbed back on his bike and continued on to Nattie Lynn's with the can in his hand. When he arrived at the house and Miss Nattie Lynn answered the door, he handed her the can and said, "I brought this for you."

Nattie Lynn took the can with a frown. "Are you wanting me to throw this away for you?" she asked.

Archie smiled and said, "It's yours. You can do whatever you want with it."

Nattie Lynn, still frowning and looking Archie up and down, opened the door wider and told him to come in. "You need a bath, young man," she said, leading him into her living room and setting the Coke can on a table in the hallway.

The house was dark, with oak woodwork everywhere, and it felt to Archie like a very masculine house, large and square, with heavy furnishings and dark, thick curtains drawn in all the windows. The only things feminine in the living room were Miss Nattie Lynn and the collection of antique dolls she had placed on the mantelpiece.

Nattie Lynn told Archie to have a seat, and he chose an oversized chair with lion paws carved in wood for arm-rests. She sat across from him, her plump body filling out the chair, and picked up her knitting from the backpack that sat on the floor by her feet.

"I just wanted to tell you how much I appreciate you coming out to check on me every now and then," Archie said, beginning the conversation.

"Well, that's exactly what I wanted to talk to you about. We never actually see you anymore, do we?" Nattie Lynn replied, smiling and tilting her head as though she had said, "Won't you please have some candy?" "We see that note you tacked up on your door telling us you're up on the mountain, but it's the same old note every time. For all we know you've fallen and broken your leg, like you did that time with the Armory Mitchell boy. We leave you food and we come back a few days later and it's still there, and I can see for myself that you aren't eating much. Why, you're as thin as a prisoner."

"I don't eat meat anymore, Miss Nattie Lynn," Archie said. "But as you can see, I'm alive and well, so next time you visit my grandmama, please tell her this."

Nattie Lynn worked quickly with her needles, not even bothering to look at her work. Instead she watched Archie. "What do you propose we do, Mr. Archibald? Do you want us to lie? Because surely, if I told her you were well, I would be lying."

"No, ma'am, I don't." Archie paused and considered what he should say. "What if I make out a new note for you each day to let you know where I am? And if you want to bring me food, which I do appreciate, then if you would bring me vegetables and bread, things like that, I will most gladly eat it. That way you'll know I'm all right and you can give my grandmama a good report. You see, until she's well, I don't think I should visit because my presence upsets her."

Nattie Lynn stopped knitting. "Sounds like you've got it all figured out now, don't you?"

"Yes, ma'am," Archie said, believing he was behaving like Clare, the way he spoke to her and shone his loving eyes on her.

But Nattie Lynn leaned forward in her seat and with a glaring expression said, "Well, I don't like it. I don't like it one bit. Give your grandmama 'a good report'? Based on what? A few scraps of food left in the garbage, a fresh note tacked on the door? You must think I'm some kind of fool, but I can assure you, I'm not."

Archie held up his hand. "Wait a minute. It's not what you think. I'm not up to anything." As he looked at her, Archie tried to hold on to the loving feelings he had felt for all man- and womankind up on the mountain. He smiled a syrupy smile.

Nattie Lynn scowled at him. "Archibald, you must think I just fell off the turnip truck this morning. Of course you're up to something. And telling me that it would be better if you didn't see your grandmama! What kind of fool notion is that? If you want her to stop worrying, you'll put on some clean clothes, pack your bags, and get yourself on down here. Then you will go visit your grandmama every single day, like a good and decent grandson should."

Archie tried another tack. "Miss Nattie Lynn, you remember what my granddaddy said before he died?"

"Of course I do; I was right there with him. Heard it with my own ears."

"Well, I believe he meant it. It was a prophecy. And now, I must be about my Father's business."

Nattie Lynn drew in a deep breath, and with her lips pinched tight and her finger pointing at Archie she said, "Don't you be quoting Jesus at me, young man. 'About my Father's business,' indeed! What, may I ask, might that 'business' be?"

"Prayer mostly."

Nattie Lynn raised her hands, then thrust her knitting down on her lap. "'Prayer'? Good gracious, boy, you can do that anytime, anywhere. You can certainly do that in this house if you've a mind to it."

Archie squirmed back into his seat and looked at the dolls staring at him from the mantelpiece above Nattie Lynn's head. "Truth is, I'm planning on going on a pilgrimage."

"A pilgrimage? To Jerusalem? Lord have mercy, what put that idea in your head?"

"Not Jerusalem, someplace closer. Clare says going on a pilgrimage is a way of deepening and proving our faith. She says it can be a life-changing experience."

"You want 'a life-changing experience'? If your grand-mama doesn't make it, you'll have yourself a life-changing experience, all right!"

Archie felt as if the room had just tilted. He grabbed the armrests and blinked several times and told himself that his grandmama would be just fine. Just fine! He stood up. He didn't want to listen to anything more. "Excuse me, Miss Nattie Lynn, but I think I had better be going now."

Nattie Lynn stood up, too, leaving her knitting on the seat of her chair. "You leaving on that pilgrimage right this minute, are you?"

"No, ma'am," Archie said, backing out into the hallway and trying to remain calm.

Nattie Lynn followed him. "And do you plan to just leave your grandmama in the hospital, in her serious condition, while you're on that pilgrimage of yours?"

Archie stopped. He clenched his fists. "The pilgrimage will be for her, too. People have been healed on pilgrimages. I will be praying for her all the time."

"Archibald Caswell, I hate to say it, but I'm ashamed of you. Your grandmama needs you there at the hospital, and she needs to know you're all right."

"Miss Nattie Lynn, don't you believe in the power of prayer?"

"Indeed I do, but nothing shows off the power of prayer better than the power of love, and showing that love by being there when your grandmama needs you."

Archie turned and walked toward the front door. He didn't want to argue with her anymore. Her words were pulling him away from God. As much as he tried to feel only love for Nattie Lynn, he had felt an ugliness creeping up inside him, especially when she had tried threatening him by using his grandmother's illness. He wanted to get home and climb his mountain, where he knew God waited for him. There his mind and heart could rest in God, but in town, with Nattie Lynn and his grandmother, he felt angry and upset and unholy. The visit had made him realize that he should not be around people who did not understand his mission. He decided he would not ride into town again. He would not ride his bike anywhere ever again. If he needed to get somewhere, he would walk. That was the way a true pilgrim of God would get around.

He stopped at the door and said to Nattie Lynn, "I want to thank you for what you have said to me. I feel even more strongly that what I'm doing is right." Then he remembered something Clare had told him and added, "It says in the Bible that we must seek *first* the Kingdom of Heaven, then everything else will follow. That's what I'm doing. Putting God first."

"Child, don't you start preaching to me about the Bible. I know full well what's in that book. Maybe instead of reading and preaching from it, you ought to try to understand it better."

"Yes, ma'am, that's exactly what I am going to do and what I hope my pilgrimage will help me with. So, if you'll excuse me, I'd better be going."

Archie didn't wait for her to open the door. He pulled it open himself and bounded down the steps toward his bike. He popped his helmet on his head, hopped on the bike, and raced down the drive, not even bothering to fasten his helmet strap until he had ridden far away from Nattie Lynn's house.

# CHAPTER

# 15

ARCHIE HAD SET OUT for home, but then, realizing
that it had to be close to time for Clare to get out of school,
he decided to meet her there. He needed to see her. He knew
that she could make him feel better again. He turned his
bike around and rode back toward town.

There were more tourists arriving in town every day.
The large flower baskets had been hung on hooks from the
antique lampposts that were set every twelve feet along the
edge of the brick walkway in front of the shops on Main
Street, signaling the early beginning of the tourist season.
Archie barely noticed them, or the shoppers milling about,
wandering in and out of the stores and eating corn dogs
and ice-cream cones. His mind was still on his conversation
with Nattie Lynn, thinking of all the things he should have
said to her.

*How dare Nattie Lynn try to scare me by telling me
Grandmama might die,* he thought. *What's wrong with the
woman, anyway? And how dare she tell me she's ashamed
of me.*

Archie couldn't pedal to the school fast enough. He wanted to see Clare's smile and the light in her eyes when she looked at him. He wanted her to touch him, hug him, even, and tell him that everything was okay; his grandmother would be all right. He tried to quiet his mind and feel God's presence, God's assurance that all was well and he was doing the right thing by staying up on his mountain and praying, but he couldn't do it. He felt too upset. Then he got angry at himself. *It's stupid,* he thought. *It's stupid to be this upset. They were just words, that's all. Grandmama's going to be fine. I'm too emotional about everything all of a sudden. Some saint I am. I stink!*

Archie turned onto the long, steep road that led to the school, shifted into high gear, and kept pedaling, his thoughts keeping pace with his spinning legs.

*I need to get away. I can't be a saint with people bugging me all the time. Phone calls. Notes. Visits. I can't wait any longer. I need that pilgrimage. I need Clare. She makes me feel... She'll lead me to God. As long as I'm with Clare.*

Archie came to the bottom of the hill and turned onto School Street. He saw that the buses were pulling out and leaving. He dismounted and walked his bike onto the grass and watched the buses. Faces stared out at him as the buses passed, and some of them Archie recognized from church and baseball and other activities he had been involved with over the years. He turned away and walked his bike toward the school. It was a modern-looking building, long and flat on top. The land that surrounded the school was once a farm owned by a good friend of Archie's grandfather's. When the owner had died, his widow had sold the property to the town and the school was built. Before then children from the town had to travel twenty miles or more to attend the county school.

From the start Archie's grandfather had predicted doom for the new building. He didn't believe in public education and he didn't like all the "foreigners," as he liked to call the newcomers, moving in and turning a quiet mountain village into a "rich man's playground with all of its fancy-shmancy shops." "If they want a city, why don't they go back to where they came from?" he said.

The first school did burn down, and Silas Caswell cried out to all who would listen, "I told you so!" The fire marshal and the police never could find enough evidence to pin the blame for the fire on him, but everybody believed he'd done it, anyway, and Archie had always felt guilty by association.

Archie wheeled his bicycle over to the bike racks, where a girl was crouching down and sorting through a pile of papers. She glanced up at him and then did a double take, looking him over. She stood up and backed away a little. "You looking for someone?" she asked.

Archie saw Clare's bicycle still in a rack, so he nodded. "Yeah, Clare Simpson. Do you know her?"

The girl followed Archie's gaze and said, "You mean the girl who owns this bike?"

"Yes," he said, setting his own bike into the rack.

A worried look flashed across the girl's face. "You mean Doris, right?"

Archie blinked. "'Doris'?" Then he remembered Nattie Lynn calling her by that name, and he said, "Yeah, Doris. I call her Clare. She's a friend of mine."

The girl smiled. "Join the crowd," she said. "Everyone

loves Doris," and then glancing sideways a second, she looked back at Archie and her worried expression returned. "At least almost everybody," she added.

"You know where she is?" Archie asked, beginning to feel anxious.

"I think so," said the girl. She grabbed Archie by the arm and pulled him over to the edge of the building and pointed out toward the woods. "She's there, I think. She went with a couple of guys—John and Hal. They all looked friendly walking together down the hill, but I don't know. She's so trusting and all, and John and Hal, they're bad news. Of course Doris can . . ."

Archie didn't let her finish. He took off running, and the girl called after him, "She's probably fine."

As Archie got closer to the woods, he heard voices. He slowed down so that he could hear them, stopping just at the edge of the woods. Then he crept forward, searching ahead for Clare. He heard her voice.

"I'm not afraid of you," she said. "God is with me, even here. God is with all three of us." He heard laughter, and then Archie spotted her, trying to get past two boys who grabbed her and pushed her back against a tree.

"Are you wanting to hurt me?" Clare asked with surprise in her voice.

Archie crept closer, hoping to catch them by surprise. He could feel his anger rising.

The shorter boy moved in on her. "You think Jesus is going to save you, sugar pie?"

"I'm already saved," she said. "I think Jesus is going to save you. Even if you hurt me, he will love you."

The taller boy said, "Yeah, but it's your lovin' we

want." He leaned forward, placing his hands on either side of her, against the tree.

"I love you," Clare said, "but I don't love what you're doing."

The taller boy took his hands from the tree and ran his fingers up her arm to her collar. Then he grabbed the collar.

Archie saw the movement and charged the two boys, his fury exploding. "Get away from her!" he yelled. He came at the taller boy sideways and tackled him. They wrestled each other to the ground, and Archie scrambled on top of him. The shorter boy jumped on Archie's back and tried to pull him off. Archie went wild. He snapped his head back, butting the shorter boy in the face, making good contact with the boy's nose.

The boy cried out and let go. "He broke my nose!"

Archie could hear Clare talking to him, but her voice seemed far away and he couldn't hear what she was saying. He kept fighting the taller boy, trying to stay on top and punching him anywhere he could. "I'll kill you," he said to the boy, and he knew he meant it. He wanted to rip him apart.

"Not if I kill you first," the boy said, struggling to throw Archie off of him.

Archie had thought the shorter boy had left, but then he felt a kick in his back; the boy was still there. The kick enraged him. He grabbed the taller boy's throat and squeezed. "You touch me again and I'll kill him; I swear it," he said to the shorter boy. "I'll kill him. Get out of here! Now!"

The taller boy was gasping for air and trying to speak,

clawing at Archie's arms, but Archie just gripped tighter, choking the boy.

"All right," the boy behind him said. "I'm going. Okay? I'm going."

Archie kept his hold on the taller boy's throat and listened to the other boy's footsteps retreating. He heard Clare behind him praying, "Lord Jesus Christ, have mercy." Her soft, calm voice sounded out of place there in the woods. He wanted to tear the boy apart. Her voice made no sense. Her words matched nothing inside him, no emotion he felt. The boy beneath him still struggled for air, and again Clare spoke, "Lord Jesus Christ, have mercy. Lord Jesus Christ, have mercy."

Clare came forward and crouched next to Archie and the boy. Still praying she reached down and took Archie's hands, pulling them with gentle force from the boy's throat.

Archie gave a deep sigh and let go. He climbed off the boy and stood up. A sharp pain shot through his back where he had been kicked. He stood over the boy, who had sat up and was coughing and spitting onto the ground. "Get out of here," Archie said, his voice low. "Go on. Get out of here!"

The boy, still coughing and sniffing, scrambled to his feet and took off running. Archie grabbed Clare and held her tight. Clare kept praying the same thing over and over again: "Lord Jesus Christ, have mercy." Archie said nothing. He just held on to her, wrapping his trembling arms around her and squeezing her close to him.

"Lord Jesus Christ, have mercy," Clare said, her head lowered to his shoulders. Archie felt her warm breath and her words as if they were coming from his own chest. He took a deep breath and let it out. He lifted his eyes and stared up into the tops of the trees, looking for the sky.

# CHAPTER

# 16

ARCHIE AND CLARE STEPPED out of the woods with their arms still wrapped around each other. Archie was limping. His knee had hit a rock when he'd fallen to the ground fighting. His back ached and his nose was bleeding. He hadn't even noticed the taller boy punching him.

Clare asked him, "Are you all right? Maybe you need to rest for a minute." They were the first words besides the prayer that Clare had spoken.

Archie stopped walking and turned to her. "What happened there, Clare? I mean how did you—how did that happen?"

"They told me they want God in their lives. They said they want what I have." Clare looked at Archie. Her eyes were clear; she held him steady in her gaze. She wasn't shaking as Archie was; as a matter of fact, Archie realized, she looked calm, serene, even, as though she had only been out for a stroll through the woods and had torn her shirt on a branch.

Her calm state annoyed Archie. He said, "And you

believed them? They want what you have, all right. How could you go into the woods with them? Didn't your parents ever tell you to stay out of the woods with boys?"

"I trust in the Lord," she said. "You have to trust, Francis."

Archie shook his head. "Don't call me that. My name is Archie; what's yours, by the way?"

"Clare," she said.

Archie started walking toward the bike racks, and Clare joined him. "That's not what I heard," he said. "If you're Clare, then who is Doris?"

"Doris is a name that I answer to because I have to; it is not who I am. I am Clare."

Archie turned on her. "What's that supposed to mean? I want to know what's going on." He pointed toward the woods. "I almost killed a guy back there, and you stand here giving me all this peace and love and I-trust-in-the-Lord stuff. What would have happened if I hadn't come along? Huh? Would you just have let them hurt you? Is that what it means to trust in the Lord? Are we supposed to just let people attack us and not even defend ourselves?" Archie's hands were all over the place. He felt hysterical, and Clare's unperturbed expression made him feel even more so.

"Yes," Clare answered.

"Impossible!" he said, throwing his arms up.

"All things are possible through God," Clare replied.

"Shut up!" Archie turned and strode toward the bike racks. He knew he could never, ever just let someone attack him. She was crazy. She had to be. It was suicide. He didn't have that kind of faith. He didn't know if he wanted that kind of faith. He reached the bike rack ahead of Clare and waited for her, leaning against the rack with his arms crossed. He noticed he was breathing hard, and he tried to slow his breathing down, taking a couple of long, deep breaths and letting them out. When Clare reached him, he said, "So you trusted God to protect you back there, is that what you're saying? You just knew someone would come along and save you? Is that what you're saying?"

"No, I didn't know if anyone would come along. We don't know really if they would have hurt me, either. My shirt tore when you tackled John. They might have listened to me and stopped, but that's not important. It's not that I trusted God to save me; it's that I trusted God to be there with me, no matter what happened. And with God there, I knew it didn't matter what happened—I would be all right."

"You could have been killed!"

"And still, God would be with me."

"Clare! That's crazy." Archie felt exasperated.

"Don't you see, they could never touch me or hurt me, not really. And anyway, I won't use violence, but I will protect myself."

"Why protect yourself at all if God is there and you don't care what happens to your body?"

"It is the will of God that I protect myself."

"And maybe it's God's will that you fight them, too."

"Violence is never God's will. Hate is never God's will. You know that. You've said it yourself. You've felt it for yourself, God's love."

"I don't know anymore. Right now I don't feel God's love at all."

"That's because your anger is pushing God away."

Archie stood up and yanked his bike from the rack. "Look, I don't want to talk about it anymore. Come on; I'll ride home with you."

When Archie and Clare arrived at Clare's house, the house was empty.

"Where's your father?" Archie asked.

"At his shop. Haven't you seen his new shop?"

Archie shook his head and peered into the kitchen. It was a small yellow room, with white fixtures and tall windows.

"He has an herb shop. He's been very busy with it. It's between Barrett's Books and the Ski Chalet. Come on." Clare led him upstairs. "I'll get you cleaned up and give you some sweatpants to wear home."

"Who buys herbs?" Archie asked, following her upstairs and noticing the clown paintings lining the stairwell wall.

"They're medicinal. You know, instead of drugs."

"Yeah, I know they're medicinal, but my grandmama just grows them." When he said the word *grandmama,* he felt his heart clench. He was furious with Nattie Lynn for making him worry about her.

Clare led him to the bathroom, and Archie told her he could clean himself up, so Clare left him and went in search of the sweatpants.

Archie looked at himself in the mirror. It had been a long time since he had seen his reflection, and he was shocked by what he saw. Besides the dried blood on his face, his eyes looked sunken into his head and his cheekbones poked out at sharp angles. "I look like van Gogh with freckles," he said. Then he leaned over the sink and washed his face and hands. He was careful washing the blood from beneath his nose, so as not to start the bleeding again. His back hurt when he bent over, reminding him of the fight. He called out to Clare. "We need to call the cops, you know? Those guys can't get away with what they did." He dried his face and hands, and stepped out into the hallway.

"It's all right, Francis," Clare said, her voice muffled. "You don't need to call the police."

"Where are you?" Archie headed down the hallway in the direction of her voice.

"Here, in my bedroom closet."

Archie came to a room at the end of the hall. It had a high ceiling, like the rest of the house, and old wallpaper with a faded blue background and fat white flowers. There was a canopy bed with frilly white bedclothes on it and stuffed animals gathered on top. The shelves in the room were filled with books. Archie looked around, and Clare came out of the closet holding up a pair of sweatpants. "I think these will do," she said. "They were always big on me." She tossed them to Archie.

Archie caught them. "Nice room, but I thought we were going simple. You know, living like monks and giving up all our possessions?" Archie felt anger rising up in him again. Who was this Doris-Clare?

Clare smiled and took Archie's hand, pulling him out into the hallway. "I'll show you my real room," she said. "That one's just for appearances—for while my mother's here. She's staying at the Vista View Inn down the road, but every time she comes over, she checks my room and my closet and watches to see that I'm eating enough."

Archie looked Clare over. She did look awfully thin, but then so did he.

Clare led Archie to a door halfway down the hall. She opened it, and there were stairs leading up to an attic. She turned on the light, and they climbed the steps. The attic smelled of sweet wood and heat.

"It's got to be a hundred degrees up here," Archie said, reaching the top step and looking around.

"You get used to it," Clare said.

A mattress covered with a white sheet lay on the floor in the center of the room. There was nothing else except at the far end of the attic, where Clare had set up an altar. She had a table with a crucifix set in a stand on it. Written in paint above it, on the ceiling of the attic, were the words *Lord Jesus Christ, have mercy on me*. On the floor, painted in front of a kneeler, were the words *Be still and know that I am God*. A bible lay on top of the kneeler.

"You sleep up here?" Archie asked. The heat was suffocating. Sweat ran down his face. "It's like a sauna."

Clare, too, was sweating, but her eyes were shining. "Yes, it is. And it's purifying to sweat. I purify my body and my soul up here."

Archie wiped the sweat off his face with the pants Clare had tossed him. "It seems dangerous," Archie said, knowing he couldn't stand it. "I'd never get any sleep up here."

Clare crossed the room and kneeled down on the kneeler, taking the bible up in her hands. "No, I don't get much sleep up here, now that the warmer weather is here. It still cools down at night some, though. It gets hard to concentrate, too, but that's good. It's like I go into a trance up here sometimes. I like it."

Archie came up behind Clare. "We need to call the cops," he said to her.

Clare looked up at him. "No, Francis, let it go."

Archie came around to face Clare and sat on the floor, feeling the stiffness in his knee and his back. "They tried to attack you. They might have beaten you or raped you if I hadn't come along. We need to report them. They could hurt someone else."

"No," Clare said, her voice firm. "I won't speak to the police."

Archie stood up, groaning at the pain in his back. "If you won't, I will." He paused.

Clare didn't seem to be paying any attention to him. She was looking past him, at the crucifix, her expression blank.

"I need to get going now," Archie said. "It's been the longest day of my life, and I still have a nine-mile bike ride home."

Clare looked up at him and took his hand. "You'll get there, dear Francis."

Archie didn't know if she meant that he would get home or if she meant he would become a saint. He didn't bother asking her. He looked into her eyes, and they held so much love for him, he felt humbled and wanted to fall on his knees before her. He had never before felt anyone look upon him with such love. The only greater feeling was when Archie had felt God's overwhelming love for him up on the mountain. He knew she saw in him something greater than he was, something wonderful, and he wanted to be that for her. He wanted to be what she expected of him, but he wasn't sure how he would ever do it.

Clare released his hand and closed her eyes. She lowered her head and prayed.

Archie wanted to stay with her. He didn't want to leave, but he felt for some reason that he should. "Okay then, I'd better be going," he said.

Clare lifted her head and opened her eyes. She smiled, but it was not at Archie; it was at the crucifix.

Archie left her, pitching the sweatpants onto the mattress on his way out.

# CHAPTER
# 17

THE BIKE RIDE HOME felt torturous to Archie, but he thought of Clare sweltering up in her attic room and decided if she could take it so could he, and he pushed on, trying to think past the pain and stiffness in his body.

He thought about the incident at the school, and he realized he had a lot to learn still about God and faith. He agreed with Clare in principle about not using violence, but when he'd come face-to-face with the violence of the two boys, he couldn't help himself, and he knew if it happened again, he would react the same way—and he felt ashamed of that. He thought about Martin Luther King Jr. and about Gandhi and the way both had stood up to the violence of thousands and had never struck back. Could he ever become like them? Could he ever have that kind of faith? He wanted it. He wanted to be noble like that, like those two men, loved by thousands, but was it noble to let two bullies attack Clare? Could he have handled the situation any differently? Clare had wanted him to, expected him to. He had let her down, but how could he have let anyone hurt her?

Archie shook his head and brushed the hair that had slipped from under his helmet out of his eyes. He had started that morning so sure that he was well on the way to sainthood. His heart had felt full of love for the world, and then look what happened. By late afternoon he was so enraged, he thought he might kill someone. He needed to get better control of his emotions, he decided, feeling jealousy suddenly rise within him. He was jealous of Clare. He felt jealous of her relationship with God, her faith. He wanted to know God was always present, even when something terrible was happening—the way Clare did—but he wasn't sure it was really possible. The whole day had been terrible, and Archie had felt God moving farther and farther away from him.

He felt jealous of Clare in another way, too, or maybe it wasn't Clare he was jealous of but God. Yes, he felt jealous of God because Clare wanted God more than she wanted him. When she had looked past him to the crucifix, dismissing him and shining her face on Jesus, Archie had felt envy. He wanted her attention; he wanted her smile and her shining eyes all to himself, and for that, too, he felt ashamed. He knew that instead of trying to get Clare's attention, he needed to return his focus to God. As soon as he got home, he determined, he would go straight up to the mountain and pray all night. He wouldn't sleep at all. He'd show God that he did have faith, that he was worthy of sainthood.

CHAPTER

# 18

W HEN ARCHIE GOT HOME he grabbed a package of Swiss-cheese slices out of the refrigerator, filled a thermos with water, and after a quick trip to the bathroom, headed for the mountain. He set out for the trail full of hope that he would be able to get back to God and all of his good feelings. The night was humid, the stars barely visible, and the moon a sliver in the sky. It was difficult for him to see the trail, but Archie knew the way by heart and navigated it without much trouble. He got himself settled in his usual place beneath the trees at the edge of the mountaintop. He unwrapped the cheese and ate all the slices, washing them down with water. When he had finished he tucked the cheese wrapper in his back pocket, set the thermos beside him, and began his meditations, telling himself that he would not let the day's troubles interfere with his time with God. But they did.

Archie closed his eyes and prayed, and instead of getting quiet and feeling God's presence within, he felt restless and nervous. He couldn't get Nattie Lynn's words about his grandmother out of his mind, and her words led to images of his grandmother lying in the hospital, so pale and bruised. He said his prayer out loud, but that didn't help, either. Scenes of the fight with the boys flashed through his mind, and he remembered that he'd wanted to call the police. He promised himself he would call when he returned to the house, but he was determined to stay up on the mountain and pray until his prayer was on his heart, the way Clare had said it would be if he prayed long enough and often enough.

He returned to his prayer and tried to keep his mind focused on God, but instead of the usual light he felt inside when he prayed, a light he identified as God's presence within him, he felt darkness. He tried repeating the whole prayer the way he had before, then meditating on it: "Be still and know that I am God." He stayed with the prayer for a long time, but it was no use. He was nervous and restless. Something didn't feel right.

Archie opened his eyes and looked about. He couldn't see much. He closed his eyes and tried the prayer again. He didn't know how long he stayed with the prayer—it seemed like hours—and then, though he didn't know why, he felt afraid. His mind searched for God, for some feeling, some lift within, but there was nothing. He still felt empty, and it scared him. It was as though all light and spirit and faith had been recorded on a tape in his brain and someone had come along and erased it. It made him angry. So many weeks of praying all the time, and in an instant it all seemed to have disappeared. He spoke to God.

"God, how could you leave me now? How could you?" Archie cried, "What is it you want from me, God? What?

Tell me. Tell me! What is all this for, anyway? What am I doing? I'm just sitting here. And I'm scared. Is that what you want? You want me to sit here and die of fright? Okay, then I will. I'll just sit here and die. Will that make you happy? Huh? Is that what you want? You want my life? Go ahead and take it."

Archie dug his hands into the ground beneath him, pulling up pine needles and dirt. He threw it at the trees. He picked up some more and threw it, too. He closed his eyes again and cried and prayed, trembling with rage and fear and calling out to God. He berated God, then turned around and asked God to forgive him for what he had said. Back and forth he went with his emotions. Again in his mind he saw his grandmother lying in the hospital, with the oxygen tank by her bed and all the machines around her making beeping and swooshing sounds. He felt panicked. He stood up and looked around. He felt surrounded by evil. Yes, something terrible and evil was with him in the darkness. He could feel it. His body trembled, his heart raced, adrenaline flooded his bloodstream, and sweat broke out all over him. "God, help!" he cried out.

Archie heard a noise, a rustling sound coming from far away. He didn't wait to see if it was a raccoon or a bear or the devil himself—he just ran. He fled down the mountain, slipping and stumbling all the way. He ran into branches and twisted his ankle on a root, but still he kept running, down and down, flinging himself forward through the darkness away from the evil, running and running toward the safety of his home.

# CHAPTER
## 19

Archie ran out of the woods and raced toward the house and the welcoming porch light. Then he heard a voice and he yelled, stumbling over his own feet and landing on the ground with a grunt.

"Francis, it's me," Clare said. "Are you hurt?"

Archie stood up and brushed himself off. "Clare!" he said, panting. "I'm so glad." He hugged her, holding her tight, feeling her warmth.

"It's all right, Francis."

He released her and stood back. "I thought—well, I don't know what I thought, but I'm so glad..."

"Francis, it's time to go."

"What? Where? What do you mean?" Archie looked at Clare's face. He couldn't see much, but even in the darkness her eyes shone.

"Our pilgrimage. It's time to go."

"How did you know?" Archie said, thinking she must have figured out that he was in trouble.

"We'll have to take your grandfather's truck. I brought this." She held up a license plate.

Archie took it and walked toward the porch to get a better look at it under the light. "What's this for?" Archie asked, examining the plate. "Where are we going?"

"It's the license plate off of my grandmother's old Ford. I saved it after she died. We'll put it on the truck in case the police start looking for us. And we're going to New York City—to the Cloisters."

Archie's eyes widened. "New York? I didn't think we'd be going so far away. What will I tell my grandmama and Clyde and Miss Nattie Lynn and the others?"

"Nothing, Francis. This is our journey. We must take it alone. This is for God. You know they wouldn't understand that."

"But I have to do something or they'll be worried. I'll leave them a note, just to say that I'm going away for a couple of days, but I'll be back. That way they won't think I've run away or that I'm hurt. They're so old. I don't want them to worry about me."

"God will take care of everything." Clare took Archie's hand. "Come on; we have a long way to go and no time to lose." She pulled him toward the barn.

"But I don't know how much gas is left in the truck. Not enough to get us all the way to New York. We need money."

"Everything is taken care of. Trust me. Trust the Lord."

Archie didn't know what to think. It was too sudden. He didn't know the pilgrimage would be all the way up in New York. He needed to prepare and to write a note, pack, get some money and food. As much as he had wanted to go on a pilgrimage, he didn't feel ready.

"Wait," he said, trotting behind Clare. "I'm not ready. I need to think about this. I didn't expect New York. What are the Cloisters? Where in the city are they? Don't we need a map or something? Clare, we're going too fast."

Clare spoke but didn't look back. "When God calls you, do you say you're not ready? We must always be ready for the Lord. We must leave now, tonight, and we must hurry."

"Wait, Clare." Archie reached out for her shoulder and tried to stop her. She kept moving toward the barn. "What's the rush? What's the hurry?"

"I'll tell you when we're on the road. Have faith, dear Francis. Just have faith."

Archie didn't want to admit to Clare how low on faith he had gotten, and he was too confused to come up with any other plan, so he followed her. She told him to find a screwdriver so they could switch the license plates, and Archie told her there was one in the house.

"Then go get it and get the keys to the truck while you're there," Clare said.

Archie nodded. He ran to the house, grabbed two screwdrivers from the small toolbox in the hall closet, found the keys to the truck on the kitchen counter, and wrote a quick note to his grandmother's friends saying that he had gone on the Smoky Mountains camping trip and would return in about a week. He wrote that he would try to call them if he could. Then he signed the note and tacked it to the front door. When he got back out to the barn, he handed Clare one of the screwdrivers and the two of them switched the plates.

As soon as they were finished, Archie looked at Clare and said, "Now what?"

"Now I get my bundle and we get in the truck and leave. Do you have the keys?"

Archie pulled them out of his pocket and held them up. Clare nodded at them. "Good, you'll drive and I'll navigate. I could get us there with my eyes closed." She turned away. "I'll be right back. I left my bundle on the porch rocker."

Archie grabbed Clare by the arm and held her still. "Wait! You want me to drive us all the way to New York? You want me to drive on the highway? I've never driven on the highway. Clare, I'm fourteen. I don't have a license. What if the police stop us? I can't drive!"

Clare wrapped her hand around his. "Have faith. You're going to do just fine. It's all going to work out perfectly. I know it is. Now go on and get in the truck and back it out."

She ran out of the barn and returned a few seconds later with her bundle. Archie had backed out the truck and turned it around. Clare eased the barn door closed, then climbed into the passenger seat. "No lights—just to be safe," Clare said. They rolled down the driveway in the dark, waiting to turn on the headlights until they had gotten off the dirt road that Archie's house shared with Clyde Olsen's.

Archie felt like a criminal escaping from prison. When they reached the end of the dirt road, he switched on the headlights and turned onto Mountain Road. Archie looked behind him in the rearview mirror, half expecting to see the police behind them. But there was nothing, and he drove down the road, through the town, and past Clare's darkened house in silence. It wasn't until they reached the highway—and Archie, with Clare's help, got them safely on the road—that he finally spoke.

"I don't know what to think," Archie said. "What are we doing? I mean, I know we're going on a pilgrimage, and—I want to go, I do—I need it. I know that. But it's so sudden, all of a sudden. I mean, the middle of the night and all." He looked at the clock in the truck. "It's only just after two!"

"How else could we leave? It's the best way. And anyway, he told me it was time."

Archie glanced at Clare sitting up straight in her seat, as calm as usual.

"Who? Who told you it was time?"

"Jesus."

Archie sat back in his seat and thought about that for a second, then he said, "Did you really hear a voice or was it like this urging inside?"

"Jesus spoke to me, Francis."

"With a voice?"

"With a voice." Clare nodded. "Jesus speaks to me all the time. Jesus told me to give you that card at your grandfather's funeral. He's speaking to me now."

"Like right now? Jesus is speaking to you?"

"Yes."

Archie sighed. He didn't know what to think. Part of him felt jealous that she had that kind of connection with Jesus, and that she was so far along on the path while he was so far behind. He wasn't even sure he was still *on* the path. But another part of him loved her so much, loved her because she was so perfect, so good and holy, so full of the love of Christ, that he wanted to touch her. He wanted to be touched by God.

They again rode in silence for a while, with Archie on the constant lookout for police cars, checking the rearview mirror as often as he looked straight ahead, and then he asked her, "How much money do we have, anyway? Isn't New York expensive?"

"I think we have enough money for gas," she said.

Archie gripped the steering wheel. "What do you mean, you 'think'? What about food? Where will we stay? What if we run out of gas? How long are we staying, anyway? It's going to take us a couple of days to get there unless we drive all night and all day. And why the Cloisters? What are the Cloisters?"

"It's a museum."

"'A museum'?" Archie shifted in his seat and held the steering wheel even tighter. "We're making a pilgrimage to a museum? I don't get it. I mean, I love the idea of going to a museum, but how is that a pilgrimage? Tell me what's going on. What are we doing?"

Clare nodded. "We are beginning our pilgrimage. And pilgrims usually don't take any money at all with them. They rely on the kindness of strangers, and they eat when they are offered food and sleep when they are offered a place to sleep. But if we went on foot, we would get picked up as runaways, so we have to take the truck and we need money for gas. If we need any more money, we'll have to ask for it."

"But how? You mean beg? Beg from strangers?"

Clare laughed and patted Archie's leg, and Archie felt his face flush. "You worry too much, Francis. It will be all right."

A car came up behind them and Archie strained his eyes to see if he could make out lights on the roof of the car. He couldn't tell. They rode in silence for a few minutes, with Archie glancing back at the car every few seconds, certain that lights would start flashing any minute. Then the car sped up and passed them, and Archie let out a long, deep breath.

"You'll like the Cloisters," Clare said, her voice calm and soothing. "It's a museum filled with art from the Middle Ages—paintings and sculptures of the Virgin and child, angels, the Annunciation—all kinds of things. And the building is like a monastery. It's a most holy place. All the art is sacred and beautiful. You'll see for yourself, and your life will change. The Cloisters, Francis, is where I was born."

# PART TWO

"*Therefore do not be anxious, saying,*
*'What shall we eat?'*
*or 'What shall we drink?'*
*or 'What shall we wear?'...*
*But seek first his kingdom and his righteousness,*
*and all these things shall be yours as well.*"

MATTHEW 6:31-33

# CHAPTER

## 20

C LARE TOLD ARCHIE ABOUT the times when she would go to New York to visit her aunt. "My parents didn't get along, and I got so upset being around their fighting all the time that in the summers they would send me to Aunt Clare's."

"'Aunt Clare'?" Archie looked at Clare, surprised. "So she's the real Clare and your name is really Doris."

Clare shook her head. "No, I'm the real Clare. I am Clare and my aunt was Clare, too. She lived in New York, in White Plains, and she worked at the Cloisters. She took me to work with her every time I went to stay. I loved it there. It was peaceful. We would step into the building, all that stone—big, thick stone walls, with carvings of angels and saints and Jesus and animals—and I felt surrounded by love. All the cares of the world just fell away the minute I stepped inside. And when I walked through the rooms, my footsteps would echo all around me, and everywhere I looked, on all the walls, in paintings and tapestries, there were stories.

"My aunt was an art historian. Her concentration was on the Middle Ages. She was a guide there for a while, and over the years worked herself up to assistant curator. She knew everything about the Cloisters. When she gave a tour, she could barely skim the surface in telling the stories that were in each room, but after work each day she would take me to one room and we'd spend a couple of hours there, with her telling me all the stories. Then, after a few days, she would take me to another room and tell me its stories. There were hundreds of stories in every room. Even tucked up into the corners above a pillar or a window, there would be stories—the story of the Nativity carved in stone, or in another corner, the story of the raising of Lazarus. There are stories of the Bible everywhere—carved into the heavy wooden doors, in the stained-glass windows, on golden goblets. Do you like stories, Francis? I do."

Archie glanced at Clare's rapt expression, and he felt a stirring in his heart. He couldn't wait to see the Cloisters and feel the way Clare looked at that moment. When he turned back to face forward, he half expected to see the stories from the Cloisters playing on the windshield like a movie.

They became silent again, and Archie, despite his anxieties, grew sleepy. He had never driven in the dark before, and the road looked to him like a tunnel of endless night. He stared at the distant taillights of the car ahead of him. They were tiny red eyes glowing in the dark, and Archie followed them as though he were hypnotized. His lids felt heavy. He wanted to sleep. He glanced at Clare, who sat back with her head leaning against the window. "Are you getting sleepy?" Archie asked.

"No, I'm not sleepy. I'm just remembering," she said. Clare turned and looked at him. "Are you sleepy? Do you need to stop?"

"No, I'm okay."

"Let's talk," Clare said, sitting up straight and turning the air-conditioning vent near her toward Archie.

The cool air blew against his arms and he got goose bumps. The air helped. He felt more alert. "What did your mama and daddy fight about?" he asked, recalling his own fights with his grandfather.

"Philosophies, I guess," Clare answered. "Before they were married they loved to argue about things. It was fun for them. They're complete opposites. My mother is an accountant. She likes numbers and logic and order. My father likes mystery and chance and intuition. The one thing they agreed on was religion. They were both atheists. My mother and her sister, my aunt Clare, were raised Catholic. Aunt Clare got all the attention and admiration because she was so spiritual and was always praying and talking about becoming a nun. My aunt said my mother used to try to be spiritual, but it wasn't in her. She was always jealous of my aunt. Mother would pretend to be really religious to get her parents' attention, but when she went off to college, she dropped all that and she rebelled. So she's an atheist. My father rebelled against the church because he believed it was religion that causes most wars."

Archie glanced over at Clare. "But what happened, then? Isn't your father a believer now?"

"That's right," Clare said. "I was born two months prematurely and I almost died. That's when my father started praying. It just came naturally to him. One time he was in the hospital reaching into my crib and stroking my hand with his finger, and he felt God's presence. He told me it just filled the room. He knew right then that everything would be all right, and it was. He told my mother what had happened, and of course they argued about it. My mother said he was just exhausted and didn't know what he was doing. But my father ignored her and started reading the Bible and attending church. He believed that I was special, that God had given me as a gift, not just to him and my mother but also to the world. He named me Clare, after my aunt and after Saint Clare. But my mother wanted the name Doris, and that's on my birth certificate. My father still refuses to call me anything but Clare. So, anyway, they fought about my name and everything else that had to do with me."

Archie nodded. "The only times I heard my grandparents argue it was about me. Granddaddy always wanted to give me a whippin' and Grandmama didn't want him to."

"My mother thinks it's my father's fault that I'm so overly sensitive and 'dramatic,' as she calls it," Clare said.

"Then why does she let you live with your father, and why would she send you to her sister's house?"

Clare looked down at her hands and hesitated, taking a deep breath. When she spoke it was almost a whisper, and Archie had to lean toward her to hear. "My parents can get into some really bad fights. The fighting used to make me ill, they upset me so much, and that scared my parents. So they decided they needed someplace to send me, but they had only three choices. It was either to my mother's parents, and she hadn't talked to them since college; my father's mother, the palm reader, and my mother couldn't abide her at all; or my mother's sister. She chose Aunt

Clare. And my mother let me live with my father now because I kept running away from home."

Archie looked at Clare, surprised. She hadn't run when those boys threatened her in the woods, when her life might have been in danger, but she ran from her mother. It didn't make sense to him and he told her so.

She said, "There are worse things than physical pain or death, Francis. There's the death of the spirit. That's far worse. Nobody should be allowed to destroy another person's spirit."

Archie didn't know what to say, so he changed the subject. "Where is your aunt Clare now?" he asked. "Is she still living in New York? Are we going to go see her? Is that why I don't have to worry about anything?"

"She's dead," Clare said, lowering her head and sniffing. "She died two years ago. It was cancer." She looked out the window. "It's starting to get light out."

Archie glanced up through the windshield. The stars were still out. "Just barely," he said.

They became quiet again. Archie looked at the sky and thought about the times his grandfather would wake him in the early morning, before light, and they would go hunting. Sometimes they hunted in their own woods, and other times they would take the truck and join some of his grandfather's hunting buddies on trips to Alabama. They would ride on the highway, just as he and Clare were doing, and they'd watch the stars fade and a pink light streak the sky, at last catching sight of the sun.

Those trips had always excited Archie. He loved getting out on the wide-open highway. It made him feel like the whole world was before him and the possibilities were endless as to where he might end up. He loved speed and used to wish his grandfather would drive faster and pass all the other drivers on the road. He had always longed for the day when he would have his license and his own car, a Porsche, and he could speed along the highway on a cross-country adventure. This time, though, he was afraid to drive too fast, and yet he felt the familiar excitement of being out on the highway, realizing that for the first time in his life he was leaving the South. He was going to New York City. *Maybe,* he thought, *my racing heart is just excitement.*

"Hey." He tapped Clare on the leg. "We're going to New York. New York!" He rolled down his window, stuck his fist out, and shouted, "Ye haw!"

# CHAPTER
# 21

W HEN THE SUN CAME UP and they saw that the sky was clear, Clare and Archie agreed that it was a beautiful day for driving. The traffic had picked up, but Archie stayed in the center lane and drove at the speed limit. When he realized they had been on the road for almost four hours without mishap, he relaxed. He noticed that Clare was humming. It wasn't a tune. She hummed just one note, a low buzzing sound. She'd made the same sound when they had prayed together on the mountain, and Archie asked her if she was praying.

Clare turned from the window. "I'm always praying. You know that."

"Do you know you hum when you pray?" he asked.

"I'm talking to God."

Archie nodded. Why wasn't he talking to God? He tried saying his prayers, but the sun on his face and Clare's humming made him feel sleepy again. He glanced at Clare. She was humming and smiling with her mouth closed, her eyes shining on something out beyond the cars on the highway. Archie thought she looked so beautiful, he wanted to say something, tell her how beautiful she looked; but he didn't know if she would like hearing that, so he said nothing. He checked the gas gauge. The gauge was almost on empty, so at the next exit he pulled off the highway and into a gas station.

Archie got out and pumped the gas. Clare went into the little store to use the bathroom. Archie watched her enter the store. He saw her say something to a woman standing in line, then the woman turned to her with a big smile and the two of them talked.

Archie shook his head, amazed at the way people responded to Clare. He saw her head toward the back of the store and then lost sight of her. He watched the people going in and out of the store, carrying sodas and candy or sweet rolls out to their cars. Seeing them made him hungry. When Clare returned from going to the bathroom, he asked, "Are you hungry?"

"No," she answered, "are you?"

"No, I guess not." Archie set the pump handle back in its cradle and screwed the gas cap back onto the truck.

Clare looked at the pump and pulled a couple of bills out of the back pocket of her jeans. "I'll go pay. I'll be right back," she said.

Archie nodded. He watched a family pull away in a white van. They were all waving to Clare. Clare waved back with a big smile, and a little girl called out, "Bye, Clare!"

"Bye," Clare said, and watched them leave. Then she turned and entered the store again.

Archie watched for a second, but then he saw a plump

girl exit the store with a large soft pretzel in her hand and his mouth watered. He watched her climb into the back of a Ford Explorer and ride away.

When he looked back toward the store, he saw Clare coming out with a cup of coffee in her hand. When she caught up to him, she handed it to Archie and the two of them climbed back into the truck. "I don't want you to get too sleepy," she said after he thanked her.

"I hope we didn't dip into our gas money too much," he said.

"Oh, I didn't pay for that," Clare said. "Charley gave it to me for free."

" 'Charley'? Who's he?"

"The boy working at the cash register. He was happy to give two weary travelers some coffee."

Archie eyed Clare. " 'For free'? I don't think so."

"I asked him if he'd ever read *On the Road* by Jack Kerouac and he had, so we got to talking about that and I told him about our trip and he said he could really dig it. He was planning on his own trip someday."

" 'Jack Kerouac'? Who's he? What's *On the Road*?"

Clare studied him a second and Archie shrugged. "What?" he asked.

"You don't read much, do you?"

Archie pulled away from the pumps and rolled out toward the highway. "Sure I do. I read books for school and comics and stuff about art. I love reading about art and artists."

Archie watched the road, looking for his chance to get back onto the highway. Clare said, "Okay—now!" and he sped up, his heart racing. He wondered if he'd ever get comfortable entering a highway. Trucks barreled past them as he got into the slow lane, and he watched for his chance to move back to the center lane, which is where Clare had said it was safest to be. Once he moved over and got up to the speed limit, he relaxed again and asked Clare, "How long do you think it will take us to get to New York, anyway?"

Clare shifted onto one thigh and reached into the back pocket of her jeans. She pulled out a couple of PowerBars. "I almost forgot," she said. "Charley gave me these, too. They're for you."

"Thanks!" Archie grabbed one and tore the wrapper open with his teeth. He felt hungry enough to eat the paper.

"It's about fifteen hours total," Clare said, responding to his question. "That is, if we keep to the speed limit and don't stop too long for gas."

Archie bit into the bar. It tasted like heaven. "That means we should get there around five tonight," he said. "Then what? I mean, where will we sleep and all?"

Clare glanced at him. "What's the matter, Francis? You're full of worries all of a sudden. Don't you know God is looking after us? We're on God's mission now. We will be just fine. Isn't this food and coffee proof of that?"

"What *is* God's mission for us, Clare? I've been wondering that lately. What will we do when we get to the Cloisters? What will we do when we get back home?"

"What we've been doing every day. We'll trust in the Lord. God will show us our mission. This pilgrimage will show us what our next steps will be. You have to trust in the Lord, Francis. God tells us every minute, every second of the day, what we should be doing. Just listen, and you will know."

They drove for several more hours, both lost in their own thoughts. In Virginia, Archie looked out the window and saw a sign for Front Royal. He wondered for a minute what a place with the name *Royal* in it might look like. He imagined a city with streets paved in gold. He craned his neck as they passed the exit, hoping to catch a glimpse of something glistening in the distance, but it looked like all the other exits on the highway.

He turned to Clare, recalling their earlier conversation, and asked, "Have you ever listened for God and not heard anything? I mean *nothing*—like, blank—no one's there?"

Clare shook her head, her dark hair sweeping the back of the seat and making a soft swishing sound. "Never. God is always with me—always."

"Yeah." Archie sighed and watched the road.

"The first vision I ever had was at the Cloisters. That's why I say I was born there."

Archie jerked his head around. "A vision? You've had visions?"

Clare grabbed the steering wheel. "Watch the road, Francis."

Archie faced forward and slowed down, regaining control of the truck. A car passed them, honking its horn.

Archie swallowed a bite from his second PowerBar and said, "Like me, you mean. The kind of vision I had, with the trees and all. Like that?"

"Yes, I've had that, too, but this one was when I was in the Langon Chapel of the Cloisters. There's an altar there on one side of the room, and it has this high dome ceiling and these narrow windows, with arches set into the thick stone walls, and there's a stone canopy over the altar, and the light from the windows was shining down through the little pillars of the canopy onto the altar. And there, in the center of the altar, is a wooden carving of the Virgin. She's holding Jesus on her lap, only Jesus is missing his head.

"I had noticed there were lots of statues and carvings there in the museum, with plaques saying that these were statues of the Virgin and child, but the child was missing. Mary would be standing or sitting with her arms cradling the air, because at some point over the centuries Jesus had broken off. I thought it was sad that even in these statues, Jesus had been torn from his mother. So I went up to the altar and kneeled before it, and I spoke to the Virgin and told her I was so sorry she'd lost her son. Then I prayed, with my head bowed because the sun was so bright, and when I finished praying, I looked up and the sun had moved and I could see the Virgin's face. She was crying, Francis. It was real—real tears. I touched her face and it was wet. I licked my fingers and they were salty. And when we get there, if you look you'll see a crack running through the center of her eye and down her face. Her tears have left a deep crack in the wood."

"'Real tears,'" Archie said, moved by what she had told him. "I can't wait to see her."

Clare nodded. "Yes, you'll see her. I've seen her tears three times now, and each time I have I've come away changed. My eyes are opened and I see the world differently. I receive gifts."

"What kind of gifts?" Archie asked, glancing over at Clare, who stared out the windshield as if she were gazing upon the Virgin right at that moment.

"One was the gift of other visions."

Archie looked at Clare and saw a pained expression

pass over her face. A moment later it was gone. "What kind of visions?" he asked.

"I'll tell you about them sometime, but not now, okay?"

Archie shrugged. "I guess," he said, wondering at all the secrets Clare seemed to have. It seemed she was always pulling another one out from behind her back every time they had a conversation. He never knew what she would tell him next.

"So then," he said, "what about the other gifts? Can you talk about them?"

"Well, another one is the gift of extra perception, I guess you'd call it. All of a sudden I could look at people and know things about them most people would never guess. I found that I just knew things, like this one's just been laid off from work and that one's afraid his baby might be deaf."

"You read people the way your father does."

"Yes, but even more so."

"So if I see her crying, I'll be like that? I'll be like you?"

"I believe so, Francis. I hope so."

Archie sighed. For whatever reason, God had deserted him up on the mountain the night before; he felt sure that when he saw the statue, God would return to him again—and he couldn't wait. He wanted to see the tears. He would cry with her, he decided. He would mourn the Virgin Mary's loss.

"It changes you," Clare said, breaking into his thoughts. "You can't help but love people when you see inside them like that. Everybody is just trying to do the best they can with their lives. Some people make really bad, even evil choices, and others make good ones, but still, they're just trying to survive and do the best they can." She nodded to herself.

Archie shook his head. "I don't think murderers are doing the best they can."

Clare looked at Archie. "Oh, but they are. They are sick, but they are still God's children."

Archie glanced at her, startled by her vehemence. "But murder isn't the answer to anything, or rape or any of those things. That's not doing the best you can; it's doing the worst."

"Some people lose their way; they turn from God and they make the wrong choice, an evil choice, maybe, but still they're just trying to survive as best as they can."

Archie shook his head. "Hitler? Saddam Hussein? No way!"

"You don't think God loves them, too?" Clare asked.

"I don't know, maybe, but it doesn't mean I have to."

"If you hope to be like Jesus, it does."

Archie shook his head. "If that Virgin at the museum can make me feel love for those two—well, that I've got to see." Then Archie remembered his grandmother and he said, "Sometimes people get healed on pilgrimages. You can pray at a shrine or something, and the person you pray for gets healed in an instant. You think if I prayed for my grandmama she would be healed? She's so ill. I'm afraid about leaving her, really. That's the biggest thing about this pilgrimage that worries me. What if—what if she's dead when I get back?"

Clare reached up and touched Archie's shoulder. "Trust in the Lord," she said. "I used to have high fevers. I'd get them three or four times a year. I would come close to dying every time. The first time I saw the Virgin's tears was when I was visiting my aunt, and I could feel the fever building in my body. I always knew a fever was coming because everything would take on a molten appearance, as though the people and things I looked at were the ones with the fever and they were melting from it. I would become color-blind, too. I wouldn't just lose certain colors, like green and red; everything would turn to a sickly yellow-white. Anyway, when I prayed and spoke to the Virgin that first time and told her I was sorry that she'd lost her son, I saw her tears and I felt the fever leave. My body cooled in an instant, and I could see colors again. I reached up to touch the tears and to taste them, and I knew I was healed. So fear not, Francis, your grandmother will be well."

Archie felt tears welling up in his eyes. "Wow!" he said, gripping the steering wheel harder. He couldn't wait to see the Virgin and child with the missing head.

Clare patted his shoulder. "Just trust in the Lord," she said.

"Trust in the Lord," Archie said to himself, over and over, recalling his last visit with his grandmother, with the oxygen and the IVs—"Trust in the Lord."

Archie was so lost in thought, he didn't hear the siren at first, and it wasn't until it was close upon them that he saw the lights flashing.

# CHAPTER

# 22

Archie panicked. He turned to Clare. "What are we going to do, Clare?"

Clare's eyes were wide with panic, but she again placed her hand on the steering wheel to steady Archie.

"Turn on your blinker and look for a chance to pull over," she said, her voice trembling.

Archie looked to his right, but the traffic was heavy. Cars were all around him. "We're stuck! I can't get over."

Archie's hands began to shake. He looked at Clare and saw that her face was ashen. He had never seen her scared before. He checked the rearview mirror. The police were staring right at him. "Great, they're going to think we're leading them on a chase." Archie looked at the right and left lanes. Both sides were still blocked. "What are we going to do?"

"Pray," Clare said. She closed her eyes and hummed. The color returned to her face. Cars began to pull over to the side of the road and a space opened up. The traffic had slowed down. Archie signaled and got into the slow lane, then pulled off to the right side of the road behind a Toyota and stopped. He pressed his forehead against the steering wheel and prayed.

The police car sped past, its siren still blaring.

Clare and Archie looked up at each other for a minute, taking in the fact that they had not been stopped. The siren was not for them. Then they both broke up laughing, and Clare said, looking at all the cars trying to pull back onto the highway, "There are an awful lot of us guilty people on the road."

Archie took a deep breath and signaled to get back onto the highway, and soon they were under way again. They drove a long distance in silence, both lost in thought. Clare hummed and Archie watched the highway, ignoring his grumbling stomach. The PowerBars and coffee had only made his hunger worse.

The farther north they drove, the heavier the traffic became, and at one point, just outside of Harrisburg, Pennsylvania, the traffic came to a halt. Archie rolled down his window and leaned out to try to see what had stopped them. His first thought was that the police were searching all the cars for two runaways, but then he reasoned that was unlikely and he relaxed. He saw a mother in the car beside him passing sandwiches back to her children. A boy, who sat in the backseat next to the window and closest to Archie, looked between his two slices of bread and smiled at what he saw. He closed the sandwich and lifted it up to take a bite. Then he saw Archie staring at him and he rolled down his window, got up onto his knees, and held the sandwich out to him. Without thinking, Archie leaned out and took it. "Thanks," he said.

The boy put his finger to his mouth and rolled the window back up.

Archie nodded and looked at the mother, who had been too preoccupied with her other two fighting children to notice the exchange. He turned to Clare. "Look what I have, a peanut-butter-and-jelly sandwich. That kid in the blue car just gave it to me."

Clare didn't seem surprised. "God always provides," she said.

Archie bit into the sandwich and then offered it to Clare. She took a bite and handed it back saying, "You have the rest; you're driving."

"It's delicious," Archie said, biting into it again. "That kid doesn't know what he's missing."

Clare nodded and wiped her mouth with her hand. "Maybe he does and he gave it to us anyway. Think about that, Francis."

Archie did think about it. Maybe, he thought, he was becoming like Clare. Maybe the boy could see the saintliness in his eyes. He looked down at the boy in the car. They were still almost side by side. Archie signaled to him that the sandwich was good, and the boy put his hand up against the car window, his middle two fingers turned down and his thumb, index, and pinky extended. Archie recognized the sign for "I love you" and was startled. He lifted his own hand and signaled back "I love you," and tears filled his eyes. *He knows who I am*, Archie thought, struck by the boy's gesture and feeling something strange come over him. The car pulled ahead and the little boy waved, his hand still signing "I love you."

Archie smiled and waved back the same way. Traffic started moving again, and the blue car pulled farther ahead.

Archie took another bite of his sandwich and waited for the cars in his lane to pick up speed. While he waited he sat back and wondered if the only reason there had been a traffic jam was so that the little boy could give him his sandwich. Was it God's way of showing him that he wasn't alone after all? Even though he had felt abandoned by God and, worse, had felt something evil and dark inside himself, was God showing him that he was still on the path? Was he beginning to look like Clare? Did he have that light in his eyes, the way she did? Did his face seem to glow with love and devotion for God?

Maybe all the hours and weeks of praying had borne fruit after all. Maybe that was the way God worked. The boy had seen love in him. The boy had seen God in him; he was sure of it. He looked over at Clare. She seemed so content, so at peace with the world and with herself. That's what he was after, he decided. He wanted to look just the way she did, so that people would know he was a saint, a holy man of God, and they would love him for it. *That boy saw it. He loved me. He told me he loved me.* Archie drew in a satisfied breath and let it out. *Yes, this is what it's all about.*

The traffic slowed to a halt again, and Archie looked for the boy in the blue car. He wanted to practice his loving gaze on the boy, but the blue car was too far ahead. He turned his head and smiled at Clare. It was easy to look lovingly at her. He set his hand on her shoulder and squeezed it. "You know, I think this pilgrimage is already working," he said.

# CHAPTER

# 23

ARCHIE AND CLARE DIDN'T arrive in New York until after six in the evening, and Archie was tired, hungry, and cranky. The city traffic scared him. Tall office and apartment buildings loomed above them on either side of the street, making him feel claustrophobic. They were a poor substitute, he felt, for the mountains back home. Cars were everywhere, packed close together and moving too fast. Yellow cabs darted in and out in front of him, and Archie kept slamming on the brakes to keep from running into them, earning him honks from the cars behind.

When Clare tried to help him relax, Archie barked at her. "Of course you're calm; you haven't been driving for sixteen hours on no sleep and very little food. I've had hardly anything to eat, so what do you expect?" he said, knowing full well that Clare had eaten only one bite of a sandwich all day and had had as little sleep as he.

"I 'expect' you're tired and hungry," Clare replied. "We're almost there. I'll find you something to eat; don't worry."

Archie honked the horn at a man who was honking at him. "Yeah, and how are you going to do that? This was a bad idea. This whole thing was a bad idea."

"You're tired, Francis. It will all be okay; you'll see."

Archie glared at Clare. "Stop telling me how tired I am and don't call me Francis. My name is Archie. Archibald Lee Caswell, okay?"

Clare didn't reply. She pointed to a sign. "Quick, take that exit; that's us."

Archie swerved right and got onto the ramp, and the driver behind him honked his horn. "Yeah, yeah," Archie said, feeling so ill-tempered he wanted to punch something. They rode along the Hudson River for a while, and then Clare tapped Archie's arm and told him to take the next right. Archie did as Clare asked and was surprised to find that they were in a quiet city neighborhood, with tall apartment buildings in red or yellow brick in rows along the street.

"Where are we?" Archie asked. "Where's the Cloisters?"

Clare didn't answer him. She was looking ahead for something. Then she pointed and said, "There. Pull into that parking space there."

It took a few moves, and Clare's guidance, for Archie to parallel-park the truck into the space. Shifting back and forth and rolling up onto the curb and almost hitting the car behind them did nothing to improve Archie's mood.

Clare hopped out of the truck and ran toward a grubby-looking park, and Archie called after her, "Hey, where are we going?" He looked around for something that might possibly be the Cloisters, but all he saw were apartment buildings and the park, with a set of swings, benches, and a basketball half-court. There was no grass in the park, only cement. A group of young boys were playing basketball on the court, shooting into a hoop with no net. The only other person there was an elderly man sitting slumped over on a park bench. Clare ran for the swings.

"Come on, Francis, let's swing," she said, hopping onto a swing and pumping her legs.

"What?" Archie asked, believing Clare had gone insane. What were they doing in a stupid park? Where was the Cloisters? What about food, and a place to sleep? He could feel more irritation rising in him. He felt so upset, he wanted to throw himself on the ground and kick and scream and have a full-blown tantrum.

He strode over to the swings. By then Clare had pumped pretty high, and he had to stand to one side to keep from getting knocked down by her.

"What are we doing here?" he shouted up at her.

The man on the bench raised his head and looked at them.

"Francis, it's so wonderful. Come on, swing! It's just like flying. It's the closest thing to flying." Clare tossed her head back and laughed. The swing swooped forward. Her laugh was musical, her delight contagious. Archie saw the joy in her eyes when she looked at him, and he couldn't help but smile in spite of his irritation. Neither could the man on the bench. Clare pumped higher. She sang a song. It sounded made-up to Archie.

The man on the bench stood up and shuffled over to them. He was a frail-looking man, not too tall, with wisps of white hair on his head. His eyes were a dark brown but rimmed in red. Archie thought maybe he was a homeless drunk.

"That's Robert Louis Stevenson," the man said to Clare.

Archie took a step forward, wondering if they were going to have trouble. Was he calling Clare, Robert Louis Stevenson? Was he a crazy man?

Clare called out to him. "You know the poem!"

"'The Swing,' I believe it's called," said the man. "My wife used to read it to my daughter when she was a little girl."

"And my aunt read it to me. Come join me," she said.

The man smiled and shook his head, backing away. "Oh no, no, no. I haven't been on a swing in a hundred years."

Clare slowed down. "Then you must swing. It's been way too long."

The man looked at Clare. He grabbed the chain of the swing closest to him with a shaky blue hand, and Archie wondered if he was really going to swing. He wasn't sure the man could hold on. He looked weak, and Archie noticed he smelled sour. It looked as if he had worn the same old suit and tie for months. There were food spills on his shirt and tie that Archie was sure had been there a while.

Clare dragged her feet in the dirt below her and came to a stop. She stood up. "You have to use *this* swing; it's magical," she said to the man.

"Oh it is, is it?" He smiled and took a step toward her. "And why is that?"

"This is the swing my aunt always pushed me on when I was a little girl. We used to come here sometimes for lunch. I haven't been back here in years. I've been living in the South. My aunt died a few years ago. I still miss her. Have you lived here always?" Clare took the man's hand and drew him toward the swing. "Come on; sit down here."

"I've lived here forever and a day," the man said, shuffling toward her offered swing.

"Well, you don't look a day older than forever."

The man chuckled and glanced up at Clare's shining face. "Pretty girl," he said.

Archie saw that the man was caught. Just as he had been caught, just as everyone who met Clare got caught. He didn't know how she drew people to her the way she did. He watched her help the man into the swing, and then she climbed on with him, standing behind him with one foot on either side of the man's legs. She held on to the chains. She bent, then straightened her legs, pumping the swing forward and back. She talked to the man while she pumped, telling him stories about her aunt, who was like a mother to her, and how she missed her so much. She didn't let the swing get too high. She kept the ride smooth and gentle. The man told Clare that his wife had recently died. He told her that he felt lost without her. He couldn't stand going back to his apartment because everything there reminded him of Sarah, his wife.

Archie leaned against one of the swing-set poles and listened to them talk. It was as if they were alone in the world, sharing their lives, oblivious to anything but each other. Archie felt left out. He knew he could have joined in and told the man about losing his grandfather, but talking about Silas would remind him of the way he had died and his worries about his grandmother, and anyway, it was getting dark and he was hungry. More talk meant food and sleep got farther away from him.

Archie spoke to Clare. "Maybe we ought to get going," he said. "I'm hungry."

The man, who had introduced himself to Clare as Irving, asked, "Have you had your dinner yet?"

When Clare and Archie both said no, Irving offered to take them out to dinner. "I don't know if you want to spend an evening with an old codger like me, but if you would, then . . ." The old man hung his head as if he was expecting them to make up some excuse and ditch him.

By then Clare had slowed the swing down enough to get off. She did so with a backward hop, and then she leaned forward and caught the man in her arms from behind and hugged him. "There is no one we'd rather spend our evening with," she said.

Archie saw tears forming in the old man's eyes, and Archie looked away.

Irving cleared his throat and patted Clare's arm. Then he stood up. "Thanks for the ride," he said. "It *is* a magic swing."

"I told you so," Clare said, taking Irving's hand and then reaching out for Archie to take her other hand.

The three of them left the park and headed on foot toward Irving's favorite Italian restaurant. Clare asked him to tell them more about his wife, and for the duration of their slow walk, Irving told them about Sarah; as Archie listened he wondered if Clare could have planned the whole encounter ahead of time. Maybe it had been the reason for their stopping at the ugly little park in the first place. But how could she have known that a lonely old man would be sitting on that bench? How could she have been sure he would respond to her and want to take them out to dinner? Had she known he would know that swing poem? Had she known somehow that Irving was grieving over the death of his wife? Is that why she'd spoken up about her aunt, to get him to talk about his wife? Was it all that crying Virgin at work?

Archie didn't know the answer to any of his questions, and once they were seated in the cozy restaurant and he was eating manicotti and Italian bread, he no longer cared—at least for a while.

During dinner Clare and Archie told Irving about their pilgrimage, leaving out some of the details, such as the fact that no one knew where they were or that Archie had driven them, without a license, in his grandfather's truck. Archie knew if he and Clare had met up with his grandmother and had told her their story, she would have hundreds of questions for them and would be suspicious if they didn't answer them. He knew, too, that she would get after Clare for eating only a small salad of lettuce and tomatoes without dressing, but Irving didn't seem to notice or to be suspicious of anything; he just listened and told them tales about his visits to the Cloisters. He also told them about a church not too far away called the Cathedral of Saint John the Divine, which he claimed was the largest cathedral in the world, except for Saint Peter's in Rome.

"You'd be interested in this, Francis," he said to Archie. "Every year in October they celebrate the feast of Saint Francis of Assisi with the blessing of the animals. It's a real zoo—hundreds and hundreds of people with their pets. It's loud but festive and just what your dear Saint Francis would have wanted, don't you think?"

When dinner was over, the old man invited Clare and Archie to stay the night with him. They walked back toward the park to one of the yellow-brick apartment buildings, with steep steps leading up to a bright green front door. Archie was surprised by the inside of the apartment. He had expected it to feel cramped and to have only one room; instead it reminded him of his own home, with its high ceilings and cheerful rooms and the lingering smell of sweet perfume. Archie wondered if Irving noticed the smell. He was certain Irving wasn't wearing perfume.

Irving took them from room to room: living room, kitchen, two bedrooms, and a study with a sofa that pulled out into a bed. He showed them his wife's collection of fountain pens—Montblancs, Pelikans, and Watermans, each one laid out neatly in a velvet-lined wooden box—and her collection of hats of all shapes and from every era dating back to the beginning of the 1900s. He had a story to tell about each pen and hat—where it came from, how Sarah had happened to find it or buy it, and where she had used or worn each one.

Archie leaned against an oak sewing table, overcome with fatigue and dying to be shown to his bed so that he could get some sleep. He didn't know how Clare could stand it. She listened to Irving drone on and on, as if he were giving her the answer to all of life's mysteries. Her eyes were bright and looked eager, and as she listened to his endless stories, she smiled and asked questions that kept Irving talking even more. Archie sagged against the table. He didn't think he could hold himself up much longer, yet still they talked.

At last, when the tour was over, Irving showed them where they could sleep. The spare bedroom would be Clare's room, and Archie would sleep in the study. Archie thought he'd finally get to lie down, but then Clare asked Irving if he would like Archie to help him bathe and the man broke down, flopping back onto the flowered sofa in the living room and weeping into his hands. Archie and Clare sat on either side of him, and Clare put her arm around Irving, and the two of them waited for him to calm down and tell them what was wrong.

Archie waited with his eyes closed and felt himself drifting off when at last he heard Irving sigh and apologize. "I have been too depressed to care for myself," he said. "It's not that I can't bathe; it's that I haven't wanted to. I want to be with my Sarah." He cried again, and Clare patted his back. "It's so lonely without my Sarah, my angel," he said.

Clare stood up and said she would be right back. She eyed Archie and indicated with her hands that he should put his arm around Irving. Archie sighed and patted the man's shoulder. He didn't know what to say. He felt uncomfortable sitting there and looked back through the doorway, hoping Clare wouldn't be long. She returned a couple of minutes later with a large pot of soapy water and a washcloth. She set the pot on the rug and knelt down in front of Irving. "I'm going to just wash your feet, okay?" she said to him.

The old man nodded and smiled down at Clare as she pulled off his shoe.

Archie stood up. The smell was too strong for him. He stood in the doorway and watched. Clare pulled off one of Irving's socks and then did the same with his other foot. Then she took the washcloth and dunked it in the water and washed his feet.

Archie thought that washing the old man's feet was a ridiculous thing to do since his whole body needed washing. He didn't see the point in it at all, even if Jesus did once wash his disciples' feet, and he figured Clare was just trying to be like Jesus. He had never paid too much attention to the Bible stories in his Sunday-school class, but he seemed to remember the whole point of that story was to show how humble Jesus was. What was the purpose of Clare's showing Irving how humble she was? They already had a place to sleep and they were full from their dinner; what more could she want?

Irving sat back in the sofa and closed his eyes. Clare hummed her one note and washed his feet.

The sound of Clare dunking the cloth in and out of the water was soothing even to Archie, and after a while of watching the scene and listening to the water in the pot, he wished that it were his feet and not Irving's that Clare was washing.

Clare finished cleaning the man's feet, then took the small towel she had resting on her shoulder and dried them.

Irving opened his eyes and smiled at Clare. "You're a strange child," he said.

"Sarah would want you to take care of yourself," she replied.

"Perhaps you're right, there."

"I am right. Don't you think we were meant to meet, Irving?"

He nodded. "I think maybe so."

"And I think I am meant to tell you this: Take care of yourself. Sarah will wait for you, but you're not finished with your life. You've given us dinner and a place to stay for the night. What would we have done if you hadn't been there in the park? You don't know it yet, but there are people who need you, just like we did tonight."

"What people? I'm all alone. All my friends are gone."

Clare took Irving's hand. "Find out. Go find out who needs you, Irving."

# CHAPTER

# 24

When Archie awoke the next day, he could hear Clare and Irving in the kitchen, talking. He sat up in bed and looked at the clock on the desktop. It was almost eleven. The clock, like most the furniture in the room, was an antique. He thought that maybe it was broken, but he got up anyway, feeling slightly dizzy. He recalled his dreams from that night and was glad to be awake. All of the dreams had had a dark overtone to them, a gloominess or, in a couple of them, a menacing feel.

One dream was more than just slightly menacing and dark. In it his grandparents were dressed as nuns guarding the entrance to a tall stone building. They marched back and forth in front of the gate with rifles over their shoulders. When Archie tried to enter, they both aimed their rifles at him and told him he was not worthy enough to pass through the holy gates. When he asked them what he had to do to become worthy enough, his grandmother answered, "You must die." Then his grandfather shot Archie, and Archie awoke, sitting up straight in bed and staring wide-eyed into the darkness, wondering where he was. He had been so frightened by the dream, it took him a long time to get back to sleep. He tried praying, but the fear would not leave him and he could not find God in his prayers to comfort him.

While Archie made his bed that morning, folding up the lace-edged sheet Irving had given him and putting the sofa back together, he decided he couldn't wait to get to the Cloisters. He felt sure that all the dark and dangerous feelings in his dreams and prayers would disappear once he got there and saw the crying Virgin. Clare had said it was a holy place. Archie knew he needed to be surrounded by holiness, and he hoped that he and Clare could get away from Irving fast and get to the Cloisters.

The dream had also left him worried about his grandmother. He hoped that Nattie Lynn or Clyde or whoever found his note wouldn't tell her he was gone. He hoped she was getting better and not worse. He recalled that last visit with her and felt a pressure in his stomach. What would he do without her? Before he left the study, he said a prayer for her.

When he went into the kitchen, he saw that Irving had bathed and was dressed in clean clothes. He looked like a professor, in his khakis and corduroy jacket. He was spreading cream cheese on a bagel while Clare sat on the counter close by, advising him not to put any on hers. Clare was dressed in the same pair of jeans and the same blue shirt she had worn the day before, but he could tell that she, too, had taken a shower, because her hair was still wet and uncombed.

They both looked up when Archie entered, their faces beaming. Clare hopped off the counter. "Francis! Did you have a good sleep?"

"Yeah, sorry if I slept too long."

"You needed to after all that driving," Clare said. "But we have already had quite a morning, haven't we, Irving?"

Irving nodded. "That we did." He handed Archie a plate with a bagel and cream cheese on it.

"Thanks," Archie said.

Clare opened the refrigerator. "We went grocery shopping this morning because dear Irving's cupboards were bare, and while we were at it, we found Irving a job."

"Bagging groceries?" Archie asked.

"Tell him," Clare said to Irving, setting a carton of orange juice on the table and slamming the refrigerator door shut.

Irving caught the bagels that popped up in the toaster and dropped them onto a plate. "We ran into a neighbor of mine at the grocery store, and I introduced Clare to her. Her name is Lizzie Alward. She has two sons, one ten and one seven—Joel and Jacob." Irving spread cream cheese onto the hot bagels. "They go down to the synagogue a few blocks away after school to get tutored and to play games, because their mother works. It's an after-school program, you see?"

Archie nodded. He had already begun on his bagel. He had never had one before, and he liked the chewiness of it.

"I'm going to be a tutor," Irving said. "What do you think of that?" Irving turned around and handed Clare her plain bagel. "I start today at two-thirty."

Archie saw that Irving had tears in his eyes, but he knew they were different from the tears of the night before.

His whole face looked different than it had the night before, when it was gray and drawn-looking. His eyes had been red and had held a pained expression. Now his face looked pink and his eyes clear and bright. It was as though he had had an infusion of some magic health elixir overnight.

Irving sat down next to Clare and said, "I hope I do a good job of it."

Clare patted his hand. "Of course you will. And when we come back tonight, we'll hear all about it, won't we, Francis?"

Archie smiled, but he didn't say anything. He had mixed feelings about returning that night. He was glad to think they had a place to stay and food to eat, but he felt jealous of the time Clare spent with the old man. He felt jealous of the attention she gave him and jealous that she was the one who helped Irving; she was the one who could talk to him and draw him out. Archie decided that if Clare had spent her whole life surrounded by people much older than she was, the way he had, then she, too, would have little tolerance for Irving's endless stories. Telling himself that made him feel better, and as soon as he had finished his bagel and glass of orange juice, he nudged Clare and said they should get moving. Then he noticed her plate with the bagel still sitting on it. "You haven't eaten even a bite out of your bagel," he said.

Clare smiled and looked from Archie to Irving. "I'm too excited to eat; I'll take it with me."

Archie would have argued with her, but he was excited, too, and wanted to leave as soon as possible, so he agreed to her wrapping it up to take with her.

Still, it was more than an hour later before they were able to leave. Clare washed the dishes and insisted that Archie bathe before they left. Then she combed out her hair and helped Irving wash a load of laundry. She said they couldn't take off until she had put the load into the dryer.

At last they were free, and as soon as they were out of sight of Irving's apartment and walking toward the truck, Archie asked Clare, "What was that all about? I thought we were on a pilgrimage—you know, visiting a holy place and doing lots of praying. I thought we were supposed to be on our own. I know we need a place to stay, but you don't have to go overboard with it. And anyway, how did you know that guy would be in the park? It's like you knew he'd be there and you had this whole thing planned out— you'd talk about your dead aunt and he would cry and tell you all about his dead Sarah, like you knew his wife had just died. And then he asked us to dinner and all. How did you know he'd do that?"

They had reached the truck, and after Archie and Clare had both climbed in, Archie turned to her and added, "I guess what I'm wanting to know is how much of what you did last night was just so we could have a place to stay?"

Clare looked at him with surprise. "Francis, I didn't know he'd be there and I didn't know his wife had died. I wanted to swing on the swing, that's all. My aunt used to take me there. But then I saw him and I knew something tragic had happened. Didn't you?" She gazed at him with her wide violet eyes looking so innocent, and Archie felt a little ashamed.

"I guess," he said, "but how did you know he would come over? How did you know about that poem—that swing poem? Is it because of the crying Virgin—the gifts?"

"I don't know. It just turned out that way. Haven't you noticed that when your heart is on God, things just happen—they just work out like that? I was just loving him. People respond to love. Everybody responds to love."

Archie wanted to roll his eyes. Clare made everything sound so simple, and maybe for her it was, but for Archie, everything seemed hard. Why was he feeling so angry and mean-spirited? Where was God? He began to wonder what had made him believe his grandfather and think he ever was or ever could become a saint. No, it was Clare he had believed. She was the one who'd said he was chosen and called by God. He still wanted that feeling of God he'd felt on the mountain, but he believed more and more that the possibility was hopeless. He put the key in the ignition and started up the truck and prayed to the emptiness inside him that the Cloisters would change everything, just like Clare had said it would.

# CHAPTER

# 25

When Archie and Clare got out of the truck in the Cloisters parking lot, Archie noticed several school buses and cars already parked there. He hadn't expected crowds of people, and he felt disappointed. Then he turned around and looked up at the stone building and felt a little better. It looked like a castle. It didn't have a drawbridge or turrets or even the cutouts at the top where the king's men would fire on the enemy below, but it had a tower and castlelike windows and a great stone wall surrounding it. They headed toward the entrance, and Archie's heart pounded in his chest. This was it. He took Clare's hand and squeezed it. Clare squeezed his hand back and laughed. "We're here at last," she said.

They entered through a set of heavy wooden doors into a stone hallway that led to a long stairwell. The stairwell smelled damp and sweaty, the way Archie's socks did after he'd put in a hot day of work on the farm back home. A slender, bald-headed man who looked to be in his sixties sat close to the entrance. He appeared bored, but when he saw Clare he stood up and smiled broadly. "Clare Simpson! Where have you been keeping yourself?" he said, holding his hand out for Clare to shake.

Clare took his hand and then hugged him. "My old friend Maxwell! It's so good to see you." Clare turned to Archie and introduced him to Maxwell. Archie smiled and shook his hand, surprised that Clare knew the man. She and Maxwell talked for a few minutes, and Maxwell said how sorry he was her aunt wasn't still around. "Everyone here misses her. She was the bright light in this place, I can tell you," Maxwell said. Then he asked if the director knew she was coming, and Clare told him she hoped to surprise him.

"I don't know if he'll be in today, but you can ask upstairs," Maxwell said. "Tell Robert at the admissions desk who you are. He's new since you were here. He'll let you go through, though." He winked and Clare gave him another hug.

Clare and Archie climbed the steps to the main floor of the museum. Clare introduced herself to Robert, but then a guard standing nearby heard her and rushed over, and Clare repeated the same greeting she had given Maxwell, but she called the man Will. Two more people working in the gift shop across from the admissions counter ran out of the shop, delighted to hear Clare's voice. Everyone hugged Clare and shook Archie's hand, and like Maxwell, they said how much they missed her aunt.

When Clare had finished explaining why they were there, saying she wanted to give Archie the grand tour of the museum and they would be staying for several days, Robert gave them each a small tin tag to wear on their shirts. It was round and had an *M* on it. Clare told Archie the *M* stood for the Metropolitan Museum of Art.

Archie examined the tag and then looked up at Clare. "It costs money to get into a museum? I thought it was free."

The people gathered around them laughed, and one of the women from the gift shop said, "For Clare it's always free. This is her home." The woman hugged Clare again, and Clare said, "Bless you, Ally. I've missed you all so much."

After a few more minutes talking with her old friends, Clare took Archie's hand and led him through the arched stone entrance of the Romanesque Hall, and everyone else returned to their posts.

When Archie reached out and touched the stone entryway, Clare told him it had been built in the twelfth century, and brought over from Europe to become part of the Cloisters. Archie ran his hand over the stonework and imagined the stones once belonging to some ancient and great mountain. He was torn between his admiration for the structure and a secret sadness that it was not still part of a mountain. "Wow!" was all he could manage to say.

"There are even grander, more elaborate entryways inside," Clare said, leading the way into the first hall.

Archie followed her and saw to his left a fierce lion painted right onto the wall. Clare called the wall painting a fresco. It looked oriental and like something from his nightmares. It also looked as if it could have come straight out of a comic book. He looked at the plaque on the wall. The painting was from the thirteenth century, and yet it was something he was sure he would have painted himself if he had wanted a beast in his stories. He wished he had his drawing pencils and his sketch pad with him.

Farther along the hallway, guarding the entrance to another room, were two more lions, both sculpted in stone. Clare told him that the lions were sleeping with their eyes open. "In medieval times people believed lions in myths represented great Christian virtue because they could sleep like that, with their eyes open."

Archie reached out and touched the fat head of one of them. It was like touching his dreams, as if his dark dreams had brought the beasts to life. Clare took his hand and led him through open-air hallways with pink-marble arches, and Archie imagined himself a monk gliding along. "I have to show you something," Clare said.

Archie nodded, following her. "The crying Virgin."

"No, not yet; later in the day, after the crowds leave. It's better if we can see it alone."

Archie frowned but continued to follow Clare. He knew she was right about waiting, but he didn't feel he could stand it. They entered a room filled with students. A guide was lecturing to them about the enormous tapestries that hung on the walls. She pointed to one in which a man with a crown sat beside a shield with a two-headed beast on it and said, "This one is believed to be Julius Caesar and as you can see . . ." The guide recognized Clare and stopped midsentence to wave. All the students turned around to look at them, and Archie blushed. Clare blew her a kiss and waved back, then pulled Archie into the next room.

"We can talk to her later," Clare said. "When the students are gone. Nancy will be moving them into this room next, and I want to show it to you myself."

They had entered the room through a stone entryway carved with two unicorns set into an archway at the top. Inside the room were more tapestries, huge woven pieces that hung from the walls, and in all but one of the seven of them there was a unicorn.

"These tell the story of the hunt of the unicorn," Clare said, gesturing to the tapestries. "There are still so many mysteries about them. Scholars have studied them and written about them, but no one has solved all of the mysteries."

Archie looked around at the tapestries. They showed in rich, colorful detail hunters with spears and their hunting dogs, wild animals, flowers and trees of every kind, castles and fountains, and always the unicorn. They fascinated Archie. He had never imagined there could be works of art woven like rugs. He had trouble enough with his simple comics and drawings.

Clare came up behind him. "Some people believe all of these tapestries tell one story, the story of the hunt and capture of the unicorn. Then others believe, like my aunt did, these are three different sets of tapestries. One set illustrates the story of the hunt of the unicorn, where the unicorn represents a lover." Clare pointed to two narrower tapestries that hung together, one of which showed a hunter blowing his horn and the other a woman in a deep-red dress with a captured and bleeding unicorn. "And another set, these two fragments here, these they believe tell a different story, in which a maiden is used like bait to capture the unicorn." Clare led Archie closer to a tapestry in which a unicorn is stabbed and then draped over a horse and carried to a castle, where the lord and lady are waiting for it. "Then the third set shows the unicorn as Christ, and see here, in this one, the unicorn has a wreath of thorns around its neck, the way Jesus had around his head when he died.

"Some people read these tapestries like a book, beginning with the one called *The Start of the Hunt* and going around the room, and others read it starting with the one there, where the unicorn is dipping his horn into the fountain. That's supposed to represent Christ purifying the water, or the sins of man."

Archie drew in his breath. He had never seen art up close before. He had seen it only in books, unless he counted his own drawings. He hadn't realized how much more thrilling it would be to see original art. He had felt such excitement when he looked through the few art books he owned and at the books in the library. He recalled the painting of Mary and Jesus, with the angels all in fantastic blue and gold, in the book about saints, and how excited he had been by that. But he realized the feeling he had there in the Cloisters, the thrill, was ten times greater. So many thoughts raced through his mind at once. He had thoughts about the grandness of the tapestries, huge illustrations woven from simple colored threads. That alone amazed him. Then there were the rich colors and all the tiny details, like the thousands of flowers woven into their backgrounds, and there was the beautiful, mysterious unicorn hunted and stabbed and at last captured. The story touched Archie. He looked at the tapestry of the lone unicorn held captive, surrounded by a fence barely big enough to hold him, and he felt a lump form in his throat. It amazed him that something created five hundred years before could touch him so deeply.

Clare was still pointing out the symbolism in the tapestries, and Archie shook his head in wonder. "How did people ever figure all that stuff out?"

"Reading and studying the history and symbolism from back then, back in the Middle Ages, and knowing the story of Christ," Clare said. "There are all kinds of symbols and secrets in these. See the backward-looking *A* and *E* held together by a ribbon?"

"Yeah, they're everywhere," Archie said, noting the one in the tree above the captured unicorn.

"No one knows what they mean. They're someone's initials, but they don't know whose."

"They look like mirror images," Archie said. "So maybe the initials are *E. A.* and not *A. E.*"

"Who knows?" Clare said. She pointed at the *Unicorn in Captivity* tapestry Archie had been studying. "All those thousands of flowers in the background are flowers that really existed back then. They're symbolic, and the trees are, too. The pomegranate is supposed to symbolize Christ and immortality, and that Madonna lily there was a symbol of purity but also has to do with being faithful in marriage. There are lots of these flowers that mean both something having to do with Christ and having to do with love and marriage. That's why some scholars think that these tapestries were originally gifts to a bride and groom, and the *A* and *E* tied together symbolize their union.

"You could spend forever in here studying all the different meanings and secrets of these tapestries, but to me they're special because they tell the story of Christ's Passion and they remind me of my own life." Clare turned to Archie. "I brought you in this room first, Francis, so that I could tell you this."

Archie studied Clare's face. Her usual cheerfulness had been replaced with a solemn expression, and it worried him. What was she saying?

"This is my life, Francis." Clare spread her arms out to indicate the tapestries. "I have been hunted and captured so many times."

The students and the guide from the other room entered the unicorn room, and Clare pulled Archie off to the side. He felt glad to hear the normal murmurings of the students and the perky voice of the guide.

"Ever since the first time I came here with my aunt, I knew that this was where I belonged," Clare said. "I knew I would have to come back. I tried, several times. I ran away from home, over and over, but the police always caught me and brought me back, and every time they did, my life became smaller and smaller. My mother fenced me in just like the unicorn."

"So that's why you don't like the police?" Archie asked.

Clare nodded. "I never could get very far, until I was much older, but still, I never made it all the way up here to New York. My mother thought I was heading for my father's house whenever I ran away. My father thought so, too. If they had ever figured out where I had really been heading, they never would have let me spend all those summers here with my aunt. I was very careful not to tell them about the Cloisters or how I felt about Aunt Clare, or my mother wouldn't have let me return."

Clare stepped closer in toward Archie, and he stepped back. It made him uncomfortable for her to be so close; he needed space to think about what she was telling him, but Clare moved into his space again. "I belong here, Francis," she said, her voice a whisper. "I'm never returning."

"What do you mean?" Archie said, feeling even more uncomfortable. "You're not going home? You have to. *We* have to. My grandmama is there."

Clare shook her head. "I won't ever return. My mother put me on the psychiatric ward of a hospital twice because of the visions I had at home. I told her I could see the Virgin Mary standing in the center of our table—floating, really—and my mother thought I was crazy. But it was true; I did see the Virgin. Once I realized that my mother wasn't seeing her, too, I stopped telling her about the visions. I didn't tell anyone. She still thinks I'm crazy, though, and way too religious and melodramatic. That's why she watches me so closely. That's why she keeps coming up to see me at my father's house. She's spying on us. She says my father is under my spell, as if I'm a witch or something. Don't you think it's a sad state of affairs when you're thought of as crazy for loving God?"

Archie didn't know what to think. All her talk about being crazy upset him. He had trusted her. He had followed her because he believed in her. She always sounded so sure about everything when she spoke, he thought. She had such faith. God spoke to her all the time. She knew the way, the path to sainthood. He had been counting on her. He didn't want to hear about her trying time after time to run away to the Cloisters. A new uneasiness crept over him. Had she just used him and his grandfather's truck to get to New York? Weren't they there to get closer to God, to become true saints? He glanced over at the *Unicorn in Captivity* tapestry again, and again he felt the lump in his throat. He thought of Clare trapped and wounded like the unicorn and felt sorry for her. He looked back at her and saw that she wore the same loving expression she always had for him, and he felt a little better.

Clare took his hand and continued, "My mother doesn't like me living with my father."

"But it's your mama who's let you go live with him, isn't it?"

Clare nodded. "I kept running away. A friend of my mother's advised her to go ahead and let me live with my father, thinking that maybe I'd wake up and discover how good I had it at home with her and then I'd come running back. So my mother let me go, but she couldn't stop trying to control me. She would call me every day to make sure I had taken those terrible pills the hospital had given me. Then, when that wasn't enough to reassure her, she came to town and stayed at the inn, so she could spy on me. She'd come to the house without letting us know she was coming, looking for signs—like crucifixes and bibles and candles. She watched me eat, to make sure I ate enough, and spied on me when I left for school in the mornings. I would see her car parked near the school entrance, and I knew she was watching to see what I was wearing every day. The other night she found my sanctuary, my attic room. She wants to put me away again. So you see, I have to stay here. Here is where God means for me to live. My mother was keeping me from the Lord. Nothing should keep us from God, Francis."

Archie stood with his mouth open. He didn't know what to think. No matter how concerned his grandmother had been about his behavior over the years, she had never spied on him, but then he didn't claim to see the Virgin Mary hovering over the kitchen table, either. Archie heard the guide discussing the *Unicorn in Captivity* tapestry and again thought of what Clare had said. Maybe it was right for her to escape her mother's clutches, but how was she planning to live? How would they both live?

"Poor Clare," he finally said. "I'm sorry about everything, really, but we've got to go on back home. How would you live up here? You've got no money and no other clothes, nothing." Then, thinking about money, he wondered if Clare had brought only enough to get them to New York but not enough for them to return home. He felt panicked at the thought. What had he gotten himself into? He realized he wanted to go home. He needed to be there, not in New York, not this way. "This whole thing feels wrong to me, Clare," he said. "I think we should go back home tomorrow. We can go and face your mama together. We'll be a united front, with God by our side. I mean, Clare, this is great—the museum is great—but it's not right."

"What I'm telling you, Francis, is that it's right for me. I belong here. I belong in the Middle Ages. I am a child of the twelfth century, not the twenty-first. If I return, my mother will put me back in the hospital, and I can never let that happen." Clare shook her head and blinked several times, as though blinking back tears, then added, "I will never, never go back to that hospital."

"You won't have to," Archie said, placing his hand on Clare's shoulder to calm her down. "I'll be with you. I'll help you. I'll make sure she doesn't put you in the hospital, and so will your daddy, but listen, Clare, we've got to go back. See, I should have told you sooner, but this whole saint thing hasn't been working for me lately." Archie swallowed, expecting Clare to object, but she just stood, waiting for him to continue.

"I—I'm not Francis; I'm Archibald, and I don't feel God's presence in me anymore. All I feel is a dark, evil presence, if I feel anything at all. Most of the time I just feel empty. I'm not like you. I'm not good like you. I don't have what it takes."

Clare touched Archie's face. "You have been *called*, Francis. You're just being tested. Don't turn away from God."

"Clare, it's no good," Archie said, much louder than he'd meant. The students turned to look at them.

"Let's go outside," Clare said, taking his hand and waving again to Nancy. She led him to a courtyard with grass and flowers and a marble fountain that reminded Archie of the one in the unicorn tapestry. They sat down on the pink-marble wall between some pillars and talked.

"Francis," Clare said smiling, her eyes sparkling in the sunlight, "you're still learning. God has so much to show you; don't give up. You're just being tested to strengthen your faith."

"But you've never been tested like this. You said so yourself. God has always been present."

"I have been tested in other ways. My mother has been a test. The psych unit has been a test. There are always tests. Even here there will be tests for me. Our faith is tested daily. It was tested in the woods that day you decided to rescue me, and even yesterday when we arrived and needed food and a place to stay. Every day I have to renew my faith and give my life to God and serve God by loving others. That is my calling, and it's your calling, too. It's everyone's calling, really."

"Then why won't you go back home?" Archie asked, feeling the roughness of the wall with his hands. "Isn't that a test? Don't you need to learn how to live with your mother?"

"No. God has shown me that here is where I belong. I know this more than anything."

"But you can't *live* at the Cloisters. It's a museum, not a real cloister."

"I will live in the tower. I have to. I have to live here."

"'The tower'? See, that sounds crazy, Clare, because you can't. Not really."

Clare stood up and faced Archie. "I will live here. God has shown me that this is what I must do. My life, my mission, is here, and so is yours. You must stay here, too, Francis. You *must* live here with me."

# CHAPTER
# 26

CLARE ADVISED ARCHIE THAT they should pray about their situation, and she led him to the Fuentidueña Chapel, a room with a large wooden crucifix hanging above the altar and a fresco of the Virgin and child surrounded by angels high up in the domed ceiling. There was no place to sit, so they stood, staring up at the crucifix and praying, while people moved in and out of the room.

Archie knew that had he been up on his mountain, back where he'd first felt such a strong sense of God's presence, he would be able to stay still and pray for hours without thought of food or sleep and without tiring. This time was different, though. He felt stirred by the art and the architecture of the room, but Clare's story had upset him and he felt confused, too. He tried praying to God and asking for help. He told God he wanted to go home and said that he was afraid for Clare. He felt ashamed of himself for doubting her and therefore doubting God, but he had the feeling that Clare almost believed she was the real Saint Clare, who had lived back during the Middle Ages. He worried that maybe she *was* a little crazy. He tried to erase the thought and to remember his own experiences with God. His grandmother must have thought he was crazy, talking to trees and stones and rejecting meat, and in a way he felt like he was, but it seemed right and good, and it really didn't matter if he was crazy or not—what mattered was God.

What had happened? How long would this test, as Clare called it, last? How was he supposed to pass it? What was he supposed to do? Pray and keep on praying? Have faith, like Clare? He wanted to have her kind of faith and devotion, but it had become so hard. Before when he'd prayed he never seemed to get hungry or tired, but there in New York he was both most of the time. The days of fasting and going without sleep had caught up with him. He even thought of eating a thick, juicy hamburger; for a moment he was tempted by the thought, but then he felt the old familiar pressure in his stomach and the desire disappeared.

What was it God or his grandfather wanted of him? He just wanted to be left alone. His life had been so much simpler before his grandfather died and he met Clare. Now everything seemed hard and confusing. He wanted to go home. He didn't want to live in some great stone tower and wander starving through the rooms of the Cloisters every day, like a ghost haunting the place. No, he wanted to go home. If they had no money for gas, he would hitchhike home. Whatever it took to get there, he was leaving.

Archie looked at Clare standing beside him and staring up at Jesus on the cross, her eyes full of adoration, just like figures in some of the paintings he had seen in the book about saints back at the library. *She really is a saint,* he thought. He felt sorry that he would be letting her down, but he knew that at least for the time being his life and his mission were not there in New York.

Archie's feet hurt from his standing so long beneath the crucifix. He wanted to sit down and he wanted to eat something. He tapped Clare's shoulder. "I'm ready to leave," he said.

Clare turned to face him. "But we've only just begun to pray, Francis. You must pray and pray. That is the only way back to God. Have faith that God is with you even if you can't feel God's presence."

"I'm sorry, but I'm hungry. I'm just so hungry. I want to leave."

"But you've hardly seen anything."

Archie thought of the Virgin that Clare had seen crying. He wanted to see that. Maybe seeing her would change everything. Maybe that's all he needed. If he could believe and have faith in a statue crying real tears, then maybe all was not lost. He told Clare that.

"We must see that later, when fewer people are around. It's the only way," Clare said.

Archie sighed and gave in. He told Clare he would wait for her out in the garden, and he left her standing beneath the crucifix. He waited in the garden a long time. He thought about going in search of the crying Virgin on his own, but he didn't think he'd know her if he saw her, and he didn't want to hurt Clare. So he waited, sitting on the marble wall and trying again and again to pray, repeating the words *"Be still and know that I am God."* He leaned sideways against a pillar and closed his eyes. Soon he fell asleep with the prayer on his lips.

It was late in the afternoon by the time Clare came out to get him. By then Archie had moved to the grass, where he lay asleep on the ground and hidden from view by a fat bush. He had been dreaming about dragons and lions biting him on the back and about blood running from the wounds the way he had seen the blood running from the unicorn in the tapestries. He told Clare about his dream, and she said that some scholars believed that it wasn't blood but pomegranate juice on the unicorn in some of the tapestries. Archie told her it was blood in his dream, and the dream was scary. When, he wondered, would he have good dreams again?

Clare told Archie it was time to go to the Langon Chapel to see the Virgin, and Archie cheered. "All right!" he said, brushing the dirt off his jeans. "I'm ready."

He wanted to run to the chapel, but he didn't know which way to go, so he walked beside Clare, forcing her to keep pace by picking up his own and holding her hand. Clare laughed and seemed as excited as he was to get to the chapel. He realized it must have been just as hard for her to wait all day.

Archie paid no attention to the great entryway they passed through, with its sculptures of two kings, one on the left, one on the right, and angels in flight above the tympanum where Christ crowns the Virgin. His mind and his aim were focused on one thing: seeing the crying Virgin. They entered the room and Clare pointed to the altar before them. It was just as she had said; a canopy of stone stood above the altar and in the center of the altar was a wooden sculpture of the Virgin with Jesus on her lap, and Jesus was missing his head.

Archie looked at Clare, not bothering to hide his disappointment. "That's it?" he asked. "It's so small. I thought it would be much, much bigger. This—she's—it's so insignificant." He looked around the spare room and saw another Virgin and child, one with all of Jesus intact. "Ah," he said, seeing what he thought was a more pleasing sculpture. "You were kidding me. This is the sculpture, right?"

Clare moved to the altar. "See her crown? See the crack running through her eye?"

Archie came forward to join Clare. "She looks hunched over to me, and Jesus looks so flat, never mind that he's headless. No wonder she cries," he said.

A man and woman walked into the room. Clare didn't notice. She was already down on her knees, praying on the bottom step of the altar.

Archie watched the couple reading the information written beside the other sculpture. They murmured to each other, but Archie couldn't hear what they were saying. Then they started toward the altar, caught sight of Clare, and turned around and left.

Archie looked again at the small sculpture. He sighed and got down on his knees and, like Clare, bowed his head and prayed, asking for forgiveness for making fun of the Virgin sculpture. Then he prayed that his grandmother would be healed and that she would live long enough for him to graduate from college. He peeked up at the Virgin, hoping to see tears, but she was the same as before: a wooden sculpture with cracks and a missing head. He closed his eyes again and listened to Clare humming beside him. He hummed, too, and waited. He didn't know how long they stayed on their knees on the stone step, but it felt like a painfully long time to Archie. His knees hurt, and again he felt hungry and irritable. Every once in a while he peered up at the statue to look for the tears, but he never saw them and he knew it wasn't going to happen for him, not then at least.

He checked on Clare. She had remained in the same kneeling position the whole time. He had never caught her peeking to see if the Virgin was crying. She hummed along with a smile on her face, a look of expectation, her brows raised, her head lifted, and her eyes closed.

A bell rang, and a woman's voice announced five minutes until closing time. Archie jumped to his feet, startled by the voice. Clare didn't stir at all.

Five minutes later the same woman's voice announced that it was closing time, and Clare opened her eyes. She stood up and turned, smiling to Archie.

"No tears," he said.

"Patience, Francis," Clare replied, crossing herself and bowing to the statue.

Archie bowed and crossed himself as well, not sure that he had done it correctly. Then he turned and joined Clare, who had moved toward the exit.

"It's my fault," Archie said when he caught up to her.

Clare raised an eyebrow. "What's your fault?"

"That she didn't cry. I wasn't concentrating enough."

They headed down the steps and left the building through the same door they had entered earlier that afternoon, pausing often to say good-bye to Clare's friends on their way out.

It was cool outside, and the breeze coming off the Hudson River felt refreshing to Archie. He took a deep breath.

"It's almost like a fall evening instead of spring," he said. "I can smell the woodsmoke of someone's stove, can't you?" Archie looked around for a house with a smoking chimney, but all he saw was the Cloisters and a stone wall and the parking lot.

They walked to the truck, and once they'd climbed inside and Archie had started it up and backed out of the parking space, he resumed the conversation. "Clare, the truth is I can't concentrate, and when I try I just get depressed or irritable. I'm hungry all the time. I feel so lost. I knelt in front of that sculpture and I felt nothing at all. Then I looked over at you and you were so rapt. I mean, you—you really are a saint. Really, I see how you are with people, and how you are with me. I..."

Clare patted his shoulder. "Let go of it, Francis," she said. "You're trying too hard. Just let God work in you."

"But how? What should I do?"

"Let go; that's all."

"Easy for you to say," he replied.

Archie drove down Fort Washington Avenue toward Irving's home. A minivan pulled out in front of them, and Archie honked at the car, then glanced at Clare. "Just acting like a New Yorker," he said.

A few minutes later they arrived at Irving's apartment. They rang the outside buzzer to be let in, and a woman answered it. She told them to come right up, and she was there waiting for them at the door when they arrived. Two slender brown-haired boys were behind her, sliding on the wooden floor in their socks.

Clare greeted the woman with a hug, as if they were old friends, and then introduced her to Archie as Lizzie Alward, the woman she had met with Irving that morning. The two boys giggling behind her were her sons, Jacob and Joel. The boys said hi to Archie and Clare, and then returned to their game of pitching pretzel nuggets into each other's mouth. Every time they missed, they scooped up the fallen nuggets from the floor and called out, "Five-second rule!" before eating them.

Archie and Clare followed Lizzie into the kitchen, where she returned to the counter to stir something in a bowl. They found Irving standing at the stove, delighted to see them. He had so many questions for them: What did they see? What did Archie think of the tapestries and the architecture and the stained-glass windows? And was it all just as Clare had remembered? His voice was animated, and he gestured every now and then with the spatula he held.

Archie had never seen such a change in a person as he was seeing in Irving. The man who had seemed so old and frail the night before suddenly appeared spry and energetic. He moved around the kitchen, pulling spices from one cabinet and oil from another, as though he were a young man. He asked one of the boys to toss him a pretzel, and he ducked and caught it like a pro. He laughed at himself and told Archie and Clare to try to do it, too. Clare tried and got hit in the face with a pretzel. Archie didn't feel like playing. He stuck his hand in the bowl and grabbed as many nuggets as his hand would hold. He stuffed the pretzels into his mouth, and the boys, watching him, decided they would see how many nuggets they could fit into their mouths at once. Their mother told them that was a bad idea, so they went back to their tossing game.

The family stayed for dinner that night, and even Archie's mood improved when he saw how happy having company made Irving. He sat at the head of his table like a king, and told Archie and Clare all about his afternoon tutoring the children. "There are so many young boys and girls there, and they all wanted me to help them with their homework. Some of them tried to get me to do it for them, but I didn't fall for their tricks."

"Mrs. Willis will do it," Joel said. "I can get her to give me all the answers."

"Then she gets smarter and you don't," Irving said. "Don't you want to grow up and be smart?"

"I want to make a million dollars," Joel answered, stuffing a large bite of macaroni-and-cheese into his mouth.

"Then you'll need to be smart."

After Irving had told them more about his first afternoon with the children, he again asked Clare and Archie about their afternoon. Clare described the tapestries for the boys, going into even greater detail about their mysteries. The two boys sat still and listened wide-eyed while she told them about the magical unicorn, hunted for the long horn that grew in the middle of its forehead. Archie sat across from Clare and watched her, just as entranced as the boys. To him she was beautiful, even if she had grown thinner and so pale. Her eyes still looked soft and beautiful surrounded by her dark lashes. When she spoke to the boys, her face was animated, and she used her hands to gesture and emphasize what she was saying. Her movements were so graceful, Archie thought that if they were put to music it would look like a dance. He watched her all evening as she worked her magic, first on the two boys and then on their mother.

At first Archie had worried that Lizzie had been too curious about their pilgrimage. She had asked too many questions, wanting to know where they were from and what their parents thought of their going to New York all alone and how long they were staying or what hotel they were going to be staying in or did they need a place to stay.

Archie had stammered out lame replies, but Clare had handled Lizzie's questions the way she did everything else, and soon enough she had put Lizzie off the subject of their pilgrimage and onto Lizzie's own story about the way her husband had walked out on her and the boys. Clare had known just what to say, just how to love the woman and her sons, and by the end of the meal, Archie could see that they loved her, too.

After everyone except Clare had eaten the dessert of ice cream and cake, and everyone had helped wash the dishes, Lizzie cut Clare's hair. Archie had missed their conversation about hair and was surprised when they disappeared and then returned half an hour later with Clare sporting a new cut. It was a funny, bowl-like cut that looked just like Joel's and Jacob's, and Archie couldn't help but laugh at Clare. She looked like a clown, with her new thick bangs hanging low over her eyebrows. Lizzie laughed, too, and said it was the only cut she knew how to do.

Irving said Clare would look beautiful even if she were bald, and everyone agreed, especially Archie, who thought maybe he would stay in New York after all. How could he ever desert Clare? He loved her too much. He knew he'd follow her anywhere. What did anything else matter? If she had faith that everything would work out all right, then so did he. He felt honored to be the one she had chosen for her soul mate. *I must have something good in me,* he thought, *that she would choose me.*

After Lizzie and the boys left and the other three hugged and said good night to one another, Archie went off to the study at the end of the hallway and decided he would stay up and pray, no matter the emptiness inside or the demons that might be lurking.

He turned off the light and sat on the sofa, staring out the window. He thought he would see the moon and stars, but it wasn't like at home up on the mountain, where the stars looked so close and clear. There were too many street-lights, and cars still drove past the house in a stream as though it were daytime and not eleven at night. He watched the cars awhile, then turned away from the window to begin his prayers. He asked God to forgive him and told God that he would believe no matter what. He prayed for Clare and for their plans to stay, and he prayed for his grandmother and decided he would call home and let every-one know his plans as soon as he knew them himself. He knew if he really intended to stay with Clare, he shouldn't go home, even for a visit, or his grandmother would keep him there and he would feel obligated to stay. His mind flashed on the image of her lying in the hospital bed, with the oxygen tank and all the machines surrounding her, and he felt a most uncomfortable pressure in his stomach. He hated the thought of his grandmother lying in a hospital bed. It frightened him too much to think about it, and he decided it was best if he put his grandmother completely out of his mind.

Archie ignored his stomach and returned to his old prayer, *Be still and know that I am God.* He stayed with it for a time, but then his mind drifted to Clare and he felt his body go warm. He loved her, he realized, like no other person. She was like no other person, except Jesus. *No wonder,* he thought, *the disciples laid down their fishing nets and followed him.* He pictured her asleep in the guest bedroom. He had never seen her sleeping before. He thought she must look like an angel when she slept, and then he decided he had to go see for himself.

He crept down the hallway to Clare's bedroom. He could hear a soft humming sound coming from the room, and he wondered if she hummed even when she slept. Her door was ajar and the lights were out. Archie crept up to the door and peered in, searching for the bed. He spotted it in the left-hand corner of the room, but Clare wasn't in it. He opened the door a little wider and found her lying facedown, arms outstretched on the floor. She stopped humming when the door opened. She said, "Come in, Francis, we'll pray together."

Archie took a couple of steps into the room. He wondered if he should lie down like her or sit on the floor beside her. He chose to sit. He got close enough to feel her warmth beside him. He looked down at her. The lights from the street shone through the window onto her hair, and Archie couldn't help but put his hand on her head and stroke it. He leaned forward to kiss the top of her head, and then realizing what he was about to do, he blushed and got to his feet. "I think I'll go pray in my room," he said. He turned and left, pulling the door all the way closed behind him.

# CHAPTER
## 27

THE NEXT MORNING after breakfast, Archie and Clare said good-bye to Irving. He had packed them a lunch of liverwurst sandwiches and pickles, and apples and some of the cake left over from dessert the night before. He followed them to the door with sad eyes and told them he would always be happy to see them and they could stay with him anytime for as long as they wished.

Archie shook Irving's hand and thanked him. He felt choked up leaving, partly because he was so grateful to Irving for taking them in and feeding them, and partly because he was scared. Where would their next meals come from? How would they live? He was glad to know they were welcome to return. He thought they might be back soon, and it was good to see that Irving was sincere about his offer.

Clare hugged the man and said, "I love you, Irving. Don't forget, God is watching over you. And take good care of yourself; Sarah would want you to."

Irving nodded. "After my tutoring this afternoon, Joel and Jacob are going to teach me how to use my computer.

Sarah bought it, but she got sick before we ever even hooked it up. I'm going to be a real hipster by this evening." He laughed at himself and waved good-bye.

Archie heard the door close behind them, and he looked back at it and said, "Nice man. I'm glad we met him. Thanks."

"I'm glad we met him, too," Clare said, squeezing Archie's arm.

Her touch reminded him of his visit to her room the night before, and he asked her if she had stayed up and prayed all night. She never looked tired the way Archie did after a late night. She looked energetic, and her eyes were always bright.

"Oh, I got all the sleep I needed," she said.

They arrived at the Cloisters long before it opened, and Clare had Archie park his truck on a nearby street instead of in the parking lot, because, she said, they would not be coming back for it that night—they were staying at the Cloisters.

Before Archie locked the truck up for the day, Clare grabbed the bundle she had brought from home out from behind the seat and then led the way toward the Cloisters, holding the bundle tucked under her arm. Archie followed her, carrying the big sack of lunch Irving had packed.

It was a gray day. *A battleship-gray day,* Archie thought. It had rained in the early morning, so there were puddles to step over, and the trees they brushed past as they walked down the path beyond the parking lot, toward the river, sprayed them with drops of cold water, making the air feel colder to Archie. He had left the sweater he had worn on the trip in the truck, and he regretted it.

They came to a viewing deck, with a concrete floor surrounded in stone, that overlooked the river. Clare stopped
and pointed at a passing ship, its lights blinking in the fog.
Archie watched the ship and wondered where it was going.
It made him feel suddenly lonely and tired and lost. He
wondered where he himself was going. He turned around
to Clare and drew in his breath when he saw a monk standing before him. Clare was wearing a long brown robe with
a hood. "Where did you get that?" he asked, looking her
over.

Clare was busy tying a rope belt around her waist. She
looked up at Archie and smiled. "I made it," she said. She
nodded toward the ground. "I made one for you, too."

Archie looked down and saw the other robe, with its
rope lying on top. He picked them up and examined the
robe. It felt heavy in his hands. "This will feel good now,
but won't this be hot when it warms up later?" he asked.

"Put it on," Clare said. "Go ahead."

Archie pulled the robe over his head. It smelled faintly
of oil, just like his grandfather's truck. It fell all the way to
his feet. He looked down at himself and smiled. "I like it,"
he said. "I feel—I don't know—different." He looked at
Clare, who had finished tying her rope. She looked like a
boy, with her haircut. *She must have known she would,*
Archie thought. *She must have asked Lizzie for the haircut
just for that reason. It's the perfect cut.* He shook his head.
"Sometimes I don't know about you, Clare. I can't tell
when you've planned and plotted something out and when
it just happens that way."

Clare gave him an innocent look. "Why? What do you
mean?"

"Your new haircut. Did you know you would look like a boy with that cut once you put on the robe? How did you know she would give you that haircut?"

"I asked for it," Clare said. "The boys' haircuts looked like the way some monks wore their hair back in the Middle Ages. I thought it would look right. It feels right. Wearing my robe feels right. Doesn't it feel right to you?"

Archie wrapped his rope around his waist and tied it. "It's cool," he said. "I don't know how I'll feel out in public, though. And if we're going through the Cloisters like this, don't you think we'll be really noticeable? What will your aunt's old friends think?"

"I'm not trying to hide in this. I'm just being who I am meant to be. Finally I get to be the real me. I get to be Clare."

"But shouldn't you be dressed like a nun, then, or like a lady saint?"

"I've made these robes according to God's directions. God said plain and brown, tied with a rope. It's what Saint Clare and Saint Francis wore."

Archie tilted his head. "Did you really hear God? Did you hear a voice?"

"You've asked me that before. Yes, I heard a voice."

"What did it sound like? Was it a man's or a woman's voice?"

"Neither. It had no sound."

"But you said you heard it. It had to have a sound."

Clare pulled her rope tighter about her waist. "It isn't a sound or a voice like you would normally think. I hear it, and then it's gone before I can identify its sound. It can't be described; that's all I can tell you. But one day you will hear

God's voice for yourself and you will know." She pulled her hood up on her head. It framed her face, highlighting the contours of her cheeks, and she looked even more beautiful than she had before. *Irving was right,* Archie thought. *She would look beautiful even if she were bald.*

He pulled his hood up and asked Clare how he looked.

"Like a real brother. You are my brother, Francis."

Archie blushed. He could think of no better compliment. He wanted to please her. He wanted to feel chosen by her as her one true companion, her Saint Francis. He looked at her moving to the edge of the deck in her robe, her hands clasped in front of her in prayer, and he felt he would do anything for her. *It must have been the hunger and fatigue that made me think I would leave her yesterday,* he thought.

He loved the confident way Clare handled everything. He loved her devotion to God, and he wanted to be just like her. She inspired him to be a better person, to be more loving toward people, and to love God more.

Archie looked at Clare's back, long and way too slender, and shook his head. He had no idea how the day would turn out, or how they'd actually live at the Cloisters—would they ask permission or would they sneak in? And he didn't know where their next meal after lunch would come from, but he had faith; he did—he could feel his own confidence. He smiled to himself and joined Clare facing the Hudson River, bowing his head as he prayed the words *"Be still."*

# 28

ARCHIE AND CLARE remained praying on the deck below the Cloisters until Clare turned away from the river and said, "It's time to go up. The Cloisters is opening now."

Archie strained his ears, listening for sounds of cars and buses arriving, but he heard nothing. Still, he grabbed the lunch bag Irving had packed for them and joined Clare on the path. He felt clumsy in his robe. He stumbled, falling into Clare and almost knocking her off the walkway and down the embankment. She caught herself just in time by grabbing on to a branch of a dogwood tree.

"Sorry, Clare," he said, reaching out and grabbing her by the waist and pulling her back onto the path. She felt thin in his arms, too thin, and his heart missed a beat. Her frailness made him think of his grandmother. He let go of her and they resumed walking, but Archie made a mental note to make sure Clare ate plenty of lunch that afternoon. She had eaten at most only a few bites of food a day since they had left home. He knew it wasn't enough.

Archie held his robe up with his free hand the rest of the way up the path, keeping a safe distance from Clare. His fall had reminded him of when he was seven and had been in the Christmas pageant at church. He had played one of the angels, and he'd worn a long white robe and a halo made from a hanger and a golden rope of tinsel. His grandmother had made the costume the way he had asked her to, so that he couldn't see his own feet, because he believed angels didn't have feet. On the night of the pageant, he had tripped onto the stage, knocking over the girl in front of him, and the whole congregation had laughed at them. The girl never forgave Archie. He thought of that as he and Clare stepped out into the parking lot and made their way toward the entrance to the Cloisters, and he felt silly in his robe and wanted to take it off. Then Clare turned around and smiled at him, and he felt brave again.

A van pulled into the parking lot, and a mother and father and three girls climbed out.

Clare smiled at them and waved and said, "I hope y'all will visit the Campin Room. Have you been here before?"

The mother said, "I have, but my girls and Roger haven't, and the Campin altarpiece is one of my favorites. How did you know? I wanted to show my daughters and tell them all about it—that is, if I can remember everything, the symbols and all."

"There are guides and guidebooks that can tell you, if you forget—or if you'd like, I can tell you," Clare said.

The three girls, who ranged in age from about six to ten, were staring at Archie and Clare, and Archie felt their stares and blushed. He felt like an impostor. He *was* an impostor. The middle girl looked at Clare and said, "You talk funny."

Clare smiled. "I'm from the South."

The young girl studied Clare and then asked, "Are you a boy or a girl?"

The father and mother both jumped in, trying to hush their daughter and saying, "That's not a polite thing to ask."

"Why isn't it?" the girl asked.

Before either parent could answer, Clare said, "It's a perfectly natural thing to ask when you're unsure of something like that. I don't mind the question." She leaned toward the girl and asked, "What do you think I am?"

"A boy?" she said.

"You're a girl," said the older one.

The youngest daughter agreed. "You're a girl."

"I'm a mystery, aren't I?" Clare said. "I'll tell you what. You go to the museum, and you'll discover all kinds of mysteries, like the painting your mother and I were talking about and these giant tapestries that look like rugs with beautiful stories on them, and before you leave come find me and tell me all about what you saw—and then I'll tell you what I am."

The girls agreed to the plan, and the youngest took hold of Clare's hand and said, "I want you to come with us, whatever you are."

Clare kissed the girl on the top of her head and said, "That's the best answer of all. You accept me for me, not whether or not I'm a boy or a girl."

The middle daughter took Clare's other hand and said, "It doesn't matter to me, either." Clare bent down and kissed her on the head as well, and the oldest daughter crossed her arms in front of her and said, "Well, it never mattered to me in the first place."

Clare laughed and dropped the two girls' hands to grab the oldest sister and give her a hug. Then the other two wanted a hug, and the parents, watching, invited Clare to join them. They noticed Archie standing behind Clare, with the brown lunch sack in his hands, and the mother added, "Your brother, too. Is that what you call him?"

Clare turned to Archie with her radiant smile and said, "That's exactly what I call him."

The three girls led Clare toward the Cloisters, and the parents and Archie followed behind.

After a bathroom stop for everyone, Clare led the family and Archie from room to room, telling them story after story and pointing out details they never would have noticed on their own. Her stories were so interesting and her manner so engaging that more and more people joined them as they moved from object to object.

There were several children in the group, and they all had questions for Clare and called out, "What does this mean?" and "What's this over here?" Clare made up games for them, like find-the-hidden-rabbit or who-can-guess-what-this-story-is-about. Even the adults enjoyed playing.

By noon Clare had ended the tour, announcing that it was time for lunch. Many people had brought picnics, and they followed Clare across the parking lot to the lawn overlooking the Hudson. They sat in a circle on the grass, which was still slightly damp from the early morning rain, and shared their food with one another. No one wanted to share the liverwurst sandwiches, and Archie was glad to have them all to himself. People passed him raisins and orange slices and cookies, and Archie gave away his pickle and apple and felt it was a great sacrifice. He had been looking forward to the pickle. He had never before seen one so big and fat. His grandmother only made pickle chips. She never kept the cucumber whole, like the pickle was. He had never eaten liverwurst before, either, and he decided it had to be an acquired taste. He liked it better the more of it he ate, but the first bite had shocked him. It was the first bite of meat he had eaten in a long time. He noticed that Clare didn't eat anything; she was too busy talking. He passed her one of the sandwiches and some cookies and slices of orange, but she passed them on to someone else and paid no attention to the food.

Archie played catch with a small boy after lunch. It felt good to be a part of things somewhat, but he wasn't comfortable in large gatherings, so he was silent most of the time, speaking only when spoken to. Most people were looking toward Clare and wanting to talk to her, anyway. Everyone wanted to please her. The children showed off for her, demonstrating cartwheels and showing her how high they could throw the ball into the air or running as fast as they could along the grass. Most of the time Archie sat back and just watched everything, as though he were one of the crows that stood on the stone wall nearby. He felt full and contented and surprised that he hadn't felt the pressure in his stomach when he ate the liverwurst. He glanced again at Clare and wished that she would eat something. He was thinking about how he could get her to eat when a man came along and pushed himself between a woman and Clare so that he could sit next to Clare.

Archie sat up. He didn't like the guy's manner. Right away he acted too familiar with her, and he kept asking her questions—too many questions—about where she had come from and why she was wearing the robe, and did she want some of his pumpkin bread. Archie didn't like it. He wasn't sure why, but he felt it wasn't the man's place to get her to eat. He was a complete stranger, after all. What did he know about anything? Anyway, getting Clare to eat was Archie's job, and he didn't like all the attention the man was giving her. The man just plain made him nervous, although he couldn't tell why exactly. He looked decent enough. He was clean-shaven, and dressed in khakis and a short-sleeved polo shirt. Archie looked for the tin tag that proved he had been in the Cloisters, but the man wasn't wearing one. He had just drifted over and joined them. Archie tried to draw Clare's attention away from the guy, but for some reason she was drawn to him. Archie didn't like it, and during the rest of the picnic, he kept watch on the man.

When lunch was over, everyone walked back to the parking lot and people said good-bye to one another, hugging like they were all good friends. They all thanked Clare, and many offered her money as thanks for the tour, but she refused to take any. The slimy man hung about them, acting as if he belonged with Archie and Clare.

Archie tried to get rid of him. "Well, it was nice meeting you," he said, offering his hand.

The man ignored him and asked Clare what order she was from. Clare answered she was from the Order of Poor Clares, an order founded by Saint Francis of Assisi and Saint Clare in the Middle Ages. She went into great detail about the order and its dedication to poverty, humility, and faith in God. The man wasn't satisfied. He wanted to know more. "Does the order forbid food?" he asked.

Archie made a face at the man. He thought it was the dumbest question anyone could ever ask. *What kind of religion forbids food?*

"Of course not," Clare replied.

The man was standing too close to Clare for Archie's comfort. Archie got on the other side of her and took her hand. "If you'll excuse us now, we're going back into the Cloisters," he said. He squinted at the man, lifting his chin and pressing his lips together to show he meant business.

The man held his hands up as if he were under arrest. "No fear," he said. "I was just curious." He walked on ahead a little, then stopped beside a tan car Archie was sure wasn't his. Archie and Clare walked past him, and Archie could feel the man's eyes following them all the way back into the building.

When they got inside, Archie said, "I don't like that man. I don't trust him."

"He's just a lost lamb," Clare said. "He needs our understanding, not our judgment."

"Well, you can be understanding if you want, but I'm keeping my eye on him."

Clare turned to Archie and took both his hands in hers. "I don't need your protection. God is with us."

"And God gave us brains and discernment, and I have discerned that that man is up to no good. And God has put a feeling in me that says that man is bad news, okay?"

Clare shook Archie's hands. "Have faith, Francis."

Archie lowered his eyes. He couldn't look at Clare without falling in with her way of thinking, and he wanted to have his own thoughts about this. To him it was the boys in the woods all over again. How could he not want to protect her? Did his desire to protect her really show a lack of faith in God? Hadn't he been born with the instinct to protect what he loved? Didn't that come from God? Archie was tired of feeling so confused about everything. He pulled away from Clare and headed toward the bathrooms.

Clare followed him.

"Maybe I have too little faith in people," he said finally, looking back at Clare. "But maybe you trust them too much—and maybe you shouldn't."

# CHAPTER
# 29

Archie had thought that they would spend the afternoon in the Langon Chapel with the crying Virgin, but they didn't. During Clare's tour of the chapel earlier that morning, Archie had stood staring at the sculpture, waiting for tears to flow. He had wanted to be the one to discover the tears and to say to the group that stood listening to Clare, "Look! She's crying! The Virgin is crying for us." As soon as he had realized the desire, he'd felt ashamed. He knew he was just greedy for attention. Everything came so easily to Clare. Everybody loved her. All she had to do was walk into a room, and people flocked to her, while Archie stood like a stooge in a monk's costume. That's what he felt the robe was, just a costume. On Clare it was real; she was a monk or a saint—someone holy—but he was just a stooge in a Halloween costume, and it wasn't Halloween.

That afternoon Clare led Archie to the Gothic Chapel and she described some of the details of the room. He loved the stained-glass windows and the high vaulted ceiling and all the delicate cutwork in the stone around the windows, but there were tombs in the room, and they made him uneasy. They were large stone tombs, with sculptures on the lids representing the dead buried within them. Clare showed Archie one lid sculpted with the figure of a young man staring up at them, his eyes open and his hands together in prayer upon his chest. She told him that the man was a knight in the Crusades who was said to have brought back a piece of the True Cross, the cross Jesus died on. Clare ran her hand over the young man's stone face while she talked. Archie didn't like looking at him. Clare said the knight looked so peaceful, but he made Archie think of the dead and of his grandfather. He felt the odd pressure above his belly button and turned away.

Clare moved to the end of the room and stood beneath the stained-glass windows. She stood with her back to the wall, hidden from most onlookers by a sculpture of a saint. She bowed her head and prayed, and Archie tried to do the same. He stared up at the stained-glass panels of Isaiah and Mary Magdalene and tried to keep his mind focused on God, but the tombs were behind him and he felt their presence. His thoughts were dark. He thought about the man they had just left in the parking lot, and then, because that disturbed him too much, he thought about his grandfather's death and the way he had missed his chance to set things right between them. Thinking about that upset him even more than the strange man had. He felt that he had missed something so important: an opportunity for him to understand his grandfather and for them both to say what was really in their hearts. Archie supposed he had feared speaking up because he'd been afraid of what his grandfather might say to him. The two of them had never gotten along, and he knew that it was his fault. He had purposely tried to bedevil his grandfather every chance he got. He was sorry, but it was too late, and he knew that he would never feel right inside about it. He felt the pressure in his stomach and it made him angry. *What am I supposed to do about anything now?* he asked God. Then he thought about his grandmother and grew even more anxious, and his heart felt heavy with dread.

Archie tried to shake all the dark thoughts from his mind. He tried to focus on God. Every time his mind strayed back to the thoughts that filled him with anger or anxiety, he reminded himself to pray, to stay with God, to look at the windows, the pretty windows with their reds and blues and golds, but still his mind strayed. Finally he got so frustrated, he couldn't stand it, and he told Clare he was going outside to the gardens and that he'd come back for her before closing time.

Archie left the Gothic Chapel and stepped out into an herb garden surrounded by brick walkways. He sat down on some stone steps, making sure to leave room for people to get by him, and took several deep breaths. He felt much better sitting outside. He thought of his mountain back home and how he had loved to bike on the trails with Armory, rising to every challenge and risk Armory would place before him. He loved to hike to the top of it and to look out over the fields, his grandfather's fields, and see the cows and sheep and corn and wheat. Viewing his world from the mountain had always made him feel satisfied somehow, and safe. He no longer felt safe or satisfied. He felt lost, empty, even, and trotting after Clare everywhere she went didn't feel good to him anymore. Maybe he wasn't a saint, not even a saint-in-the-making. Maybe his grandfather had meant to say *sinner* instead of *saint,* or he had been hallucinating, or as Archie had originally believed, his grandfather hadn't had enough time to say it all, and what he'd really meant to say was, "Young man, even if you are a saint the rest of your life, you'll never make it up to me!"

Archie stood up, hesitated for a second, looking to see who might be watching, and then when he was sure no one was looking, he undid the rope around his waist and pulled off the robe. He folded it up as best he could and coiled the rope and set it on top. He sat back down, placing the robe beside him, and returned to his thoughts of home. He missed the mountain and his home, but most of all he missed his grandmother and felt guilty for the way he had deserted her. *What's wrong with me, anyway?* he wondered. *One minute I want to run away from it all and never think about it, and the next minute I want to go home again. Why don't I make up my mind already?*

A tour group stepped out into the arcade where Archie sat, and the guide began a speech about the herb gardens and the Italian wellhead that stood in the center. The visitors walked along the arcade and spread out through the garden, then moved back inside to the Gothic Chapel.

Archie thought of Clare in there praying. He didn't know what he was going to do. When he looked at her, all he wanted was to be with her and follow her, but when he walked away from her, he felt lost and just wanted to go home. He knew he needed to give the Virgin one more try. He wanted to at least pray to her for the sake of his grandmother, but the thought of going to the altar and waiting for the tears—and his memory of that morning, when he had wanted to get everyone's attention by bragging to them that the Virgin was crying—made him doubt that the Virgin would ever cry for him and heal his grandmother.

Archie grabbed his robe and returned to the Gothic Chapel before closing time. He caught Clare's look of surprise when she saw that he didn't have on his robe, but she didn't say anything. She was standing with a small group of people. She waved him over and introduced him to the group, and they all left the building together, moving down the stairs and out to the parking lot. They stood and talked some more out by the cars, and Archie talked a little bit, too, but he was also watching the people leaving, thinking he might see the strange man still hanging about. He noticed that the tan car near where they had last seen him was still there. A while later he saw a couple get into the car and drive off. He wondered where the strange man had gone, and if he lived somewhere nearby.

The people Clare was speaking with invited Clare and Archie to join them for dinner, but Clare declined, thanking them and saying that she and Archie had to be on their way. After hugging Clare and then, with hesitation, Archie, the people in the group left and Clare said, "It's hard being a true pilgrim. Everyone wants to feed us. We have too much."

Archie nodded, but he would have liked to have gone out to eat. The group had suggested a Chinese restaurant. Archie had eaten Chinese food only once, when his homeschooling group was returning from a weekend retreat and the group had stopped at the Peking Duck restaurant. His grandparents had never taken him out to eat. He was enjoying experiencing all the new foods.

They returned to the Cloisters, and after a quick visit to the bathrooms, Clare found Will, the guard, and asked him if they could go up into the tower to visit her aunt's old friends. Will nodded and told them they could use the staff elevator. The two of them got on, and Clare pressed the button for the third floor, where her aunt had once worked.

Clare introduced Archie to all of her aunt's old friends, and like the guards and the rest of the staff on the floors below, everyone was delighted to see her. Some commented on her robe, and several people said, "I always knew you'd want to be a nun when you grew up." Archie held his robe under his arm and felt awkward when Clare introduced him; her aunt's friends looked at him as if they were wondering what had been the point of bringing him along. He wondered himself.

After a brief visit Clare hugged them all and told them she wanted to introduce Archie to the director, but instead of going toward the elevator, she led Archie to the stairs. "No one uses the stairs here," Clare said. "We can wait in the stairwell until closing, and no one will find us. The guards will think we took the elevator down to the basement and left the building."

Archie sat and waited next to Clare on the cold cement steps. His heart was beating hard in his chest. He felt like a spy or a criminal. He didn't know how they would get away with living up on the top floor of the tower. He was sure they would get caught. He and Armory had always gotten caught at home. His grandfather had had a naturally suspicious nature, and he'd always found them out. He whispered to Clare, "Are you sure this is going to work? What if they've installed alarms in the tower since you were last here?"

Clare patted Archie's hand. "Don't worry. There are no alarms. We just need to be quiet so the guards downstairs don't hear us in the night, but even they are so far away that they're not likely to."

They waited in the stairwell a long time. The hard cement became uncomfortable to Archie. He stood up and placed his folded robe on the top step and then sat on it. The cushioning and the warmth felt better; he just wished he could find a way to make his mind feel better, too.

While they waited Clare told Archie about the times she used to play on the top floor of the tower while her aunt and other staff members sat around the conference table in a meeting. She played with her trucks and dolls on the floor of the room. "The tower's always been a happy place for me," Clare said. "Everyone is so nice here. When I got older I brought my books to read, and I got to stay up there all afternoon, reading until closing time. Some days the director didn't come and I'd have the room all to myself. I love it here. This is my home. That room is my home. It belongs to me."

Archie watched Clare while she spoke. She seemed so happy and calm, as if there were nothing wrong with sitting in a stairwell waiting for everyone to leave so that they could sneak into the top room of the tower for the night. God may have told Clare that it was the right thing to do, but it didn't feel right to Archie. He wished God would let him in on the plans for once, so that he could feel good about things. Instead he felt nervous and on edge, and Clare's happy memories and her belief that the room belonged to her did nothing to calm him.

After what seemed like hours, Clare gave Archie the

signal to follow her, and they crept up the steps toward the top floor. They climbed a long flight of stairs and came to a landing, then they turned and climbed another long flight. At the top they came to a door. Clare pushed it open a couple of inches and peered in. Then she opened it wide and let Archie enter first.

The room was huge and square, with two sets of tall, narrow windows on each wall. The lights were off, but there was plenty of light coming in through the windows. The director's desk stood to one side of the room and to the other was a conference table with chairs set around it. Behind the table were shelves filled with books. There was little decoration. There were curtains in the windows and several Oriental rugs on the floor, and that was it.

Archie went to one set of windows and looked out. He could see much of the city before him. "The view's nice," he said, moving to another set of windows and seeing the Hudson River below. He turned around and saw Clare sitting cross-legged on the floor, and he went and dropped down beside her, surprised to be safely in the tower room.

After a few minutes of silence, while they took in their surroundings, Archie asked, "So, when will we see the crying Virgin again?"

"Tomorrow," Clare said. "Tomorrow morning before the museum opens."

"But how? How will we get past all the guards?"

Clare smiled. "It will be okay, Francis, I've made arrangements."

Archie could see her shining eyes even in the dim light. He shook his head. "Nothing feels okay to me anymore," he said. Then he touched Clare's hand and added, "Except you. You have a way with people that I don't have. People love you. They flock to you like sheep. You know just what to say. I feel like one of those stone statues fastened to the wall of the Cloisters. I have nothing to say."

"Francis, it's not about you."

"What do you mean?"

"I mean that if you want to know what to say to people, you have to look at them, pay attention to them, not yourself."

"That's easy for you; you've been given the gift from the crying Virgin."

"You don't need to see the Virgin cry to be able to reach out to people and love them. You just need to pay attention and care. You have to notice them. You have to really see them, the way they're walking, their facial expressions, their body language—you can tell so much just by paying attention to them. Are their voices timid or bold? How do they use their hands when they speak? How are they dressed? Are they alone or with others? Who is with them? Is one person in charge, or are they all equals?"

"You're in charge of us," Archie said.

Clare shook her head. "You drove us all the way to New York. You got us here."

"Because you asked me to. I'd do anything you asked me; you should know that by now."

"I love you, Brother Francis."

Archie liked the sound of that. He liked being called Brother Francis, although he didn't feel worthy of it. "I'm losing it," he said after a moment's silence. "I'm no saint. That's why I took the robe off. I feel like a phony in it. I don't know; I feel so angry all the time lately, and depressed." He looked up at Clare and felt tears forming in his eyes. "I feel depressed all the time. If it weren't for you, I don't know. I'm so lost. God is—God is gone. I . . ."

Clare reached out and touched Archie's hand. "Let go, Brother Francis. Let go of yourself. Put your trust in God."

Archie pulled his hand away. "How? How do I let go? What do you mean? I try to pray and I feel nothing. You don't know what that's like. It's all 'glory hallelujah' to you all the time. It's different for me. I'm empty. The only thing I have is you. I don't even know what to do with myself anymore. I have to wait for you to tell me. I'm so—so lost."

Clare moved closer to Archie and stroked his head. "God is with you even now, Francis."

Archie liked having Clare's hand on his head. He lowered his head and sighed. "But what does it matter if I can't feel God with me, if I have no sense at all that God is here? You're here. That's all I know—all I'm sure of."

"That's God's presence working through me."

"But I want God working through me, too. How am I supposed to be a saint? I'm not a saint. I'm not anything."

"You're learning. We're both still learning. I guess we always will be."

Archie twisted away from her. "What? What are you 'learning'? You're perfect. I've never met anyone more perfect. You're so perfect you're unreal, you're not human."

"You don't believe I'm human? Francis, I ran away from home. I'm very human. I'm searching just like you. But I'm doing what you said. Remember? Didn't you say you wanted to see if you could lead a sin-free life? Didn't you want to see if you could be like Jesus?"

"Yeah, and the answer is I can't be."

"You believe you can't, so no one can? Is it not even worth trying?"

Archie didn't answer. He knew he was sounding like a jerk. How egocentric could he get? Clare was right—just because he couldn't be like Jesus didn't mean it was impossible for everyone. Clare was proof of that. The real Saint Francis had been proof of that.

"I'm sorry," he finally said.

"You don't have to be sorry for anything. I'm not perfect. I'm not trying to be, and you don't have to be, either. Just listen for God."

Archie slapped his thigh. "But God's not talking to me!"

"Keep listening. God is talking, all right. Why is it that you're so upset? Why are you unhappy because you can't reach out to people? Maybe that's God speaking to you. Maybe your unhappiness is God in you. Why do you think that God's voice is always going to make you happy?"

"Because you're always happy."

"I'm happy because I'm just listening to now, to this moment. That's where God is—in this moment. Don't you see that, Francis? You have to put your mind on the present. You won't find God by worrying over what's already happened or fretting about what's going to happen."

"Yeah, I guess," Archie said, trying to understand.

"God is speaking to me now and I'm listening. God is speaking to you, too, but you're not listening. If you won't listen to God, then listen to your anger and unhappiness. Ask yourself this: What are they trying to tell you?" Clare stood up and went over to one of the windows.

Archie stayed seated on the floor, stretching his legs out and leaning back on his hands, and thought about what she had said. What were his anger and unhappiness telling him? What had changed in him? Why had he been so happy, so blissful at first? He remembered being on his mountain, eating a lemon and looking out at the cows and the trees, feeling the sun shining down on him. His grandmother was home and her hip wasn't broken. He was drawing pictures of Mountain Mike the Mountain Biker and the Back Street Thrasher. What was God saying to him back then? Archie thought about the question and decided God had been pleased with him. So what happened? Why wasn't God even more pleased after Archie changed? He was devoting his life to God, so why wasn't God happy with him? What had he done wrong?

Archie thought about when things had started to change. When was it? Then he remembered. It was the day he had gone to talk to Miss Nattie Lynn and told her he wouldn't be moving in with them, that he had to be about his Father's business. What had been wrong with that? Isn't that what God would have wanted? Isn't that what Jesus had done? And then he had fought off those boys for Clare. Was that the problem? Was God mad at him for using violence? That was when everything had changed, all right, and he had to admit that even though it seemed like he had done everything right, he didn't feel right, even back then. He had left Miss Nattie Lynn's feeling upset with her and worried about his grandmother, and later when he'd attacked the boys in the woods, he had felt murderous and that couldn't have been right. But then, what was the answer? What should he have done? Archie sat up and bowed his head in his hands and demanded that God tell him—what should he have done?

# CHAPTER

# 30

THE NEXT MORNING CLARE nudged Archie awake and told him it was time to go to the Langon Chapel to see the crying Virgin. Archie sat up and felt the stiffness in his shoulders from his lying on the floor all night. He looked at Clare, who stood above him in her robe with its hood drawn up over her head. Her face was hidden in the shadows, and she reminded Archie of cartoon drawings he had seen of the Grim Reaper. He shuddered and got to his feet, rubbing his eyes. He had put his robe back on sometime in the middle of the night to keep warm and decided to wear it again, at least to the chapel. He pulled the hood up over his head and said, "Okay, I'm ready. What do we do?"

"Follow me."

They started down the stairs, and Archie held his robe up with both hands and followed two steps behind Clare, just to be sure he didn't trip her or himself. The steps seemed to go on forever, and he could see that the long descent tired Clare. She took her time going down them, and even so she was breathing hard and leaning into the railing to steady herself. Clare's behavior worried Archie. She was too thin. She would have more strength if she would just eat. He made a promise to himself that after their visit to the chapel, he would find them some food and get her to eat it.

They stepped out onto the second floor, and Clare whispered, "We'll wait here."

They found a couple of chairs and sat down. Archie asked, "Who are we waiting for?"

"Mr. Endly. He took over my aunt's job when she died. He's coming early to do some work. We'll have about an hour before the museum opens."

"When did you arrange all this?"

"I saw him yesterday when you were in the garden. I told him all about our pilgrimage. He was very excited about it, and he offered to get permission for us to pray in the chapel by ourselves."

Archie smiled. He liked that they had permission to be in the chapel. "That's great. That's really great," he said, feeling a spark of hope. "I've been really worried about my grandmama. I'm going to pray for her the whole time."

Clare patted Archie's shoulder but didn't say anything. She began to hum, and Archie knew she was praying. He stood up and went to the window and looked at the city view. He drew in a deep breath and let it out. He wondered where his grandfather's truck was in relation to where he stood. If he looked out of one of the other windows could he spot it? He went around the room to the other windows, trying to find it, and was disappointed when he couldn't. He understood that to Clare the Cloisters felt like home, but to him the only bit of home he had with him was his grand-daddy's truck—and he had a sudden longing to sit in it and smell the familiar, if unpleasant, odors of cigar smoke, mountain mud, and pig urine.

Archie smiled at the memory of the pig urine. A few months before Armory had moved away, Archie was show-ing off the new camera his grandparents had given him for his birthday. Armory had the great idea of posing a pig in the driver's seat of Archie's grandfather's truck, with its front hooves up on the steering wheel, so that Archie could take a picture. It took both of them to get the pig into the truck, but it stayed there only long enough to pee on the seat before leaping back into Archie's arms and knocking him to the ground. The pig ran over his head, cutting his forehead, and his grandfather said the gash served him right. He and Armory had to spend the afternoon cleaning up the urine, but they never did get rid of the odor com-pletely. Archie laughed to himself and wondered what Armory was up to. Then, remembering their last phone conversation, he felt a twinge of sadness. Maybe it was best that their friendship had ended, he decided. Armory had never brought out the best in him.

A short while later Archie heard a noise, and he turned around looking panic-stricken at Clare.

"It's all right," she said. "Mr. Endly is meeting us up here. That's just the elevator."

When Mr. Endly, a portly man with a thick mustache and a pasty complexion, stepped off the elevator, he was surprised to find them standing there.

"Now how did you get in? They said you hadn't ar-rived yet," he said, looking Archie up and down.

"They'd better step up their security around here," Clare said, giving the man a hug. Then she turned and introduced Archie, and the man offered him a sweaty hand to shake. Archie shook it, and when Mr. Endly wasn't looking, Archie wiped his hand on his robe. A minute later they all got on the elevator, and Mr. Endly led them to the chapel.

"Will you two be all right then?" Mr. Endly asked before he left them alone.

Clare nodded, and both she and Archie thanked Mr. Endly and then he left. At last they were alone in the chapel, kneeling before the solemn Virgin at the altar. Archie bowed his head and prayed for his grandmother. He prayed that she had been moved to the rehabilitation center, and he prayed that she believed the note that he had left behind saying he was on a camping trip. He prayed for her happiness and asked for forgiveness for any way he may have hurt her since his grandfather's death. He knew his death had been hard on her, although she'd never said anything about it. He had seen the sadness in her eyes. Even when she laughed with her friends it was there, and there was worry, too. Had she just been concerned about the pain in her leg?

Archie lifted his head and stared at the Virgin. No, he knew what she had been worried about. Even before she broke her hip she had been worried about him. She was frightened she would die, too, and Archie would be all alone. She was frightened. Archie knew it. She was frightened still, and he had abandoned her. What had he done? He had been scared, too. He knew he couldn't face another death, not yet, not hers. But it had been stupid to run off. He glanced over at Clare. Her face was lifted to the windows. Her eyes were closed and she was smiling. She looked so contented, and it reminded Archie that he didn't belong there. The Cloisters was Clare's home, not his. The memories and people were hers. He belonged in the country, not the city. He needed the mountains and the country roads and the South, where people didn't talk funny, the way they did in New York. Archie blinked up at the Virgin and made his final decision: With or without Clare, he was going home and he was leaving that very day. His grandmother needed him, and, he realized, he needed her.

## CHAPTER

# 31

ARCHIE HEARD CLARE GASP. He turned his head and saw her staring wide-eyed with her mouth open. She raised her arms toward the Virgin, and her body went rigid. Her arms were held straight out, her fingers splayed and stiff but shaking as though electricity surged through her body. Archie stood up, frightened.

"Clare? What is it? Clare?"

He looked at the sculpture, but nothing had changed. He saw no tears. He felt Clare's shoulder, and it felt like stone, hard and cold.

He shook her and spoke again to her. "Clare? Are you all right? Say something."

Clare gasped again and then again, as though she was trying to breathe but couldn't draw in enough breath. He got behind her and wondered if he should try to lift her up. He was afraid she was having a seizure. He looked back at the sculpture, and still he saw no change, yet Clare stared as though she was seeing something. Archie leaned over her. "Clare, can you hear me? Are you okay? Clare?"

He moved around in front of her, blocking her view of the Virgin, hoping to break the spell. He took her outstretched hands in his. They were still stiff, and cold to the touch. He didn't know what to do. He rubbed her hands, trying to warm them, to wake them or her up. He looked at her face, still with its startled expression. He wondered if she was dying. Could someone die kneeling like that?

Archie kept rubbing Clare's hands, wondering if he should call for help. Her hands began to feel warm, and he believed his rubbing was helping. He saw her blink once, then again. He kept rubbing, and Clare's hands got warmer and warmer. Then he felt something wet, and he looked at his own hands and saw blood on them. He looked at Clare's hands, and she, too, had blood. He grabbed her hand and saw a wound in the center of it, where blood oozed and trickled down her palm. He looked at her other palm, and it, too, was bleeding.

Tears ran down Clare's face. She pointed at the Virgin. "Do you see, Francis? Do you see the angels?"

Archie looked at the sculpture. It was as it had always been. He turned to Clare. "No. No, I don't see anything. Clare, there is nothing there."

Clare was not listening to him. Her face was beaming. Tears streamed down her cheeks. The sight before her eyes enraptured her. "O blessed Jesus!" she cried out, lifting her palms up toward the ceiling.

Archie felt as if he were in the dramatic death scene of one of those Shakespearean tragedies his grandmother liked to watch on public television. He looked again at the sculpture, moving closer and examining its eyes and the altar space around her. "Clare, there is nothing there." He grabbed her chin and forced her to look at him. "Clare, it's nothing. You've had a seizure or something. You're sick. You need help. Okay? Let's go now."

Archie let go of Clare's chin and tried to get hold of her arms and lift her up, but she grabbed his robe and clung to him, using all her weight to hold him still. She cried, pressing her face into his stomach, and Archie leaned over her and rubbed her back, trying to calm her. He wondered where Mr. Endly was and how soon the museum would open. He needed help. Again he tried to lift Clare, and he succeeded in pulling her to her feet. More blood oozed from her hands, and when she stood up and faced him, she grabbed her chest; Archie saw that blood had seeped through the side of her robe, leaving a small wet spot.

"What's happening? I don't understand," Archie said, wrapping his arm around her and feeling her warm, thin body fall against him. He led her toward the exit, taking one small step, then pausing before taking another. He wanted to grab her and run, but Clare felt so fragile limping along beside him. He looked down and saw blood coming from beneath the straps of her sandals. He stopped walking and turned to her. "Your feet are bleeding. Everything is bleeding. I need to carry you. I'll take you to the truck. We should get to a hospital. Where's a hospital around here?"

Clare lifted her face to Archie's. "Don't fret, dear Francis. Don't you see? Jesus has united me to him forever. I share in his Passion. I bear his wounds." She showed Archie the palms of her hands, where several more trickles of blood ran from the centers.

"How—how did you do that?" Archie took her by the wrist and led her toward the door. She moved with him, walking faster than before. Clare spoke and her voice sounded stronger. "I have done nothing but meditate on Christ's Passion. It is Christ who has done this."

Archie could hear voices in the hall beyond the room. The museum was open for business. He wanted to get out of there, and he didn't want to be seen. What should he do? He shut his eyes for a second and prayed for help. Then he felt Clare tugging on his sleeve. "We must go now, Brother Francis."

Archie opened his eyes and followed Clare through the hall, surprised by her sudden energy. Archie saw a few people staring at them, but no one stopped them or asked what was wrong.

Archie guided Clare down the steps toward the exit and the parking lot. Once they were outside, Archie took a deep breath, happy to be free of the Cloisters. He told Clare that he would go to get the truck if she wanted to sit down and wait for him. Clare surprised him by agreeing to the plan, and Archie took off at a gallop. He wasn't gone more than five minutes, but when he returned he saw that the awful man from the day before was with Clare. Archie pushed down on the accelerator and pulled up right beside them. He jumped out of the truck and told Clare to hurry up and climb in. He ran around to where the two stood, and he saw that the man had Clare's wrists in his grip.

"Hey, back off!" Archie shouted.

The man let go of her and raised his hands. Archie watched him back away, and he decided the man had eyes like the comic-strip cat Garfield, heavy-lidded and lazy-looking. He didn't like the guy at all.

"That's the stigmata!" the man said to Archie, lowering one hand to point at Clare's hands.

Archie glanced at Clare, and then back at the man who had started coming toward him. Archie grabbed Clare's hand and Clare said, "It's all right, Francis."

Archie knew he didn't want another episode like the one he had had with the two boys in the woods at the school. The man was far bigger than Archie, both in height and weight, so he tried to seem relaxed and friendly. "Look," Archie said, "we'll have to talk another time. We've got some business to take care of. So if you'll excuse us..."

The man blocked the passenger's side of the truck. "She needs help," he said, glaring at Archie.

Archie gritted his teeth. "I'm taking care of it, so would you mind getting out of the way?"

The man turned around and opened the door of the truck. Archie thought the guy was going to get in, and he prepared to reach out and grab him, but the man just held the door open for Clare and bowed.

Clare thanked him and climbed up into the seat. Then the man turned back to Archie and said, "Go to Irving's. She needs help."

Archie was startled. How did he know Irving? When did Clare tell this nutcase about the old man? He felt confused. He didn't know what was going on.

He closed the door on Clare's side of the truck, then moved around to the other door, still glaring at the man, and said, "I'm handling things, so just leave us alone." He climbed into the truck and pulled away looking back at the man in the rearview mirror. The man stood with his hands on his hips, shaking his head the way Archie's grandmother used to do whenever she found that he had gotten himself into more trouble than he could handle.

# CHAPTER

# 32

When Archie had turned out of the Cloisters parking lot, he said to Clare, "We need to find a hospital. You're not well. We need help."

He saw panic flash in Clare's eyes when he said the word *hospital,* but then she smiled at Archie, her face beaming, and said, "I'm fine. I don't need a hospital. God is all I need."

"I don't know what to do," Archie said. "I don't know where to drive. Clare, I'm scared. I think we should get you help and then go home. I need to go home. We haven't eaten in so long. You haven't eaten. Maybe if you ate. Maybe that's what you need. No sleep and no food—that's why you were hallucinating back there."

Archie had driven in a circle and was coming up on the Cloisters again.

Clare lifted a palm to Archie. The wound was still there, but he saw no fresh blood. "Is your faith so small, dear Francis, even now?"

Archie felt the pressure in his stomach. He wanted to cry. He was too young to deal with the situation. Was his faith "so small"? *Yes!* he wanted to shout. *I'm not you. I'm not Francis.* But he kept silent, clenching his jaws. He turned onto Fort Washington Avenue and headed toward Irving's house. "I'm taking us to Irving's," he said. "He'll know what to do."

Clare didn't say anything. She closed her eyes and hummed. A pained expression crossed her face, just for an instant, and Archie saw her jerk her hand up toward her chest. Then she stopped and let it fall back in her lap, and her expression was blissful again.

Archie had a hard time finding a place to park when they arrived in Irving's neighborhood. At last he found a space seven blocks away. "I hate the city," he said, trying to fit into the tight parking space and getting no help from Clare. When he had maneuvered the truck well enough to keep it from getting hit by passing cars, he turned off the ignition and let out his breath. He rested his head a moment on the steering wheel and said, more to himself than to Clare, "When I get home I'm never driving again." Then he lifted his head, and turning to Clare he said, "Come on; we're here. Let's see if Irving can help us."

"Francis, you go. I'm very tired. I'll stay here and wait."

"But you're the one who needs help. You need food and a shower and sleep. Clare, you need to get yourself cleaned up."

Clare shook her head. "I'll never wash the blood of Jesus from my body. You go on. And find out how to get to the Cathedral of Saint John the Divine. We're supposed to go there."

"We are?"

"Jesus has told me that we must go."

"But you need..."

Clare closed her eyes and hummed.

Archie sighed. "Okay then. I won't be long."

Clare nodded. Her face glowed; her expression was still one of rapture, but Archie could see that her face was too pale. He knew she needed food and water. She had gone too long without both. He was afraid she might die if he didn't get her to eat. She had felt so thin when he had put his arms around her earlier and helped her out of the chapel. He had felt her ribs through the two layers of clothing she wore.

Archie took one last look at Clare and repeated, "I won't be long." Then he ran down the sidewalk toward Irving's house. He arrived at the apartment out of breath, and he leaned against the wall of the building a minute to rest before pressing the buzzer. He had felt so weak running, he couldn't imagine how Clare was even sitting up. He had eaten much more than she had over the past few days. She hadn't eaten enough to make up even a single meal. He hoped he could get her to eat something; otherwise, he decided, he would take her to a hospital. He didn't want her dying on him.

Irving answered the buzzer, and Archie told him who he was. Irving sounded happy to hear from him, and when Archie arrived at his apartment door, the old man was waiting. He smiled at Archie, taking in his robe but saying nothing, and then looked beyond him for Clare. Not finding her he drew his brows together and said, "Where is Clare? What's happened?"

"Can I come in?" Archie asked, stepping inside.

Irving backed up. "Yes, yes, certainly, come in." He closed the door behind Archie and led the way to the living room. "Is everything all right? Where is Clare?"

Archie sat down on the sofa, and Irving sat across from him. "Clare is waiting in the truck. I parked it about seven blocks from here. She won't come in. She's praying. We—we went to the Cloisters early this morning, and we went to pray in the chapel with the Virgin—there's this Virgin Mary with Jesus, only Jesus' head is missing, and we were praying and then Clare said she saw angels, but there weren't any and then she started bleeding."

"Oy," Irving said, moving forward in his seat and frowning. "Where did this blood come from?"

Archie shrugged. "I don't know. From her. I mean, I didn't see her get cut, but she's bleeding from both of her hands and somewhere, like her ribs, and her feet—both her feet were bleeding. This guy—this guy we met called it something like—like *stigma*."

"The stigmata?"

"Yeah. I mean, that's the same word this guy used. This guy saw us and he said that word—*stigmata*. What is that?"

Irving shook his head. "I don't know too much about it, but I do know it's nothing dangerous, just very rare. She's not gushing blood, is she?"

"No, just some oozing, like a few trickles. I can't tell about the wound in her ribs. I guess it's not too bad."

"They're the wounds of Christ, right? You've got the hands and feet and the ribs. Holy people get the stigmata."

"You mean, like saints?"

"I believe so." Irving stood up and shuffled over to a bookshelf. He ran his finger along a row of encyclopedias and pulled one out.

Archie, feeling calmed by the slow, gentle way the man moved and spoke, joined him and waited while Irving flipped through the pages.

"Here we go," Irving said, pressing his index finger on a page and reading the paragraph. Archie leaned forward and read over his shoulder.

"Says here ecstatics bear the marks of the Passion of Christ," Irving said, running his index finger beneath the words as he read. "That's Clare, an ecstatic."

"What's that?" Archie asked.

Irving twisted toward Archie. "You know, has fits of ecstasy."

Archie nodded, recalling his own feelings of ecstasy. It seemed like a lifetime ago.

"Says the stigmatic feels the suffering of Christ and suffers with him for the sins of the world."

"But what do we do about it?" Archie asked, leaning closer to the book.

"Nothing. Nothing to be done. Look here." Irving pointed to a paragraph. Archie leaned even closer, so that their heads were touching, and followed Irving's finger as it ran along the page. "Says physicians cannot heal the wounds. But it's not blood. See, they don't think it's blood but an oozing from the pores. Don't seem to know what it is, do they?" Irving looked up at Archie, and Archie pulled his head back.

"No, but look at this," Archie said, pointing to another paragraph. " 'The divine malady of the stigmata ends only in death.' What do they mean? Will she die?"

"I think it means it never leaves her—the stigmata. She'll have it always, until she dies."

Archie nodded, feeling only slightly better, and returned to the book. It cited examples of stigmatics, Saint Francis of Assisi and Saint Catherine of Siena and others. It told of one girl, Louise Lateau of Belgium, who lived in the nineteenth century and who ate no food for twelve years, except her weekly communion at church, and who drank only four glasses of water a week. She never slept but kneeled at the foot of her bed and prayed.

Archie read about the girl and pointed the paragraph out to Irving. "Here, this is Clare. This is just like her. She's like this Louise Lateau."

Irving read the paragraph, then raised his head. "It doesn't seem possible," he said.

"But that's just how she is."

Irving eyed Archie. "And you? What about you?"

Archie took a step back. "Me? No, I'm not like this. I don't know what I am. I just want—I don't know what I want."

Irving nodded and closed the book. He set it back on the shelf and turned to Archie. "So, you must pull the truck up to my door and drop Clare off. Then you can park it again. We need to take care of her."

"She won't come. She says we have to go to that Cathedral of Saint John the Divine. She says Jesus told her. Maybe afterward I could get her to come here. Really, I just want to go back home." Archie said the word *home* and felt his throat constrict. He could tell he was about to cry. "I'm hungry and tired, and I don't belong here the way Clare does."

Irving nodded and ran his hand through the white wisps of hair on his head. "What do we do?" he asked, speaking more to himself than to Archie. He looked at Archie. "You must get her to come here; that's all there is to it."

"I will. We're staying at the Cloisters, in the tower. That's where we were last night."

Irving shook his head. "No, no, no, no, no. You come here. No more of that."

"We will, I promise; but first we have to go to that cathedral. I know her. She's stubborn. Maybe if you gave me some food—she just needs something to eat. Then she'll be all right until we get back here."

Irving hesitated, then nodded. "Come on. Let's see what I've got in the kitchen."

Archie followed him to the kitchen and sat down at the table. Irving pulled out a waxed-paper sack and opened it. "I've got three bagels—could you use those?"

Archie nodded, hoping he'd get some cream cheese with them. "Thank you. We would love them."

"And some fruit and cheese. You need protein. Let's see if I've got any more liverwurst." Irving opened the refriger- ator door. "My two young friends cleaned me out the other day, but they left my liverwurst alone."

"Thanks, Irving," Archie said. "I'm sorry I'm cleaning you out, too."

"Shush!" Irving grabbed the liverwurst, a block of hard cheese, the cream cheese, and some mustard, and then closed the refrigerator door. Archie jumped up to help him carry it all to the counter.

"You don't have to worry about me. I've got Lizzie shopping with me now." He set the food down and hunted for a knife. "Here we go."

"So the tutoring is going well with the kids then?" Archie asked, unwrapping the block of cheese and eyeing it, wanting to take a huge bite.

"Yes, very well, and I've made some more friends at the synagogue, young and old. I'm going to my first poker game next week. We don't play for money."

Archie nodded.

"And I'm hooked up to the Internet. Don't know what to do with it yet, but I'm connected. The boys are going to show me more tonight. Maybe you'll join us. Tell Clare to join us."

Archie remembered Clare and thought he should hurry. He didn't know what she might be doing back in the truck. "Irving, can I use your bathroom and clean up a little?" he said.

Irving pointed the knife in the direction of the bathroom. "Sure, sure."

Archie left Irving with the food and hurried to the bathroom. He studied himself in the mirror and wondered how Irving had dared to let him in. He looked terrible. His hair was down to the middle of his neck, greasy and stringy and straight. His face was smudged with dirt and blood, and his freckles covered his face in big brown spots, having come out more from all the time he'd spent in the sunny garden at the Cloisters. His eyes were watery and his lids puffy. He looked down at his fingernails and found that they were black. He turned on the faucet, grabbed the bar of soap off the sink, and scrubbed his hands and face well. Then he scooped the running water in his hands and took several swallows of it, scooping the water up over and over again. He thought he could spend all day drinking, but he was worried about Clare, so he dried his hands and face, grabbed as much tissue as he could stuff into the pockets of his jeans beneath his robe, hoping to clean up Clare with it, and returned to the kitchen.

Irving was just putting the food into a grocery bag. Archie saw that he had added two large bottles of water and some cookies to the pile. He felt like crying, he was so grateful. He came up behind Irving and without hesitating gave him a hug. "Thank you, Irving," he said. "You're saving my life."

Irving turned around. "You saved mine."

"No, Clare saved yours. I just came along for the ride."

Irving handed Archie the bag. "You take care of her, now."

"Yes. Yes, I'll take very good care of her. And I'll bring her back here after we visit the cathedral."

"Make sure you do." Irving nodded.

Irving gave Archie directions to the cathedral and walked with him to the front door of the apartment building. He opened it and looked down the street, as though hoping to see Clare.

Archie stepped out onto the stoop and turned with his hand extended. Irving shook it, and Archie gave the man another hug.

"Yeah, yeah," Irving said, patting Archie's back and then withdrawing. "You'll come back here tonight."

Archie nodded and smiled. Just being in Irving's presence had made him feel so much better about things. He turned and trotted down the steps. He waved one more time to Irving, and then ran back down the sidewalk to Clare.

# CHAPTER

# 33

WHEN ARCHIE RETURNED to the truck, he saw that Clare looked the same as when he had left her. She sat with her eyes closed and her head lifted toward the roof. She was still humming. He looked down at the palms of her hands, which rested in her lap facing up. The blood had begun oozing again. He set the grocery bag down in the space behind the seat and struggled to take off his robe. Then he pulled out the tissue he had stuffed into his pockets and dabbed at Clare's palms with some of it.

"Looks like it started up again. When will it stop, I wonder?" he asked Clare, but she didn't seem to hear him. He wrapped some of the tissue around her hands, and then reached back for the food. He couldn't wait to eat. He opened the bag and pulled out the bagels with cream cheese wrapped in plastic. He tried to hand one to Clare, but she wouldn't take it. He unwrapped it and ate it himself as fast as he could. When he had finished the bagel, he pulled out another and again tried to make Clare eat it. Again she refused. He got out a bottle of water, opened it, and offered it to her. "Please," he said, "for me."

Clare nodded and took several gulps. Archie believed he was making progress. He unwrapped the second bagel and broke off a piece. He waved it under Clare's nose. "For me," he said again.

"More water," Clare said.

Archie handed her the water and waited while she drank from the bottle. He offered the bite of bagel again, but she refused.

"We must go to the cathedral and take part in the Holy Eucharist," Clare said.

Archie didn't want to go. He had had enough emotional upheaval for one day. He thought again of home and wished he were there. "Why 'must' we go?" he asked.

Clare shook her head. "We just have to, that's all. God is calling us there."

Archie didn't feel God calling him; he didn't feel God at all, and he hadn't seen the Virgin cry or the angels Clare had seen. He thought about rebelling, telling her no, he wasn't going to take her to the cathedral. He thought about insisting they go to Irving's, or the hospital, but then he looked at Clare's face, beautiful and vulnerable, and he knew he would always do what she asked.

Archie followed the directions Irving had given him. He drove back onto the parkway and looked for the 125th Street exit and Amsterdam Avenue. They didn't have far to go; they were there in minutes. There was no parking at the cathedral, so again Archie drove up and down the streets looking for a space. He thought maybe they wouldn't be able to find one close enough and Clare would decide it was better to go back to Irving's, but then, at last, he saw a car pulling out of a parking space. Clare was in luck; it was only a couple of blocks from the cathedral.

Again Archie struggled to parallel-park the truck, backing up onto the curb to get into the space better. He was sweating by the time he had finally straightened out the pickup and turned off the engine. He looked at Clare. She seemed so frail, it scared him. He wanted to take her to a hospital. He knew she had said she would never go back to the hospital, but he couldn't bear to look at her this way. He mentioned the idea of going to a hospital to Clare, and she shook her head and gripped Archie's arm.

"Never, Francis. Please, you promise. Never."

Archie looked at Clare's desperate expression and nodded. "Okay, I promise."

Clare released her grip and smiled. "Anyway, Jesus wants us here. We must go inside the cathedral."

"Well, okay then. Let's go," he said, deciding that the sooner they went the sooner they'd be through and he could at least get her to Irving's house.

When they reached the cathedral and Archie looked up, he could not believe his eyes. He had never seen anything so huge and majestic in his life. As they approached the entrance, with its stone sculptures and ornate designs towering above them in arches and circles of stone, they came to two sets of immense bronze doors divided by a statue Archie guessed was of Saint John the Divine. Each door showed scenes from the Bible set in huge square panels. Archie recognized some of them. He identified Adam and Eve in the garden of Paradise, the animals entering Noah's ark, the Last Supper, the Three Kings visiting the newborn Christ, and the Crucifixion.

Archie thought he could stand and study the doors all day. He reached out and touched the panel that showed Jesus kneeling and surrounded by angels. He felt a lump form in his throat as he ran his hands over the raised bronze. The humble Jesus of the scene touched him, and he, too, wanted to fall to his knees. But it wasn't only the scene that moved him; it was the artwork itself. He felt a desire so strong within himself to possess those doors, to have created them himself, that it made his heart ache to look at and touch them. He saw Clare approach the panel with Jesus' Crucifixion, and he wondered what she might do, but then the door opened and a group of people came out of the cathedral and Clare stepped inside.

Archie hurried after her, hating to leave the doors, but once inside he looked down the great length of the cathedral and up to the great heights of the vaulted ceiling, and he was overcome with awe. He had never in his life seen anything so magnificent. He decided that being in the cathedral was what being inside a great mountain might be like, if such a thing were possible. He could not believe that human hands had created it. He knew that only God could have inspired its creation. He thought about his own artwork. He had believed giving it up would bring him closer to God, but seeing the great cathedral made him change his mind. He looked down at his own hands, thin and rough, with knobby knuckles, and he wondered if God would ever inspire him to create something so great. Maybe he could use his art as a way of celebrating God, the way the cathedral builders had.

The cathedral was filled with people milling about or seated in chairs or kneeling and praying. People whispered, and their voices carried through the cathedral and up into the high vaulting, up to the heavens. Everything drew the eye up to the heavens—the piers and columns, the stained-glass windows, the great height of the ceiling. Archie looked at all of it and felt humbled and ashamed and overcome with a love for God. Forgetting Clare he stepped out of the aisle and sat down in a chair. He bowed his head and spoke silently to God:

*How do I show you that I love you, Lord? I want—I'll do anything. I'm yours. Use me. I want to show you my love. I want to build a great cathedral and prove to you how much I love you. I want to be worthy of your love. God, I want you back in my heart. I want to be good for you. I do. I want to be a good person, like Jesus, like Clare, like Irving, even. He made me feel so good and loved just by making me a bagel with cream cheese, just by being there when I needed him. I want to do this for people. I want to do it for Grandmama and her friends. I've been so selfish, thinking only about what I want. Lord, I want to be a good person. A really good—*

Archie looked up from his praying. His mind had flashed back to a time when he was six years old and was in his church at home. He was standing with his Sunday-school class at the front of the church, waiting to receive his first bible. He remembered the excitement he had felt when the minister put a bible in his hands and the Sunday-school teacher placed a silver cross on a black rope around his neck. Later, when he had showed the bible and cross to his grandfather, Archie had said to him, "Granddaddy Silas, I want to be good, just like Jesus. I want to be really, really good." He had clutched the cross around his neck and added, "I can feel Jesus in my cross. Feel it, Granddaddy. Feel Jesus."

His grandfather had examined the cross and tousled Archie's hair. He said, "Why, you just a little saint, ain't ya, young man?"

Archie hadn't known what a saint was back then, but his grandfather had looked pleased with him, so he nodded.

Archie was surprised by the sudden memory. *Why didn't I remember this before?* he wondered. *Was that why Granddaddy called me a saint? Was he remembering that day when I got the cross and the bible? Why had I forgotten it? When did I stop wanting to be good?*

He had been good—a saint, an angel. He remembered how happy he had been pleasing his grandparents, doing what they told him to do, helping them with the chores, saying his prayers every night and every morning, and going off happily to church and reading his bible. His grandparents had been proud of him—for a while. Then Archie noticed a change in his grandfather. It was a subtle thing at first; a look would come over his grandfather's face now and then that was almost a look of disgust when Archie acted so willing and obedient. Then his grandfather had started making comments like "I reckon if I told you to go roll around in pig stink, you'd do it for me, eh, boy?" and "Don't you be turning sissy on me, child, you hear?"

Archie hadn't known what to make of his comments. His grandfather didn't say them often, and most of the time he was pleased that his grandson was so helpful and good, but the comments had hurt Archie and made him feel ashamed of his goodness. Then, too, the other kids in his home-schooling group and on his soccer team and even in his Sunday-school class used to make fun of him and call him Goody Two-shoes and coach's pet.

It wasn't until he met Armory that things changed. At seven years old Armory was already a big child, with broad shoulders and large hands and feet. He was a tough kid nobody messed with, and Archie knew his grandfather liked him, so Archie liked him, too. The first time he invited Armory over to the house, they were all eating dinner when his grandfather asked Armory how he liked going to the public school. Armory said, "I hate it. My teacher is a witch with a capital *B*."

Archie had looked up at his grandfather, who had paused with a forkful of corn in midair. He knew that it was wrong to say something bad about another person, especially an adult, and he wondered what his grandfather would say. But his grandfather had laughed, spilling the corn back onto his plate. " 'Witch with a capital *B*'!" he had said. "Very clever, very clever."

Archie had been shocked. What was clever about it? Armory hadn't made the expression up. Archie had heard it from other kids many times before.

His grandfather had beamed at Armory all night, as though he was as proud as could be of him, and Archie had felt small and unimportant in his grandfather's eyes. After that first visit his grandfather was always asking when Armory was going to come over again. So, wanting to please him, Archie kept inviting Armory to the house. Soon they became best friends, and Archie learned to follow Armory's lead, joining him in all his crazy schemes and forgetting all about his own desire to be good.

From that time forward Archie and his grandfather never got along. It seemed that Archie, good or bad, could never please his granddaddy Silas, and Granddaddy Silas could never please Archie.

# CHAPTER
# 34

ARCHIE WAS SURPRISED by the old memory coming back to him all of a sudden after hiding in the dark for so many years. He felt sorry and sad. He wished his grandfather were still alive so that he could tell him that. He wanted to say, "Let's start all over. Let's be friends this time." He knew it was impossible. His grandfather was dead and there was no way now to make it up to him. Archie bowed his head and cried for his loss. For the first time since his grandfather's death, he realized what a loss it really was.

Someone jostled him from the seat beside him, and Archie looked up. A young woman said, "Excuse me," and slid down onto the kneeler in front of her seat to pray. Archie looked around and saw that the cathedral had filled up. The seats had all been taken and people stood in the back, crowding together and facing forward as though they were waiting for something. Archie wondered what was happening. Then he remembered Clare. He looked left and right, but she wasn't there. Archie stood up and searched for her, casting his gaze over the crowd. He couldn't see her anywhere. He felt panicked. He made a move to leave, but then everybody stood up and turned, and Archie saw that the Holy Eucharist service had begun; men and women dressed in robes were proceeding down the aisle.

The service seemed to last forever. Archie kept searching for Clare, craning his neck to see over the heads in front of him, hoping to spot her dark head among all the others. It was useless. He could not see her anywhere and his panic grew.

When the service ended, Archie pushed his way out of his row and fought the crowd to reach the exit. He decided that Clare must have gone back outside, but the grounds were as huge as the cathedral itself, and it seemed impossible that he would ever find her. He returned to the cathedral and searched the bays and the radiating chapels, his anxiety mounting. Where was she? What had happened to her? Had she fainted somewhere? Why hadn't he taken her to the hospital?

As he moved from bay to bay and chapel to chapel, the beauty of everything he saw captured his eye: the stonework, the statues, the stained glass, the marble altars, the tapestries and wood carvings—all of it spoke to him. He knew he would have to return someday, but he couldn't stop to look; he needed to find Clare. Where was she?

At last he found her in the chapel of Saint James. He spotted her kneeling at the front of the chapel, and without thinking he called out to her, "Clare!"

Heads turned and eyes glared at him, and Archie whispered, "Sorry," then he crept with his back against the wall up to the front. Clare turned to him and looked up, smiling. He was relieved to see that she was all right, but then he felt angry and said, "Where have you been? I've been searching all over for you. Do you know how hard it is to find someone in this place? You missed the service. You said you wanted to go to the service. You said Jesus..."

Clare put her finger on Archie's lips. "We came here for you, Francis, not for me. This is for you."

Archie was stunned. "What? What is? What do you mean?"

"I mean it is you who needs to be here. Don't you understand that?"

Archie looked about him, catching sight of a painting of the head of Christ with his crown of thorns. He thought of his grandfather and his heart felt heavy. He turned back to Clare. "Yes, I do understand," he said.

Clare blinked at him and smiled. "I will be right here. You have the whole afternoon."

Archie took her hands in his and examined her palms. The bleeding had stopped again. He looked at her face. She seemed better. Her eyes shone the way they usually did. Maybe she was going to be all right after all. He let go of her, and Clare got down on her knees again and bowed her head. Archie heard her low hum.

Archie spent that afternoon wandering through the cathedral and walking the grounds around it, his heart full of the desire for God and goodness. Everything he saw, everything he touched, filled him with that desire and a sense of holiness. Kneeling at the front of the cathedral before the High Altar, with its Great Cross of the triumphant Christ, Archie reviewed his life and saw that his reluctance to be baptized, his refusal to go up to the front of the church and be "saved," and his indifference to the teachings in his Sunday-school classes had been a way of getting back at his grandfather for shaming him—and a way of proving to himself that he wasn't a Goody Two-shoes. He realized that he didn't need to do that anymore, and his desire for goodness and to love and serve God overwhelmed him. Kneeling in the great cathedral, he no longer felt the ambivalence he had felt about God and religion for most of his life. He remembered what Clare had said the night before: He needed to stop thinking of himself and pay attention to others. He needed to really see them.

For once Archie was seeing things from his grandfather's point of view. He recalled his grandfather's drunken prophecies and understood for the first time his grandfather's own struggle for goodness. The man had gone about town preaching hellfire and damnation to the sinners—the tourists and rich people who had moved into town, threatening his grandfather's way of life and his very farm with their ideas of expansion and growth. His grandfather had been unable to accept the changes and the way the town grew around him, surrounding his farm and littering its boundaries with Taco Bell wrappers and Styrofoam cups. His prophecies and his drinking were his only defense against the people who mocked him.

Archie's grandmother had told him many times of the way life had been when they were young and people listened to Granddaddy Silas. Back then most of the valley was farmland, and no one could read the earth the way Silas could. He was able to look at the stars and the clouds, study leaves on the eastern side of a tree, feel a breeze, experience any number of things, and know what was coming weeks in advance. He knew when heavy rain or a freeze was coming. He knew when there would be floods or tornadoes or drought. His knowledge had been important once, when his friends were all farmers, too, and depended on him to protect their crops with that knowledge. But then the weathermen on television became more accurate, the farms were all sold off, and the tourists came, and people stopped listening to Silas Caswell. Silas and his predictions were no longer needed. That's when he had begun drinking in earnest and roaming about the town preaching to the sinners.

Archie realized his grandfather was ashamed of his drinking. His liver got damaged from all the alcohol, and yet he still couldn't stop, not until it killed him. Clyde had been right—the alcohol killed his grandfather; not Archie, and not his grandfather's anger about the still. His grandfather had been furious with him, angrier than he'd ever been. He had said Archie was in the clutches of the very devil himself, and Archie knew that if he hadn't vomited on him, his grandfather would have beaten him with his belt. He would have beaten him harder than he ever had before. Archie realized, though, there in the cathedral, that all his grandfather really had wanted to do was to beat the devil out of his own self, and Archie forgave him for that. He knelt before the altar and forgave the man for everything, and in turn he felt his grandfather's forgiveness. He believed his grandfather's dying words had been words of acceptance of who Archie had wanted to be all those years before, and who he might someday become. Realizing that, Archie bowed his head and cried with relief.

# CHAPTER
## 35

ONCE THEY HAD RETURNED to the truck, Archie told Clare all about his discovery in the cathedral. He had pulled out the liverwurst sandwiches and the apples Irving had packed for them and was trying to eat while he explained his new feelings toward his grandfather, but he was so overcome with emotion that he couldn't swallow and gave up trying to eat.

Clare listened, nodding as he spoke, as if she knew everything already, and even when Archie told Clare that he felt the best way he could serve the Lord was to return home, and that he believed his life, his future was there, she did not appear surprised or object to his decision.

Archie thought that meant Clare would be going home with him, and once they were on the road, he suggested that they spend their last night at Irving's.

Clare drew her brows together and looked at Archie. "I don't understand. What do you mean by our 'last night'? Last night of what?"

"Our last night of staying in New York," Archie said. "Our last night before we return home."

"But the tower is our home. Isn't that what you meant when you said you wanted to return home?"

"No," Archie said, feeling alarmed. "I meant our real home in the mountains, with my grandmama and your daddy."

"The Cloisters is our 'real home,'" Clare said, turning back to face the windshield, her eyes wide, as though she, too, felt alarmed.

Archie glanced at her and saw how pale she looked. Even her lips looked white. It frightened him. Their conversation frightened him. "The Cloisters is not my home," he said. "Those offices are not my home."

"Of course they are." Clare smiled, still staring wide-eyed out the windshield.

Archie turned off the parkway and drove up the hill toward the Cloisters. "Clare, we can't stay here forever. We need food, for one thing. And we need to go to school or get jobs or something. We can't spend the rest of our lives just hanging around a museum, can we?"

"This is our home, and we will live here always."

"Doing what?"

"Loving and serving the Lord. We're saints, aren't we?"

Archie drove into the Cloisters parking lot. He parked the truck and turned to look at Clare, studying her. She sat leaning against the door, with her pale face still turned toward the windshield. Her hair looked thin. Her wrists and fingers and neck looked thin. He touched her hand and felt a tremor. He squeezed her hand, and Clare looked at him. Her eyes seemed feverish. He turned her hand over and saw that it had begun to bleed again. Had squeezing her hand caused that? He noticed her robe had dark stains on the front from where she had wiped her hands, as well as the stain on the side.

"Clare, you know how you told me that I don't look at people? I don't really see them? Well, this afternoon I looked at my granddaddy, really looked, just the way you said I should, from his point of view, and I saw him, and now I'm seeing you." He patted her hand this time. "I know you hate hospitals, but..."

Clare jerked her hand away. "No! I told you, never again. They make me take pills. They watch me. They won't let me pray. They hate God. You promised me, Francis, no hospitals."

"But you need help, Clare, and I can't do it. I can't help you. I'm scared. Looking at you now, I'm scared. This isn't our home. We can't live like this, and if you can't see that, then—I—I think you need help."

Clare looked into Archie's eyes and shook her head. "Where is your faith, Francis? Do you trust God so little? God will provide everything we need. Jesus speaks to me and he tells me that we must stay here, together. Saint Francis and Saint Clare must always stay together."

Archie let go of Clare's hand. "But we *aren't* Saint Francis and Saint Clare," he said with force. "I'm Archie." He pointed to his chest. "I'm Archibald Lee Caswell."

Clare blinked at him. She screwed up her face as though she was about to cry. He couldn't stand it. He reached out and pulled her to him. "I'm sorry, Clare," he said hugging her. "I have no faith—not like yours. I *do* look ahead. I want to know where my next meal is coming from. I want to sleep in a bed, and I want to feel safe. I don't feel safe here. And I don't know what to do. I don't know if you're right and you're just following God or if you're—you're..." He couldn't finish the sentence. He couldn't bring himself to say the word *crazy* out loud, not in reference to her. He let go of her and sat back, closing his eyes. "God, what should we do?" he whispered.

"We must return to the tower," Clare whispered back.

Archie felt confused. Irving was expecting them. He wanted to at least take her there, if not to the hospital. He wanted to hand her over to Irving and then collapse in the nearest chair. The worry over Clare exhausted him. Then, thinking that, he felt guilty. Hadn't he prayed in the cathedral for God to use him? Didn't he say he wanted to prove his love to God? Wasn't loving Clare a way of doing that? What did he know, after all? God spoke to Clare. God was with Clare all the time. He wanted to follow God's will for him, and maybe staying with Clare in the tower was it. Clare seemed so sure. Wasn't it better to follow her? She had the stronger faith. And wasn't he acting just like her mother, wanting to put her in a hospital because his own faith wasn't strong enough to understand hers? He loved Clare. He couldn't imagine his life without her. They belonged together. Clare was right; they were soul mates and would be forever. Archie sat up in the seat and opened his eyes. He turned to Clare. "All right, we'll stay here tonight," he said.

Clare smiled at him, and Archie shook his head and wondered how many times he would go through this, always questioning and never trusting.

They rode the elevator up to the third floor, just as they had done the day before, and then waited in the stairwell for closing time. Clare sat leaning against the stone wall with her eyes closed and her body shivering. Archie reached out and grabbed her wrist to feel her pulse. It felt fast to him, much faster than his own. It worried him. When it was time to climb the two long flights of steps to the top floor, Clare stood up and swayed with dizziness. Archie grabbed her before she fell forward, and he suggested they go back out into the offices and then take the elevator to the top floor.

Clare shook her head. "A guard might notice; we're better off using the steps."

"Then why don't we just stay here on the third floor for the night? You don't look too well."

Again Clare shook her head and started up the steps, but she had to rest several times before they reached the top. Archie thought about carrying her on his back, but he feared losing his balance and falling backward down the cement steps.

By the time they reached the top, Archie was exhausted from his anxiety over Clare. He had brought along the bag of food Irving had packed for them, and he tried to get Clare to eat, but she wouldn't.

"Too much food keeps us separated from God," she said. Then she got down on her knees and crossed her arms over her chest and said, "I now share in the suffering of my Lord, Jesus Christ." Then she began humming, and Archie lay down on the floor, using his arm for a pillow, and watched her. Her face looked ghostly in the moonlight shining in through the window. It frightened him and so did her words. What did she mean by sharing in "the suffering of Jesus"? How far would she take that? Jesus had died. Is that why she wouldn't eat? Is that what she expected for herself? It seemed to him she was halfway there already.

He recalled the first time she had come to his house. She had been so vibrant, and her body had looked strong and muscular. She had looked healthy and beautiful, and she had been so full of the joy and love for God. He had wanted that for himself. But did he want this, he wondered? Did he want to become the way she was? Would following God lead him to that? Would following her? He closed his eyes and prayed to God. *Is this your will for me, Lord? If I follow you will I end up like this? Is that what it means to follow you?*

Archie felt the familiar pressure in his stomach just above his belly button. He had always believed that the pressure was a message, a warning from his grandfather, but he had come to understand that it wasn't. He had realized back at the cathedral that his grandfather had forgiven him. That's what his dying words had meant. No, the pressure he felt was not some warning from the grave of his grandfather, he realized, but his own gut feeling. It was his body trying to tell him what his mind kept ignoring. He opened his eyes and sat up. He looked at Clare and saw her suffering and knew that it was wrong. This was not God's will for her; this was something else. He knew, too, that as much as he loved Clare, he could not follow her anymore. Following her was leading him away from God. Where she was going, he could not follow.

It reminded Archie of when Armory and his family had moved to Washington, D.C. He had wanted so much to go with his best friend. He didn't know what he'd do without him. All his life he had followed Armory. Armory would hatch the schemes, and Archie would follow along. Armory would come up with the challenges, always something he knew he could do better than Archie, and Archie would try to meet them. When his friend moved away, Archie had felt empty, and then his grandfather died and Archie had felt lost. Then Clare had come along, and he had someone new to follow.

Archie shook his head and looked at Clare still on her knees, her body shaking with the effort of kneeling. No, he couldn't follow her. He couldn't follow anyone anymore, not Armory and not Clare. It was time he listened to his own voice, listened to God's voice inside him. He didn't need to hear a real voice the way Clare did to know that living in the tower was wrong and that Clare starving herself was wrong. He bowed his head and asked God, "What should I do?" Then he stayed up all night and waited for the answer.

# CHAPTER

## 36

Archie waited until the early morning before he nudged Clare and said, "Come on; it's time to go."

Clare lay facedown on the floor, humming. When Archie nudged her again, she didn't move, so he bent down and lifted her up. "It's time to go," he repeated, this time with more force.

"All night I saw Christ's Passion before me. Did you see it, Francis?" Clare asked, allowing Archie to pull her up onto her feet.

Archie examined her hands, relieved to see that the blood had dried and crusted over. "No, I didn't see anything. Now come on; climb on my back and I'll take you down the steps." Archie turned his back to her and crouched down, waiting for her to climb on.

"But I can't. I must stay here. We must stay up here, Francis."

He turned back around to face her. "No, Clare. We have to leave now. This is *not* God's will for us."

Clare's eyes widened. "What?"

"That's right; this is *your* will. It was your will that brought us up here, not God's."

Clare shook her head, but Archie continued. "What I know, what I believe, is that God's will would never hurt anyone, and staying here, running away the way we did, that hurts a lot of people."

Archie saw the pain in Clare's eyes. Her body started to sink down to the floor, and he lunged forward and grabbed her by the wrists and pulled her back up. He shook her arms. "Listen, I stayed up all night thinking and praying about this, Clare, and I realized that I've hurt all the people back home who care about me. Most of all, I hurt my grandmama. She's in the hospital with a broken hip and pneumonia. She could be dying, for all I know, or—or dead, even. I left her. I fooled myself into believing that it was right to go on this pilgrimage because I was so scared and couldn't face the possibility of losing her, not after what happened with my granddaddy. And you, Clare, you fooled yourself into believing God told you to come here because *you* wanted to be where all your good memories are." He shook her arms again. "Don't you see it? You ran because you couldn't take your mama spying on you all the time. You're afraid she'll put you back in the hospital, but Clare, I'm afraid, too. I'm afraid you're killing yourself— on purpose."

"No!" Clare said, struggling to get away from Archie. "That's not true!"

Archie gripped her wrists harder and continued. "And— and I'm angry. I'm angry because you chose me to help you do it—to help you kill yourself. All this time I felt so special because you—beautiful, wonderful, perfect Clare—chose me as your partner, your soul mate. But now I see what I have really been chosen for, and it makes me angry. This isn't God. This is you, Clare, desperate for a way out—and so was I. Now, I don't know what will happen to me if my grandmama dies; all I know is I need to have faith in God—leave it to God. You showed me that. But, Clare, you need that faith, too. You need to go back home, not starve to death up here."

Clare sunk to her knees and bowed her head. Archie let go of her wrists, and she looked up at him and said, "Don't you see, even if I die God is with me. Death is the ultimate union with the Lord. We become perfect in death. We are united forever with God—just like Jesus. Didn't you say you wanted to become just like Jesus?"

"This isn't what I meant!" Archie said. "You just said that even if you die God will be with you, and yeah, I know, you said that before, when I fought those guys in the woods. You thought I was wrong to protect you. Well, okay, the violence was wrong. Like you said back then, God's will is never violence. But, Clare, starving yourself is violence against your own body, and God wouldn't will that, either. You know it. And okay, if you die, God will be with you—great. But does that mean I'm supposed to let you starve yourself and do nothing about it? Is that really faith in God? I think faith is trusting in God to help you. It's acting in faith, but in order to do that you have to *act,* Clare. That's God's will for us, I think. We act, we step out in faith, and then, like you said, God is with us all the way."

Clare closed her eyes and lowered her head. She hummed. Archie felt she was trying to block out his words, but he continued, talking above her humming.

"I don't know, maybe you don't realize what you're doing. Maybe you're—I don't know. You hear voices and have visions and that stigmata thing. I don't get what that's all about, whether it's for real or if you're..." Archie crouched down in front of Clare. "Look, all I know is that I don't have what it takes to figure it out, okay? I don't know. Maybe nobody does. Who can judge? Am I crazy? Are you? Who isn't? I don't know, and I don't have to. I just think that if we stay here, you'll die, and I can't lose you—I won't. I love you, Clare."

Clare looked up at him with tears in her eyes. "God is the only one who loves me."

"Everybody loves you," Archie said, surprised by the conviction in her voice. "Everybody adores you. You know that. Now, come on." Archie reached under Clare's arms and lifted her up again. "We're leaving. We're going home."

Clare squirmed in his arms and with desperation in her voice said, "No, Francis! No! If you love me, then leave me here. Just trust in the Lord and leave me here. Why is that so hard for you?"

"Loving you shouldn't mean that I have to do every-thing your way and give you everything you want. Espe-cially not when I know it hurts you. God doesn't love you that way and neither will I."

Archie let go of her and stood back with his hands on his hips. He didn't know what to do. Clare lay down on the floor and began humming again. He needed help. He thought about the guards who kept watch over the museum at night. They were still on duty. He could go down and get them. He wondered what they would do when they discov-ered he and Clare had been sleeping in the tower. He de-cided not to think about it. He walked over to the door and looked back at Clare, expecting her to call out to him and stop him, but she didn't. She just kept praying.

Archie headed down the steps, his legs shaking from the fear of going against Clare's wishes. He prayed to God for help, reciting to himself, "Be still and know that I am God." The words comforted him and he knew God was with him. It wasn't an ecstatic thing, just a certain knowing feeling in his gut, right where the pressure in his stomach used to be.

Archie reached the third floor and stopped. A new idea had come to him. It scared him even more than his first idea of getting the guards, but he believed it was the right thing to do. He stepped out into the room on the third floor and went over to the phone on one of the desks. With his hands trembling, he picked it up and made a collect call to Scott Simpson.

"Mr. Simpson, this is Archie, Archie Caswell," he said after the operator told him to go ahead.

"Archie? Where are you? Do you realize the manhunt that's been going on around here? Is Clare with you? Where are you, Archie?" Mr. Simpson's voice sounded alarmed.

"Yes, she's here. We're in New York. I'm sorry." He tried not to cry over the phone. He swallowed hard and said, "Could you—could you get up here? Clare's in trouble. I'm scared she's . . ." Archie couldn't finish the sentence.

Mr. Simpson asked, "Where in New York are you?" and before Archie could answer him, he heard a woman's angry voice saying, "Let me talk to him.

"Hello. This is Mildred Simpson, Clare's mother. What's going on? What's happened to Clare? Tell us where you are."

"Yes, I—I was just saying—we're in New York, at the Cloisters, a museum, and Clare—she isn't eating and she's seeing things, having visions, I mean, and I—I don't know, but I think she needs to go to a hospital. I think you need to come up here."

"We'll take the next flight out. Where will you be? Will you stay there?"

Archie swallowed again and said, "I'm—I'm going to try to get her to a friend's house—Irving's. You could meet us there."

Archie gave her the address, and Clare's mother told him again that they would take the next flight out. Then she said that he had done a very foolish and dangerous thing and hung up.

Archie put down the receiver and stared at the phone a long time. He wanted to call the hospital and talk to his grandmother, but he was afraid. What if she was dead? How could he stand it? How would he live with his guilt? Again he prayed for God's help. He took a deep breath and picked up the receiver. Then he heard a noise behind him. He whipped around and saw three people stepping out of the elevator: the strange man from the parking lot, Lizzie Alward, and one of the night guards.

# CHAPTER
# 37

Archie didn't waste much time with explanations, nor did he ask for any. He hung up the phone without making the second call and told them Clare was up on the top floor and he needed their help to get her to go with him to Irving's home. He told them he had called Clare's parents.

When the four of them arrived by elevator on the top floor, Clare was just as Archie had left her, lying on the floor humming. When Lizzie spoke to her, Clare lifted her head and smiled as if she had been expecting her all along. Lizzie suggested that Clare come with them to Irving's house for a visit, and Clare nodded and got willingly to her feet. She looked at Archie and said, "I'm glad we're staying, Francis. You'll see; everything will be all right."

Archie couldn't look her in the eyes. He felt guilty for deceiving her, but he said nothing to correct her impression that they were just going to Irving's for a visit and would return to the Cloisters in the afternoon.

It felt like a party when Archie, Clare, Lizzie, and the man who had introduced himself as Albert Winkler arrived at Irving's house. Irving was so happy to see everyone, and his pleasure made Archie feel welcome and safe. Lizzie's two boys, dressed in pieces of Irving's old army uniform, were running around the living room playing soldiers. It reminded Archie of the days when he and Armory used to play like that, and he thought maybe he would join them for a while, just to keep his mind off Clare and what was going to happen when her parents arrived. Before he could join them, though, Lizzie asked him if he would help her fix sodas and coffee for everyone.

Archie followed Lizzie into the kitchen, happy to have something to do and anxious to find out about that morning. He dug a tray out of a cabinet beneath the sink and asked Lizzie, "So what happened? I mean, why were y'all at the Cloisters? How did you know? And what's that Albert guy doing here? I thought he was trying to kidnap Clare or something. He kept hanging around us at the Cloisters."

Lizzie put on water for the coffee, then turned around to face Archie. "You promised Irving that you and Clare would come spend the night with him. You never showed up and he got worried. In the morning he called me to say you still hadn't showed up and that you had told him you had been staying in the tower." Lizzie placed a sugar and creamer set on the tray and continued, "I thought maybe Irving had gotten things mixed up. I didn't believe it was possible for you two to stay in the tower without getting caught. So I called Albert, and he said he thought it was likely because he never saw you two come out at closing.

Then we went over to the Cloisters and talked to the night guard, Johnson, and he let us go up."

Archie asked, "So is Albert a policeman or detective, or something?"

Lizzie grinned. "He's a friend of mine. He lives right near the Cloisters, so I asked him if he would keep an eye on you two. I knew you were runaways, and I was worried about Clare. I had a sister with anorexia, so I know the signs."

"'Anorexia'?" Archie said.

Lizzie nodded. "Starving herself, no desire for food, hiding her body in that big old robe."

"But she isn't trying to get thin because she thinks she's fat; she's trying to..." Archie couldn't finish the sentence, so he let it drop and stared down at the wood floor.

"It doesn't matter what her reasons are," Lizzie said, "the results are the same, aren't they? Anyway, I was worried, so I told Albert to keep an eye on you two."

Archie nodded, and they both grew silent for a couple of minutes while they put ice in some glasses and poured the Cokes. Then Albert came into the kitchen, asking if he could help.

Archie went over to him and held out his hand. "Sorry, about everything," he said.

Albert shook his hand. "Hey, I should have done something sooner, but I didn't know where you two were staying until Lizzie told me what Irving had said."

"Sorry I didn't trust you. You were creepy with all your questions, though, and watching Clare the way you did. I thought you wanted to hurt her."

Albert nodded. "You took good care of her."

"Not really," Archie said. "Not good enough. I thought she knew what she was doing. Actually, maybe she did. I was the one who didn't know."

All morning long the group of them sat in Irving's living room and talked. Everyone but Clare knew that her parents were coming to get her, and the conversation sounded forced and Archie grew more and more uncomfortable. There were frequent lulls during which everyone sat trying not to appear to be listening for the buzzer or watching the door. Archie sat in a chair across from Clare and watched her. He didn't know what to think. She seemed almost like her old self again. Her voice was animated and all the things she said made sense. She had sipped her cup of coffee with sugar, and a bit of color had returned to her cheeks. Watching her made him feel so sad and sorry for what he had done. He still believed it had been the right thing to do, but he knew, too, that he had betrayed Clare.

At noon Albert went out for pizza and brought it back for everyone to eat. Clare said she couldn't eat a bite, and Archie felt too nervous to eat. He knew her parents could arrive at any minute, but he took a slice and set it on his plate. They were still in the kitchen when the buzzer sounded and everyone but Clare jumped up. Clare looked at them all, surprised, and asked what was going on. Then Irving answered the buzzer, and Mildred Simpson's voice came over the speaker. Clare heard it and stood up. She looked at Archie and, with her hands gripping the back of her chair, said, "I put all my trust in you, dear Francis, my soul mate, and you betrayed me."

"Clare, I had to. I couldn't let you starve yourself."

Clare and Archie stood facing each other across the table, both of them blinking back tears.

The others left them alone, leaving the kitchen to go wait for Clare's parents.

"You promised no hospitals," Clare said when the others had gone.

"But, Clare, look at you." Archie pointed at her.

"I was just trying to be like Christ," she said. "The only problem is, no one will let me. No one trusts it."

Archie lowered his head. "I'm sorry, Clare."

Clare let out a sob. "I want love, not hospitals."

Archie stepped forward and held out his hand toward Clare. "I'm sorry. I do love you. It's because I love you that..."

Clare's face twisted up and tears spilled from her eyes. She blurted out, "Why won't they love me?" She looked at Archie with pleading in her eyes. "Why won't they love me?"

Archie stood with his mouth open, trying to understand what she was asking. Her parents burst into the room, and Mrs. Simpson rushed over to Clare and hugged her. Then Mr. Simpson hugged her while Mrs. Simpson began examining her, lifting her eyelids, checking her fingernails, and examining the palms of her hands. Both parents were talking at once, asking her how it had happened and what did she think she was doing. Then Mrs. Simpson raised her voice and said they needed to get Clare to a hospital immediately, and she pulled her out of the kitchen toward the door to the apartment.

Clare didn't say anything or show any emotion during all of it. She allowed herself to be examined and then led by the hand through the living room. And after the Simpsons' brief expressions of gratitude to everyone for looking after Clare, the three of them left for the hospital, and Irving closed the door behind them.

Archie stood in the center of the living room and stared at the closed door. Everyone had gone silent. Archie waited, expecting to feel a wave of sadness wash over him, or to feel lost or empty, but he felt none of those things. He stood facing the door and from deep within him he heard the words *Be still and know that I am God,* and he felt comforted.

# CHAPTER
# 38

ARCHIE TRIED SEVERAL times to call home, trying first his own house, in case his grandmother had gone home, and then Clyde's and Nattie Lynn's homes, but no one answered. He sat at the desk in Irving's study, the same room where he had slept just a couple of nights before, and made his calls. When he failed to get anyone at home, he wondered if they were all at the hospital visiting his grandmother. He thought about calling the hospital, but then he had the dreadful thought that perhaps they were at her funeral. Archie didn't know how he would ever forgive himself if his grandmother had died while he was gone. He had thought he couldn't face her death, especially after losing his grandfather, but he realized sitting there in Irving's study that running away from it and abandoning her when she needed him most was going to be even harder to face and live with, especially if she had died.

Archie didn't want to return to the living room just yet, so he stayed in the study and prayed, first for his grandmother and then for Clare.

Sometime later he heard a knock on the study door, and Lizzie poked her head in. "There's someone here to see you," she said.

Archie stood up, wondering if Clare had escaped from her parents again and had returned. Then Lizzie opened the door wider, and there stood Clyde Olsen, dressed in a suit and tie.

"Clyde?" Archie said, feeling a catch in his heart. Tears welled up in his eyes. He felt so choked up, he couldn't say another word. He scooted around the desk and rushed to him and hugged him. It was so good to see a friendly face from home. Then Archie stood back and looked at Clyde. He was dumbfounded. "How—how did you get here? How did you know where to find me?"

"That Mr. Simpson called me and told me everything," Clyde said. He frowned at Archie and shook his head. "I don't know what we're going to do with you, son. This has to be the craziest stunt you've ever pulled. It near 'bout killed your grandmama to hear you'd run off, and in your granddaddy's truck, too."

"You mean—you mean, she's still alive? Is she okay?"

Clyde nodded. "She left the hospital two days ago. She's at the rehab place now."

Archie hugged Clyde again and then said, "I'm so sorry. I know how wrong I've been—and stupid. I just— I just couldn't face losing Grandmama, not after losing Granddaddy. I hated seeing her in that hospital, all hurt and sick and all. I was just scared."

Clyde patted Archie's shoulder. "She's going to go someday, you know. She's no spring chicken."

Archie lowered his head and Clyde added, "But you'll be well taken care of, don't you worry. It's been agreed upon that I'm to look after you, if ever anything should happen to her."

Archie looked at Clyde.

"We get on right well, don't you think?" Clyde said. "Think you could stand living with me?"

Archie smiled and shook his hand. "Yeah, I could stand it real well. Thanks, Clyde."

Archie and Clyde spent the afternoon with Irving, and Archie was pleased to see how well the two of them got along. Irving invited them to stay the night, and Archie and Clyde made plans to leave in the morning, with Clyde driving the truck. Archie was more than happy to leave the driving to him.

Before dinner Archie called his grandmother at the rehabilitation nursing home and spoke to her. He spent the first half of the conversation crying and telling his grandmother how happy he was to hear her voice and how sorry he felt about all the trouble he had caused her and her friends. Then he said, "Don't you worry, Grandmama, when I get home I'm going to look after you real well. I'm going to look after all your friends. And I'm going to do a good job of it, too."

"No indeed you're not!" Emma Vaughn said, sounding cross.

"But, Grandmama, I want to. I do. I love you. And I want to show you that. I've been selfish, and I want to show you I've changed."

Emma Vaughn said, "Now you listen to me, sugar. I did wrong getting you to drive me places with you underage and all. And I did wrong making plans to move in with my friends. That's no place for you, running a nursing home.

Don't you see, Archibald, I was scared, too, when your granddaddy died—scared I would be next and where would that leave you? I just wanted you taken care of. I'm getting on up there in age. And then I had this leg, you see. I knew something was bad wrong with it, and I just kept ignoring it, hoping it would go away. I've been foolish. I knew better, but fear makes a person do stupid things."

"It sure does," Archie said.

Emma Vaughn continued, "You've been too isolated up there on that mountain. When we get back home, you're going to go to that high school and meet more people your own age."

"I'd like that, Grandmama, but I'd also like to stay on the farm and not move into town. I love the mountains. I love our mountain. I found something special up there, and I'm not ready to leave it."

"Oh, you'll live on that farm all right, sugar. And you'll help Clyde run it, too. I want you back working again. Clyde's hired a few other boys from the high school to help out, so you'll have plenty of company. Besides, you owe him the price of a plane ticket."

"Yes, ma'am," Archie said, delighted to hear his grandmother's voice sounding so strong.

Archie went to bed early that night, exhausted from the events of the past several days, but before he could turn out the light, he heard a knock on the door and Mr. Simpson entered the study.

"Mr. Simpson!" Archie sat up. A sudden wave of guilt washed over him.

Mr. Simpson went over to Archie's bed and put his hand on his shoulder. "How you doing, son?"

"How's Clare, sir? Is she all right?"

"She's dehydrated and her kidneys aren't working as they should, but she'll be all right—she's a strong one."

Archie looked down and rubbed his legs. "I'm sorry, Mr. Simpson," he said. "I know what you must think. You must hate me. I'm so ashamed of myself."

Mr. Simpson pulled the chair out from behind the desk and sat down beside Archie's bed. He leaned forward. "So it's all your fault, is it?" he asked.

Archie nodded, looking straight into Mr. Simpson's eyes. "Yes, sir. I'm sorry. I should have taken better care of Clare."

"No," Mr. Simpson said, "I should have. I should have paid more attention to her. I pride myself on my ability to read people, but I couldn't even read my own daughter. I guess I was blinded by my anger with her mama. I wanted to give Clare her freedom. I thought that's what she needed. Her mama watched her all the time. She put her in that mental hospital and made her take the pills the hospital gave her. Those pills changed her personality. I felt like I was losing my Clare. I couldn't bear it. So I let her throw the pills down the toilet. I even encouraged her by giving her the attic room to use for her prayer ceremonies, and helping her hide what she was up to from her mama. I was using my own daughter to get back at my wife, and I'm ashamed of myself for it—we've both been using Clare." Mr. Simpson nodded at Archie. "So don't blame yourself for my mistakes."

"No, sir. But I was the one who drove us here. I did whatever she told me to, like I didn't have a mind of my own."

Mr. Simpson smiled wistfully. "She's a hard one to resist. She's got strong convictions. She knew exactly what she wanted, and she went after it."

Archie nodded and gazed up at Mr. Simpson. "So then, all her visions and the stigmata and stuff, is that just some mental illness? Is none of it real?"

"All of it's real to her, Archibald. I don't know if they're gifts from God, if that's what you're asking. Nowadays they've got other explanations for those kinds of things. And I don't know who's right, the scientists or the religious people, but her love for God is real, and I believe God's love for her is real, too. I believe that."

"Yes, sir, so do I," Archie said, "but I think maybe she sometimes confused her will with God's, because she was so desperate to get up here to the Cloisters. I think she was real unhappy, Mr. Simpson, if you don't mind my saying. I don't think she believes y'all love her." Archie looked down at his hands remembering Clare's words, *"I want love, not hospitals."* And *"Why won't they love me?"* Then he looked up and continued, "And I think she fooled herself into believing God wanted her to suffer and die like Jesus. That's how unhappy she was. I think she believed if God wanted her, then she wouldn't be committing a sin, she'd just be dying for the love of the Lord. She fooled herself, you see, and she fooled me—I mean she always looked so happy, didn't she? She never let on that she was hurting."

Archie looked at Mr. Simpson and saw such pain in the man's face, he had to look away. He felt sorry for what he had just said and decided he shouldn't have said it.

Mr. Simpson bowed his head and said, "I hope God can forgive me for what I've done."

Archie thought of his grandmother and his own need for forgiveness, and he swallowed hard. Then he said, "Lord Jesus Christ, have mercy on us."

"Amen," Mr. Simpson said, nodding. "Amen."

# CHAPTER
# 39

ARCHIE COULDN'T WAIT to get back to the mountains, but he was sorry to say good-bye to his new friends, and when everyone had gathered around the door to bid him and Clyde farewell—Irving, Lizzie, her two boys, and Albert—Archie turned to Irving and said, "Now that you've got your computer hooked up, let's stay in touch. I'll e-mail you."

Irving nodded. "Good, good. I'd like that."

Archie smiled at the old man, noticing the way he then stood up so straight and the way his eyes sparkled, and he said, "You know, I thought we were just helping you out a little—actually, Clare was—but then it turns out you helped us so much more." He looked at Lizzie and Albert and added, "All of you have. I feel like a real fool."

"Nonsense," Irving said. "That's just the way it works. Any time you give, you get. It doesn't matter if you don't want anything, you still get. It's just the way it works."

"Well, thank you," Archie said.

"Sure, sure." Irving waved the thanks away.

"Thanks to all y'all," Archie said, nodding at Lizzie and Albert.

The three of them laughed at Archie's expression, repeating it to one another, and then they hugged him and shook his hand, and everyone said good-bye.

On the ride home Archie and Clyde were slowed in traffic near Front Royal, Virginia, and Archie remembered the trip up, when he had looked for a road paved in gold as they passed the Front Royal exit. *That was stupid,* he thought to himself, and then he thought that the whole trip had been about his looking for some golden highway to enlightenment. He had wanted visions like Clare, and to hear the voice of God. He had wanted to live in a constant state of bliss, and to believe that God had chosen him, that he was special—that he was a saint. *When,* he wondered, *did it become more about me and what I want for myself, and less about God?*

Archie looked out the window at the car beside him. The man in the driver's seat seemed impatient with the delay. A young boy sat in the backseat of the car. Archie smiled and waved. The boy stuck his tongue out at him. He remembered the other little boy on the trip up, the boy who had handed him his sandwich and lifted his hand in the "I love you" sign. Archie had thought that the boy had seen saintliness in him. He had believed the boy had looked at his eyes and face and had seen them shining the way Clare's always had. But, he realized now, the boy probably just saw a starving person and had given away his sandwich as an act of kindness. *He was the saint,* Archie thought, *not me. Maybe that's all it really takes to be a saint—those simple acts of kindness.*

OVER THE NEXT SEVERAL months, Archie went often to visit Mr. Simpson, who gave him updates on Clare's progress in the hospital. He had told him that Clare's mother had taken her back to North Carolina to the mental hospital there, and that she was doing very well on her new medication. He said the doctors and the staff at the hospital called her Doris.

Archie had written several letters to her, still calling her Clare, but she had never answered any of them. Over Christmas break he rode to North Carolina with Mr. Simpson and got permission from him and Mrs. Simpson to visit Clare by himself.

Archie felt nervous following the nurse through the locked doors of the mental ward. She led him to a large room where tables had been placed in the center in rows, and couches and chairs sat off to one side in front of a television set. There were groupings of people all over the room, of all ages and colors. The room smelled of ammonia. Archie looked around for Clare and found her with some of the other patients, sitting at a table and listening to a man reading from *Time* magazine. As he approached the table, he hoped that she would recognize him and that she had forgiven him for what he had done. He could see that she had gained some weight, and he was pleased about that. It made him feel that his betrayal had done her some good at least. She was dressed in a pair of jeans and a red sweater instead of the robe, and that worried him although he knew that it shouldn't. It was a sign that she was getting better, wasn't it? But he wondered, *Is there anything of the old Clare left anymore?*

He walked over to the table, and several faces looked up at him, but his eyes were only on Clare. Would she recognize him?

Clare smiled at him, but the smile didn't light up her face or reach her eyes, and Archie's heart sank.

The nurse who was with Archie said to Clare, "Mr. Caswell has come to visit you, Doris. Why don't you take him to the private corner and talk?"

"Yes, ma'am," Clare said, her voice quiet and slow.

Archie felt so sad, he wanted to run away. Where was his old Clare? He walked with her to the far corner of the room, noticing the shushing sound the slipper-socks she had on her feet made. They sat down across from each other, and Archie fidgeted with the torn plastic on the armrest of his chair.

"How are you, Archibald?" Clare asked without emotion.

Archie nodded. "Good. I'm real good. I'm at the public high school now, taking advanced courses. I guess my granddaddy taught me pretty well, after all." He scratched the back of his neck. Clare didn't look as if she was even listening.

"Uh—I'm doing a lot more drawing now, cartoons and other stuff, like faces," Archie continued. "You really taught me how to look at people—remember?"

Again Clare smiled, but she wasn't looking at him. She was staring at the piano.

"So—uh," Archie said, scratching his ear, "the art teacher at school says I've got real talent. Maybe someday I'll create something as beautiful as some of those paintings at the Cloisters."

"Have you ever heard me play the piano?" Clare asked, turning to face him finally.

"Oh—uh, no. So—you want to play something for me?"

Clare stood up and shuffled to the piano, and Archie followed her.

They sat down together and Clare played a waltz. She sounded good, and it made Archie feel better. Maybe she wasn't a complete zombie.

"So, how are you?" Archie said, studying Clare's profile. She wasn't looking at her hands but over the top of the piano, at the wall.

"I'm doing very well," she said. "The meds they give me are very good."

"That's great," Archie said, his own voice sounding dull. He knew he should feel happy for her, but he couldn't help it, he wanted his old Clare back.

"I'll be leaving here in a few more weeks," Clare said.

"Great," Archie said again. "Then what will you do, do you know?"

Clare sped up her waltz. "I'll live with my mother and finish up school."

"That's good." He looked around at the other patients in the room. He wanted to leave. He knew he had been there less than five minutes, but seeing Clare that way felt like torture to him.

"I—I've been praying for you, D-Doris."

Clare played louder. "Have you?"

"Yes. I've started going to church, the Catholic church, with Clyde." Archie cleared his throat and then said, "So, do you—have you prayed for me? I mean, are you allowed to pray here?"

Clare played a little faster. "Not really. It's frowned upon."

"So then that's over—all that. You don't hear voices and have visions and stuff because..."

"Of course not. Do you like my music?" Clare asked.

"Yeah, sure. It's nice."

"Listen, Francis," she said.

Archie smiled. She had called him Francis.

"Are you listening?"

He listened to the piano music and nodded, and then he heard it and his heart skipped a beat. Clare was humming. She was humming to the music.

Archie slid over closer to Clare, hope rising in his chest. "Do you play the piano a lot here—Clare?" he asked.

Clare nodded. "As often as I can. I've come to love music so much."

Archie looked over his shoulder and noticed one of the staff people looking at them. He nodded at him and turned back to Clare, who said, "Even when I'm not playing the piano, I'm humming a tune. We're allowed to hum here."

Clare glanced at Archie and smiled, and he saw, for the briefest moment, a flicker of the old light in her eyes.

## AUTHOR'S NOTE

The crying Virgin in this story is a sculpture of the enthroned Virgin and child from Autun, Burgundy, in France, dated 1130–1140. It is usually on display behind the altar in the Langon Chapel at the Cloisters; however, when I visited there in October 2002, the sculpture had been removed temporarily for conservation purposes. The other sculpture mentioned in that room, the Auvergne Virgin and child, had been moved outside the entrance to the Langon Chapel and is now encased in a clear container. I believe that the Autun Virgin will return encased as well.